THE SURVIVORS

Also by Kristin Hunter

GOD BLESS THE CHILD

THE LANDLORD

For Children:

THE SOUL BROTHERS AND SISTER LOU

BOSS CAT

GUESTS IN THE PROMISED LAND

Kristin Hunter

THE SURVIVORS

CHARLES SCRIBNER'S SONS
NEW YORK

1 3 5 7 9 11 13 15 17 19 H/C 20 18 16 14 12 10 8 6 4 2
Printed in the United States of America
Library of Congress Catalog Card Number 75-612
ISBN 0-684-142015

For Jackie (John, Jr.) and Andrew Lattany:
May they survive and prevail

THE SURVIVORS

One

On Monday morning, Miss Lena Ricks was in a great hurry to get to her shop and make sure nothing had happened to it over the weekend.

For a small person, she moved very fast when she wanted to, taking big strides in her high-laced boots with their hidden arch supports. Her seven-league boots, she called them. Necessary for walking downtown to the fabric district and uptown to the shops that sold buttons and trimmings. Indispensable for getting to sick customers' apartments for fittings, and to the street-stall markets for fresh fruit and vegetables. She owned pairs of boots in many colors, because she walked everywhere. Walking was healthy. Besides, Miss Lena was convinced no mere bus or cab driver could take her anywhere as fast as her feet could.

She was probably right. Her seven-league boots covered six city blocks in seven minutes.

At the corner, she was relieved to see that the square window which displayed a different Custom Design by Lena every week had not been broken. Her old-fashioned sign still swung gently from its curly black iron standard above the door.

Things to Wear by Lena
Dressmaking—Alterations
CUSTOM DESIGNS

—The most important part of the sign, in solid capital letters.

The blue door was closed, as were its inside shutters, and its brass knocker in the shape of a woman's hand gleamed like gold in the early morning sun. The single square window, which displayed a different Custom Design by Lena every week, had not been broken. Everything was exactly the way she had left it.

Or was it?

Miss Lena closed her eyes and opened them again. She was sure she had not put her trash out on Saturday night. That was something she never did. Too many things could come along to overturn trash cans in thirty-six hours: stray cats, hungry dogs, thirsty tramps, devilish boys. Yet there they sat at the curb, both her green plastic trash cans, ready for the nine a.m. collection.

Miss Lena darted across Berkeley Street, causing brakes to squeal and horns to honk, and bent over her cellar door. Whoever had put out her trash had to go down in the basement and come up again. But the combination padlock was on the hasp, exactly as she had left it.

She should be glad, Miss Lena told herself. Carrying out trash was a chore she hated, and some kind person had done it for her.

But who? Janitor service did not come with low rent, and Miss Lena was too happy about hers to complain about carrying trash cans that weighed next to nothing anyway because they contained only scraps of fabric and snips of tissue-paper patterns. Suspiciously, she studied the early-morning crowd of shabby black women waiting for the bus with shopping bags and thin, smartly dressed white ladies walking pedigreed dogs on leashes.

Tenth and Berkeley was a changing neighborhood—changing for the better, in Miss Lena's opinion. Every day, more rich white people moved in from the north and more poor black folks were pushed farther south. Four years ago, when Miss Lena had signed her lease, this had just begun to happen. So she had cheap rent, which had never been raised, plus an ever-increasing stream of rich, idle ladies passing by. It was the best deal in town on the best location in town.

Or was it? Miss Lena knew the poor black people did not like being forced out of their crowded, run-down places to make room for renovated town houses and tall, gleaming apartment buildings. In a way, she did not blame them. How could she? She had been poor and overcrowded herself once, and she was still black. But some of the people who were being Urban Removed were angry enough to smash or burn or break in and rob any place that looked like it belonged to someone better off then they, and Miss Lena did blame them for that. She had worked hard for what she had. Why couldn't other people struggle and sacrifice to get something better for themselves, like she had? And if they wouldn't, why take it out on her? Miss Lena had already been robbed twice, and she was always afraid it might happen again. That was why she locked up her shop carefully every night before she went home, and why it took all her self-control to keep from worrying about it every minute until she got back.

The uneasy feeling that had crept over her grew as she inspected her window. This week's Custom Design, a purple velvet Short Dress that buttoned over matching Short Pants, looked better than ever on its headless mannequin. Last week it had glowed, as a costume for which she planned to charge a hundred and fifty dollars should, but this morning it shimmered like twice as much money.

Miss Lena had to touch the glass to make sure it was

still there. When she did, nothing came away on her white glove. There was no doubt about it. Someone had washed her window. A professional, too, who had left no streaks or smudges. Her white steps also looked freshly scrubbed.

What was that chill creeping from her scalp down the back of her neck to her spine? Fear? *Nonsense,* Miss Lena told herself. It was the October breeze, and even though the man on TV had said today would be mild and fair, she should have had better sense than come out without a neck scarf. Miss Lena took out her keys, opened her outside Yale lock and her inside chain lock, and marched into the warm, cozy waiting room which she called her "salon".

It deserved the name. Everything in it was French, from the full-length pier glass that tilted in its carved gold frame to the oval cream-colored rug with its pattern of softly colored flowers to the curvy-legged coffee table in front of the plump little green velvet love seat. Even the fashion magazines that were spread out on the coffee table were French: *Elégance* and *Elle.* The salon was in perfect order, ready for her first customer, the way it was supposed to be every morning.

But unless Miss Lena was losing her mind, her first chore this morning had been to give it a thorough cleaning.

She had worked very late Saturday night on Miss Van Wyck's wedding gown. Miss Lena never talked about her customers to other people, but to herself she said that Miss Van Wyck's fiancé, whoever he was, had better be a strong man. Otherwise he was really going to catch hell. Every seed pearl on that gown had to be sewn in a perfect *fleur-de-lis* shape. Every perfect seed-pearl lily had to be in its exact place to form a regular overall design. And the places kept changing because Miss Van Wyck kept wanting the seams taken in to make her waist look smaller. Miss Lena had worked until midnight Saturday, an hour past her bedtime, to make sure today's fitting would be the last. Afterward she had been too tired and sleepy to pick up the scraps from the floor.

But, over the weekend, the scraps had disappeared. The pins and seed pearls had been neatly collected and put in the ashtray, which had been emptied and dusted first. (Miss Van Wyck smoked like a chimney, and whenever she coughed, a seam would burst on the skin-tight gown, and Miss Lena would have to sew it all over again.)

Parting green velvet drapes, Miss Lena went back to her work room and sat down hard at her sewing machine. She was not going crazy, not at all. She was as sane as ever. Everything in her shop was the way it was supposed to be on a normal morning, yet everything was a little bit different, as if the rooms had tilted slightly. For instance, she never put pins in the ashtray. Only a stranger would put them there, someone who did not know her pins were kept back here, in the blue pin bowl, until she found time to stick them into the green velvet pincushion on her cutting table.

A good stranger, it seemed, because nothing but trash was missing from the salon or the work room. Her clock radio still sat on its shelf beside her portable color TV. Her bolts and lengths of fabric, which were worth much more, had not been touched either. And when Miss Lena rose on shaky legs to hang up her coat, she saw that all the clothes that hung in various stages of completion on her garment rack were still there, even the coat into which she was sewing a mink lining for Miss Allinson.

Someone good, then, who could get in and out without disturbing padlocks, Yale locks, chain locks, window locks, or burglar alarms. A good fairy? A friendly elf?

Miss Lena did not believe in fairies—except the human kind, men who wanted to look like women and paid her twice as much as lady customers to design and make elaborately padded dresses that helped them achieve this look. Nor did she believe in ghosts, demons, imps, witches, booger men, spells, or any of the other invisible things her family had frightened her with to make her behave when she was little. She had decided at fourteen that a spirit would be a fool to inhabit such a small, shabby house with so many poor people in it. If *she* had supernatural powers, she knew *she* would certainly not be there. Therefore she had put such things out of her mind forty years ago, and she would do the same now. Sooner or later she would find out what flesh and blood person had been here, and then she would know what to do about it.

In the meantime, there was work to be done. Miss Lena looked at her watch, then at her calendar. It was eight forty-five. At eleven she was expecting the Hippo (Mrs. Reverend Johnson, so called by Miss Lena because she had such big hips) to pick up the hostess gown Miss Lena had designed for her At-Home party. The gown was actually a caftan, a loose-fitting robe sewn only partway down the sides. (What else could a Hippo wear, except a tent?) But she was a nice, smiling, shiny-black Hippo whose husband pastored a rich church, and she deserved to be treated just as well as skinny, selfish Miss Van Wyck. Better, in fact. Ladies with perfect figures were not steady customers. Why should they be? They didn't need Custom Designs by Lena or anyone else. Oh, they might pop in now and then to order something for a special occasion, but most of the time they could just snatch any old thing off a rack in a store and walk out wearing it.

A Hippo, though, was a regular customer. She needed Miss Lena just as much as Miss Lena needed her.

Sometimes, just sometimes, Miss Lena wished there were someone she could say these things to and trust not to repeat them. But there was no one, so instead she turned on a TV talk show and let the voices make conversation for her.

Talking to herself was a dangerous habit. Someday she might do it out loud when someone was there. And her lips had better not slip today and say anything about *hips*, unless she wanted to lose that good steady money. "Mrs. Johnson, Mrs. Johnson, Mrs. *Reverend Doctor Johnson,*" she said aloud three times, to replace the bad habit with a good one, as she deftly stitched the side seams of the caftan to end just above the knee. Like so many ladies of Nilotic extraction, the Hip—oops, *Mrs. Johnson*—had slender, graceful legs. Miss Lena had observed that descendants of the tall, slim tribes of the Nile, who resembled storks in Africa, tended to put on weight in America on a plentiful diet of pork—but only above the knees. In this dress, Mrs. Johnson's legs were all of her that would show—those and her face and her pretty, jeweled hands.

My mouth tastes like some coffee, Miss Lena thought as she hemmed the silk caftan, emerald green to match the Hippo's engagement and wedding rings. Her craving was right on schedule. It was nine-thirty, the time when Miss Lena allowed herself her first cup of the day. But while she was making up her mind whether to heat water for a cup of instant or go to Foot-Long's on the corner for a cup of real, someone knocked at her front door.

Miss Lena frowned. The Hippo was an hour and a half early. Oh, well, at least the caftan was almost ready. She would invite Mrs. Johnson to have a cup of instant with her while she finished it by hand.

But when Miss Lena opened the top shutter, no one was there. She shrugged and turned back toward her work room.

There was a second knock, louder than the first. And still no one visible through the top shutter.

Standing cautiously behind the door, Miss Lena opened it a few inches without unfastening the chain. She had trained herself to keep it on whenever she opened the door, in case of unpleasant surprises.

This was one. Instead of her customer, a small, strange creature stood on her doorstep. Miss Lena would call it a demon or an imp if she believed in such things. Instead, she called it a dwarf. It was either that, or a very short old man.

Miss Lena was barely five feet tall, and she was looking half a foot down at a head of beaded hair, full of dust and lint, which had not been touched by a comb in weeks. Below it were a raggedy sweater and a pair of wrinkled pants that looked like they had spent the night in an alley. Instead of forming straight columns to support his body, the little man's legs were bent and twisted under him. When he tilted his chin to look up at her, she saw that his dark brown face was also twisted, and lined, too, from bad habits or old age.

Roth, she decided, and started to shut the door against the unpleasant sight.

Before she could, though, he smiled. With that smile

—crooked lips, snaggle teeth, red eyes, and all—years dropped from him.

Why, it was only a little boy.

"I brought your coffee, Miss Lena," he said.

Two

He held out a foam cup on a paper tray. "Black with extra sugar. That's right, ain't it?"

Miss Lena had to admit, after the first sip, that it was. Hot, sweet, and strong enough to strip paint off furniture. It was her only vice, and she only drank it after she had lined her stomach with a good breakfast.

But how did this boy she had never seen before know exactly how she liked it? Or exactly when she took her first cup? Instead of these or the half dozen other questions that were buzzing in the back of her mind, she asked, "Where did you get the coffee?"

"Over to Foot-Long's."

Of course. Foot-Long was most famous for his oversized hot dogs, but for Miss Lena, his reputation rested firmly on his always-freshly-made coffee, the best in town. She reached behind her for her purse. "How much do I owe him?"

"Nothing," the boy said. "See, I carried out Foot-Long's trash for him this morning, so he gave me the coffee free. He gave me this besides."

He held out a sooty palm on which a dime and a nickel gleamed.

"Did you carry out my trash, too?"

He flinched and dropped his eyes. Long lashes that any woman would envy swept his grimy cheeks. Miss Lena looked away from his embarrassment and saw the wind sweeping a snowstorm of papers down the street. She was getting chilly, standing in the half-open door.

And he was trembling in that holey sweater.

"Well, come on in," she said crossly, "before you let all the heat out." She was cross with herself for extending that rash invitation. Boys were dangerous these days. Even the young ones were running wild, robbing, fighting, and killing. Watching him limp inside, she felt better. This one was small and crippled besides. Defending herself against him, should it be necessary, would be no problem.

"Are you hungry?" She kept a jar of diet cookies for herself and tea biscuits for her customers in the back room.

"No ma'am. Foot-Long gave me my breakfast."

Soda pop and potato chips, probably, she thought. She knew what most of these kids considered to be a meal.

As if he had read her mind, he added, "Grits and eggs."

"Doesn't your mother give you breakfast?"

"I ain't got no mother, ma'am."

"Everybody has a mother," she contradicted. (Except imps, demons, and other offspring of Satan?)

"I mean she's dead, ma'am. Since Christmas."

"Oh, excuse me. I'm sorry." Miss Lena felt herself begin to flood with sympathetic feelings that matched her words. Check that, she reminded herself. Before you get involved.

"Don't feel bad," he said. "I don't no more. She was old. *Real* old."

How old could she have been, to have a boy this age? But than, what *was* his age? He looked anywhere from eight to eighty. All of us come in this world wrinkled, same way we leave it, but this one's wrinkles never went away, she thought.

Once more he responded as if he'd heard her question. "She was sixty-three. She got me on the change, when she was fifty. Least that's what I heard tell. What's the change, Miss Lena?"

She covered her embarrassment with a crisp, direct answer.

"It's the time of life when ladies begin to get old. *Some* ladies," she amended.

"You mean it don't happen to all ladies?"

"I mean—I mean it doesn't affect all ladies the same way. Never mind *what* I mean. There's a bathroom in the basement. You run down there and wash your face and hands, and maybe I'll have something sweet for you when you get back."

It disturbed her to see him head instantly for the door at the back of her work room without asking directions. He knew exactly where the basement entrance was, then. Just as he seemed to know everything else about her, including her thoughts.

But at least she knew his age now—thirteen—and understood his prematurely old appearance. She'd heard that children of older mothers were frequently born old, and malformed as well. And there were other legends, to which she gave less credence, about change-of-life children. They were said to be as old and wise as they looked. Not children at all but diminutive ancients, with the entire memory of the race stored in their shriveled skulls. With the power to read minds, predict the future, and become invisible at will. Miss Lena did not want to think about whether they were expected to live very long. She would not think about it. Miss Lena had very firm control of her mind at all times.

The temporary removal of his funky presence from

her salon was another relief. As he stood over the heat register, the stench had risen from him in practically visible waves. Hand and face washing wouldn't do much for those clothes or what was under them, though.

Something has to be done about cleaning him up, she thought. A bath, some clothes. And then: Check it. You don't need any responsibility besides yourself. What you have to do is get rid of him fast, then fumigate this place.

He was back suspiciously soon.

"Let me see those hands," she commanded.

He held them out one at a time, shifting his precious coins from one fist to the other. His hands were clean, all right; the gray palms had become pinky-beige, the backs medium brown. But a darker line at the wrists showed where the soap and water had stopped. As for his face, it was a grotesque two-toned mask—a clean brown oval in the center, framed by a sooty black rim. She was almost afraid to look at his ears.

His eerie ESP was still operating. "I couldn't see in your mirror," he apologized. "It's up too high."

"Well, you can *feel,* can't you?" she scolded. "Even blind people get themselves clean, you know. And you're liable to end up deaf if you don't dig the dirt out of those ears. There's enough in there to plant sweet potatoes."

"I can hear all right, ma'am. I hear you fine."

"Well, you won't for long, if you don't clean your ears out good. What you need is a bath."

"I know," he said, ducking his head. "But I ain't got no clean clothes." Then he headed straight for the cookie jar concealed behind her pattern books as if he had been dipping into it all his life.

"Help yourself," she said drily. But she was wondering if she had been too rough on him.

She was sure she was right when he withdrew an empty hand and said, "No thanks, ma'am. I ain't hungry."

"Who takes care of you, now that your mother's gone?" she asked more gently.

"Nobody. I takes care of myself," he said proudly. He even seemed to grow a couple of inches as he said it.

"Don't you have a father?"

"Oh, yes ma'am. But after my Mom died, he was so sad he started drinking, and pretty soon they laid him off his job. He has lots of big plans about goin' in business for hisself, but he just lays around the house drunk most of the time."

Miss Lena shuddered. Some people should not be allowed to have children. Most people, in fact. If Miss Lena had her way about it, the government would test everybody to see if they were right in the head, and sterilize all the unfortunate, irresponsible ones.

"He say he gonna have his own store, a big store," he volunteered. "I don't believe him though. He don't never stay sober enough to run no store."

"Well," she said, trying to find *something* hopeful to say to this boy, "at least you have a home. Where?"

"On Mole Street. It's kind of an alley between Ninth and Tenth."

"I know where it is," she said, and didn't ask for any more details. She had wandered through Mole Street once by mistake, thinking to take a short cut to the fabric stores. Once had been enough. She would never go back to that narrow street of abandoned cars and condemned, boarded-up houses where there were more rats than people, who indeed lived in there like moles, hiding from the daylight and the law.

"What does your father call you?" she asked next.

"He don't call me nothin'. Told you he's 'sleep most of the time. When he wakes up he's subject to be mad. Then he calls me Boy."

"I mean, what's your name?" she said impatiently.

"B.J."

"That's all?"

"Yes ma'am."

"You mean it doesn't *stand* for anything?"

The wrinkles in his forehead became trenches. "Let me see can I remember. I think my mother said she named me for a sign that was the first thing she saw when she woke up in the hospital and looked out the window."

"And what did the sign say?"

"I think it said 'Bond Jewelers'."

Miss Lena sighed at the hopelessness of it all. What hope could there be for people who had so many babies they ran out of names and had to resort to initials? "I'll just call you 'B.J.', then, like everybody else."

"Ma'am, could I ask you a favor?"

Miss Lena stiffened herself to refuse what was surely coming next. In her experience, "a favor" always meant "Will you lend me some money?" And, to the folks who asked, a loan always meant a gift. Schooled hard and early in the art of survival, she had learned its main lesson well. Never grant favors, not even to your closest relatives. *Especially* not to them. They always thought you owed it to them anyway.

But instead B.J. held out his morning's earnings and said, "Will you bank my money for me?"

She stared, unable to speak.

"I mean, will you keep it for me till I need it? See,

there's lots of big tough kids around here, and I don't want none of them taking it off me. Besides, I got holes in both my pockets." He pulled two deplorably torn pouches from his pants. "See?"

Miss Lena almost cried. Almost, but not quite. With all the force of her considerable will, she practically sucked the tears back into her eye sockets.

"Of course I will," she said.

"I makes lots of money, doing work and running errands for people," he said proudly. "Not just Foot-Long. *Lots* of people around here."

"That window-washing job was worth at least a quarter," Miss Lena said.

First he dropped his lashes in that shy way that was so appealing. Then he raised them and gave her a steady, defiant stare. "Miss Sylvie at the hardware store always gives me fifty cents to wash *her* window."

"Don't get greedy with me, you tricky devil. Miss Sylvie is Miss Sylvie, and I am Miss Lena. She is who she is, and I am who I am. Understand?"

"Yes ma'am."

"Besides, I didn't ask you to do it, so I don't *have* to pay you anything."

She peered in her handbag and found an empty coin purse. "Put your money in here." After he did, she let him suffer several seconds of suspense before she added a quarter of her own.

"This will have to be your bank till I can get you a real one. A glass one, so you can always see exactly how much you have."

"You don't have to do that. I trust you, Miss Lena," he said.

"Why? You shouldn't trust anybody. *I* don't." She was immediately sorry for having answered him so harshly.

It was the nicest thing anyone had said to her in years.

"You might as well take off your pants now," she said in the same gruff tone, "so I can mend those torn pockets."

"Uh, ma'am," he said, "my underwear ain't so clean."

"I didn't expect it to be."

"What I mean is, I ain't got *on* no underwear."

"You think I never saw a little boy with no clothes on before?"

"To tell the truth ma'am, no."

"And why not?"

" 'Cause you ain't got no husband or children."

I will *not* let him make me mad, Miss Lena resolved. No one is going to stir up my blood pressure today, especially not no child. But, come to think of it, he was not really such a *little* boy, except in height. He was a teen-ager. Miss Lena grabbed the nearest thing at hand, a two-yard length of flowered silk, and tied it sarong-style around his waist.

"For your information," she said, "I could have had all the children I wanted. I did have a husband once. I saw all of him I wanted to see, until I got tired of looking. And before that, I had four little brothers which I helped raise. So I don't think you can show me anything I haven't seen before." Miss Lena paused. For breath, and to wonder why she was telling all her business, things no one else knew about her, to this strange boy. She had better stop that right now. "But you can keep that wrap on anyway, and take your pants off underneath."

"What happened to your husband?"

"He died," she said to cut off all further discussion. For all she knew it was true. James Ricks was dead as far as she was concerned, anyway. She could not have survived the last twenty years without killing him off in her mind.

The pants needed disinfecting. So did B.J., probably. As well as, now, that ten-dollar length of silk. Nevertheless, Miss Lena machine-darned the pockets as carefully as if she were altering Miss Van Wyck's bridal gown.

B.J., meanwhile, was fingering the emerald robe. "This for the fat lady, ain't it? The preacher's wife."

"Don't touch that!" she cried.

"But," he whimpered, "you *know* I just washed my hands."

Seeing drops of moisture on his lashes, she softened her voice and lied, "I just meant because it's not finished yet. I only put it together with basting. It might fall apart."

"What's basting?"

"Big loose stitches you put in by hand, so they're easy to pull out later."

"I thought so," he said. "But why would anybody *want* to pull them out?"

"In case the dress doesn't fit exactly right when the lady tries it on, and I have to take it in."

"That lady don't need you to take nothing in. She needs you to leave plenty room in her clothes to let them *out.* She gets bigger every week."

"I know," Miss Lena said, and giggled. He laughed too. The way laughter brightened his old, sad face made her relax. She let the bars down again.

"B.J.," she confided, "you know what I call her sometimes? 'The Hippo'."

"I know why. She looks like one of them big slick things what floats around in the water. Bet she got a bathtub home big as that pond they live in at the zoo."

Miss Lena laughed so hard that time, first picturing

the Hippo getting stuck in an ordinary-sized bathtub, then doing a slow stately paddle around a giant one, that she began to cough.

B.J. slapped her on the back till the coughing stopped, then said, "And her husband, the preacher, *he* looks like a alligator. Always grinning, and he got about a hundred teeth."

Miss Lena regained her composure and her primness at the same time. "B.J., it's not nice to talk about people's looks."

"Why not? It's fun. Besides, if I was rich as him I'd grin all the time too. I'd buy *extra* teeth from the dentist so I could grin all around my face, even in the back of my head. And I'd eat so much I'd be *twice* as big as her. I'd have pork chops for breakfast and a quart of ice cream three times a day. I'd get so big I couldn't even walk through your front door. I'd have to come in through the cellar."

Miss Lena had been doubled over her machine in another fit of laughter, but she straightened suddenly. "How come you know so much about my cellar?"

"I was just down there," he answered quickly. Too quickly. And changed the subject even more quickly. "How come you don't have no children?"

"How come you don't know why?" she parried. "You seem to know all my other business."

"I didn't mean to be newsy, Miss Lena. Don't get mad. I'm just out here all the time, watching who comes and goes. I knew this dress had to be for the preacher's wife, 'cause she's the only lady who comes here what's big enough to wear it. You ain't mad, are you?"

"No," she said, cutting the threads on his trousers.

"I keep an eye on your place all the time."

She was keeping an eye on him. "Why?"

"I watch lots of people's places around here, so they won't get robbed or nothing. Most times they pay me to do it."

Miss Lena waited silently, refusing to react to the hint. It suggested a threat, echoing the shouts of other street kids: "Watch your car, Mister?" Miss Lena knew about the car-watchers, a midget Mafia. If not paid in advance, they would slash tires, scar paint, steal hubcaps or even an entire car.

"I watch this place for you 'cause I know you been robbed twice already. But it ain't happened since *I* been around. Not since May."

"Do you know who robbed me in May, B.J.?"

"Yeah," he admitted, and dropped his eyes.

An abyss of doubt opened in front of Miss Lena's feet. What were B.J.'s real motives for hanging around her shop? To earn quarters and dimes? Or to case it for a gang of thieves, perhaps the same thieves, and set her up for a third robbery? A small, handicapped kid would be the ideal choice for such an assignment. He could easily gain her sympathy and entry into her shop. Miss Lena wished she had not been so gullible.

"Why didn't you tell the police?"

" 'Cause," he said, "them guys got arrested that same day for robbing somebody else. They still in jail right now. You don't have to worry about *them* for a long time, Miss Lena."

Miss Lena sighed. Was he lying, and if so, how much, and why? But all she said was, "Here are your pants."

While he was trapped, stepping into the stinking, wrinkled things and carefully untying the silk sarong, she made her move.

"Now I want to ask *you* something. How come you

have time to run errands, and watch people's stores, and be out on the street all day? Why aren't you in school?"

"They put me out last term. Said they couldn't teach me nothing more. Said I was a retard."

The answer had come as quickly and directly and convincingly as all the others. But Miss Lena wondered about it. Truly, she wondered about it more than all the other puzzling questions put together. She didn't know anything about I.Q. tests or whatever else teachers judged children's brains by. And she wasn't sure she knew anything about this boy B.J., either. Except one thing. He was smart, smart enough to run circles around most grown people.

Including Miss Lena Ricks, if she wasn't much more careful in the future.

Three

Miss Lena loved her apartment. But she had only lived there eight months. Before that there had been the long, lean winter when she first quit her garment-factory job and opened her shop, and could not afford to live anywhere but in its basement. Fortunately the building had housed a church before, and the congregation had left a complete kitchen and bath down there. Miss Lena had only had to add a cot. It was dark in the cellar, but warm and cozy, except when it rained or snowed. Then it was damp, with a chill that seemed to penetrate her bones. That had been a wet winter. So Miss Lena had kept a cold until spring came, bringing customers and money along with sunshine and better health.

Before that there had been a series of rooms in the houses of difficult landladies who would not permit her to cook, or do laundry, or make phone calls, or open her windows for fresh air. Rather than go back to another of those rooms, Miss Lena stayed on in her basement another three years and saved her money, using it first to fix up her shop, then to furnish the apartment she had dreamed of all her life.

She still could not quite believe it was hers. As if she expected an evil genie to turn her four lovely rooms into a small, dark cave while she was away, she always took a little tour as soon as she got home, patting velvet cushions, smiling at vases and pictures, until she felt reassured. Her tour would end at the modern kitchen, where she would take a piece of meat from the freezer to thaw for her supper. Then she would carefully hang up her clothes, slip into a pretty hostess gown (no sloppy housedresses for Miss Lena), and read her mail and the evening paper until she began to feel hungry.

But today she neglected her routine. The only thing in her mailbox had been a letter from her brother Lester. It could wait, along with the newspaper. Nor did she pay any attention to her clothes or her surroundings. She just dropped her gloves and coat on a chair, pulled off her boots, and sank into another chair. She had to think, to try to make sense out of her crazy day. But the more she tried to piece its events together into a sensible pattern, the more they refused to fit together, and remained a puzzle.

Who was B.J., anyway? How had he found her and his way into her shop? More important, *why?*

And how did he know so much about Miss Lena—her schedule, her habits, her tastes, even her thoughts? Unless B.J. was psychic, which she doubted, he had been studying her every move for months. He was up to something—but what?

She would rather not think about B.J. and his strange fund of knowledge. Usually Miss Lena was very good at not thinking about things. But she loved her privacy even more than her apartment, and it made her uneasy to discover that a complete stranger knew almost everything about her. It was like learning that these solid-looking walls were really glass, allowing all her neighbors to observe her when she thought she was alone. Perhaps that was why B.J.'s old-young face with its pointed chin and sad expression kept floating in front of her eyes, and why his clever tricks kept teasing her mind to come up with explanations.

For instance, Miss Lena had never mentioned the time of Mrs. Johnson's appointment. Then how had B.J. known to leave exactly five minutes before the Hippo arrived? His misshapen form had disappeared around the corner just as her long black Lincoln Continental eased up to the curb.

And five minutes after Mrs. Johnson had departed, delighted with her gown and planning to tell all her friends and church members who had made it, B.J. came limping back with Miss Lena's lunch. Lean corned beef with all the fat trimmed off, on dark diet bread, and some more of Foot-Long's good strong coffee.

Miss Lena could tell by the crisp pickle that the sandwich had come from the good delicatessen, Harry's. Not from Max's, where the pickles were soggy and the prices too high.

Since B.J. had known exactly what she liked for lunch and where to get it, she almost assumed that he had pulled off another miracle like this morning's. But she asked anyway, "How much do I owe Harry?"

B.J. surprised her by answering, "Eighty-five cents. But you can pay him tomorrow. I told him it was for you, and he said he'd trust you."

"Pay him *now,*" she'd said, and reached for her purse. "I never ask people to trust me."

"You don't have to, Miss Lena," he said, his wise old eyes opening wide until they were young and innocent. It was disturbing, the way he kept changing from old man to young boy and back again.

Miss Lena chose to think he was talking about her good financial rating. "That's because I always pay people right away," she said. "You do the same. Credit has a way of catching up to you and running past you till you can't catch *it.*" She held out a dollar. "Now take

Harry this, and get yourself something with the change. No, wait a minute." No wonder he didn't grow. The Lord knew a boy couldn't get a meal to grow on for fifteen cents. She dug out another dollar. "Get yourself a good sandwich."

As before, pride straightened his spine and made him grow taller before her startled eyes. "I have my own money," he said, and showed her a quarter. "I made this running errands today. Plus, I have forty cents in my bank."

"That's right, you do."

"What's a good sandwich I can get for sixty-five cents?"

"You also have," she reminded him, "the fifteen cents change I said you could keep."

"That's *eighty* cents. Man!" So much wealth made his eyes brighten. Then they darkened and became serious. "I don't want to spend it all, though. I want to spend fifty cents and bank thirty."

She approved of his thrift. "Good. You can get an American cheese sandwich for thirty cents, and a carton of milk for twenty."

"I think I'd rather have baloney and a grape drink."

The cheap, insubstantial tastes of the ghetto were already a part of him. Still, if Miss Lena had shed the craving for spongy cakes and Kool-Aid, so could he. She explained firmly, "There's no nourishment in baloney. It's mostly junk, not meat. And grape drink is just flavored water. Cheese and milk are much better for you."

Scowling, he considered this information, then decided to accept it. "I'll get cheese and milk, then. Even though I don't like 'em. I have to grow up big and strong."

Yes, poor baby, you do, she thought. It's rough out

here for all us black folks, but the small, weak ones like you have even less of a chance. But then, B.J. already knew that. He also knew how to add, she observed—and in his head, too, not on paper—and wondered again about that teacher.

Wondered, too, whether anything less than a miracle could make B.J. grow into a big, strong man. Miss Lena had more faith in calcium and protein than in miracles, though. Let others rely on the healing waters of Lourdes or the laying-on of preachers' hands; she would advise B.J. on how to eat properly and see whether it would do any good.

After they ate lunch together, B.J. did his magic vanishing act again, ten minutes before Mrs. Weinberg's appointment, giving Miss Lena time to sweeten her shop with air freshener. Not that Mrs. Weinberg deserved special preparations. She was a fool. What else would buy English tweed here, at three times what it cost over there, and have it made up here into a suit to wear on a Thanksgiving trip to London, where tweed suits were as plentiful as plastic raincoats and almost as cheap?

Miss Lena did not enlighten Mrs. Weinberg, though. There were too many advantages in letting her remain ignorant. Keeping her as a customer, for one thing. For another, Miss Lena intended to give Mrs. Weinberg a book of swatches before she left, and ask her to bring back a luscious supply of British and Irish woolens from the duty-free shops. She would pay for them, of course—exactly what they had cost Mrs. Weinberg. Miss Lena often made such arrangements with her traveling customers. This saved her both the expense of going on foreign buying trips and the high cost of paying for imported goods in American stores. Often, the unsuspecting customer would fall in love with one piece and ask to have it made up for her as a special favor. Miss Lena always granted the favor, but very reluctantly, until the customer agreed to pay a high price for it. Oh, it paid all around not to tell the Mrs. Weinbergs of this world about their foolishness.

Instead, though that was not wise, either, she told B.J., who knocked at her door and was admitted exactly five minutes after Mrs. Weinberg left. She hadn't expected him to understand. Only to listen.

But he had done both. "Stands to reason," he said, "if you buy something where it comes from, it's cheaper. 'Cause they have to pay the boat to bring it all the way 'cross the ocean, and you have to pay for *that* along with the cloth."

"That's right, B.J."

"Like the time my Aunt Bessie sent us a big basket of oranges from Florida. We couldn't afford to buy oranges in the stores up here, but they didn't cost her nothing. Oranges *grow* in Florida."

After learning that B.J. hadn't had an orange in the year since his Aunt Bessie's death, Miss Lena advised him to look for the Reduced-for-Quick-Sale counters in the big food stores. "They usually have plenty of fruit there that isn't spoiled yet, just soft or a little bruised, and it's very cheap. You ought to have a piece of fresh fruit every day, for the vitamins." She had also said to herself, I will go and talk to his teacher tomorrow.

"I will not," she said now, firmly and very loud. "I am not his mother or anyone else's. Not by chance but by *choice.*

"And why," she continued in a self-scolding tone, "were you babbling your trade secrets to that tricky child? Things you've never told anyone. *He* might tell the whole world. Is it old-age softening of the brain? Old-maid loneliness? What?"

Since Miss Lena knew she was not really suffering from either, she smiled and felt better. And, though she still did not know how B.J. had gotten inside her shop to clean it that morning, and nothing else that had happened today made any more sense than it had when she first sat down to think about it, she had at least reached a decision. And that allowed her, finally, to get up and begin her normal routine.

For the first time since she'd come home, she paid attention to her surroundings. She looked around her modern living room, which was all white with touches of hot pink and orange, and saw that everything was where it belonged. Then she inspected the frilly white bedroom, the pretty blue dining room, and the cheerful red and white kitchen with its shining appliances. Everything was in order. Miss Lena took a small, choice steak from the freezer and went back to the living room for her clothes.

She hung her dress up to air, put her boots in the closet, and set a bath running. There had been a damp chill in the air today. Best get good and warm in a hot tub *now* instead of waiting till bedtime. Miss Lena took very good care of herself. As she said to everyone, "If *I* don't, who will?"

There had been someone once, so long ago that B.J. was the only person in her life now who knew Miss Lena was not really a Miss. But James Ricks had not taken care, not at all, so she had put him out of her mind along with all other unpleasant things.

Age, for instance. Growing older was one of the unpleasant things Miss Lena refused to think about. Bathed, dried, and dressed in a long Empire-waisted robe of pale blue crepe, the small person in her mirror looked a shade over thirty. Possibly thirty-five.

At fifty-four, Miss Lena had pure black hair without a strand of gray, clear brown skin without wrinkles, and a perfect size 7 figure. Also, if you counted the caps put on by the dentist, all her own pretty teeth.

Miss Lena believed she stayed so young-looking because growing old was one of the subjects she never allowed to enter her mind. People who thought old became old, was her theory. Miss Lena ignored age the way she ignored most unpleasant things, such as the war, and bad weather, and taxes, and other people's misery. Those things were always around, and since there was nothing she could do about them, there was no point in her thinking about them.

She set her brother Lester's letter aside and picked up the newspaper. She always read it from back to front: first the comics, then the amusement section, then the television listings and the women's page. She read her horoscope, too, but only took it seriously if it was favorable. Last she riffled through all the pages to glance at the ads and see what styles were being featured by the department stores. As soon as she saw an unpleasant headline—tonight, something about the robbery and murder of a woman who lived alone—she put the paper away, as she always did.

Miss Lena had her steak broiled with all the fat removed, boiled carrots glazed with honey, and a green salad with lemon juice and herb dressing. With her dinner she drank a cup of tea sweetened with honey instead of sugar. No fattening bread or butter. No cigarettes. Miss Lena did not smoke. Nor did she drink anything except a very good wine, now and then, with a very good dinner.

Above all, she did not worry. Worry, Miss Lena knew, was harder on a person's health than all the other vices put together.

That was why she could not let herself get too interested in B.J. A child like that was sure to be a source of worry.

It was also why she was not looking forward to reading her brother Lester's letter. She already knew what it contained before she opened it: a long list of troubles, ending with a request for money.

My sorry relatives attract hard luck the way molasses attracts flies, Miss Lena thought. But she did not believe it was really a matter of luck, but of the way they chose to live: recklessly, foolishly, without planning or common sense, as if the Lord would always provide and tomorrow would never come. That was why she had decided to leave them strictly alone, with their bad debts, and their bad habits, and their bad health, and their hordes of needy children. She could not save them all; she could only save herself.

Miss Lena had seen too many unfortunate examples of people who had lost everything by trying to do the opposite. Junior Harris, for instance, whose small grocery store was supporting him nicely until his sisters moved in with their children and began eating up more stock than he sold from his shelves. Nell Jones, who lost her restaurant when her nephew began helping himself to both the profits and the food. And Bessie Gumby, whose paid-for house was sold for unpaid taxes after her relatives moved in and forced her paying guests out.

Miss Lena had eight brothers and sisters and forty-one nephews and nieces, all living in a constant state of emergency. But her shop could not support fifty people; it could only take care of one. Her business was like a small, buoyant raft floating her along on the surface of the deep, dangerous waters of life. It supported her very nicely now, but it was a one-woman raft, and she would drown if she took on any passengers. Even *thinking* about her family's troubles would be the first step to suicide. Miss Lena turned the TV dials instead.

But the program that had sounded, in the TV listings, like a pleasant foreign love story, turned out to be a gruesome tale of spies and murder, and the other shows were even worse: a war movie, a panel discussion about drug addicts, and a film about starving black people in Alabama. Why couldn't they give people something cheerful to look at on at least *one* channel? Miss Lena sighed and opened the letter.

Sister,
I sure hope you can do me a little favor. I got a misery in my back again & can't work, so am behind on the mortgage pay't, also the heat & light bills. Plus Little Sister and Reggie both had to have their tonsils out and the Dr. wants his money. Otherwise all are well. Sugar is expecting again (Hope a boy this time) & sends love. If you will just send us Three Hundred Dollars ($300.00) we can get straight and will pay you back by Xmas.
Yr. devoted brother,
Lester

Miss Lena could feel her blood pressure rising. Anger tightened her head like a hot water bottle filled to bursting. Since when was three hundred dollars a small favor? And what about the even larger "favor" she had granted Lester five years ago, without ever getting a penny back? He hadn't mentioned it in his letter. Nor, come to think of it, had he inquired about her health. He had only told her about *his*. Devoted brother, indeed. Miss Lena remembered the dark, lonely winter of her own hardship, when she had written to Lester for help. He had not even bothered to answer. Well, she had lived through it somehow, fighting off pneumonia on tea and crackers and determination. Let Lester and his wife and their seven (soon to be eight) kids do the same.

Fat chance she had of getting her money back by Christmas, anyway, with him out of work and all those children expecting presents. Had the nerve to be hoping for another boy. What did he want, a basketball team? *May your tribe increase.* Maybe it was a blessing to those white folks back in Bible times, but to Miss Lena, it sounded like a curse. She did not believe the Lord must love poor black folks because he kept making so many of them. Quite the opposite. She tore up the letter and tried to compose herself for sleep.

Her mattress was Super Firm Foam, good for the back. Miss Lena had a very straight back, and she always slept on it without a pillow. Sleeping on your face on a pillow caused wrinkles. Kneeling on her fluffy white rug, she said her prayers:

"Lord, please help Lester with his troubles, 'cause You know I sure can't, and please help all my brothers and sisters to take care of the babies they have, and to stop having more babies they can't take care of, so they won't have to go on pestering me. Also please help me to stay self-supporting and independent and keep my self-respect, for which I thank You. And please look after B.J. Amen."

That last part was a surprise to Miss Lena. How had it crept into her prayer? She thought she had put B.J.

out of her mind four hours ago, and when Miss Lena put something out of her mind, it usually *stayed* out. But, thinking back, she realized that she had been wondering, while she enjoyed her steak, whether B.J. was eating a good dinner. That she was wondering, even now, whether he was warm and cozy tonight as she was beneath her down-filled quilt. And wondering, also, whether she still had that piece of tan gabardine that could be made into a new pair of pants for him.

"You'll do no such thing," she told herself aloud, very firmly. "He's a little crook. Walks crooked, talks crooked; how can his head be straight? Where's your sense? Don't let him in again."

But he, or someone, had already been inside her shop over the weekend. A light shudder of fear rippled her skin. *You've got to find out what his game is. Let him keep coming back till you do. But don't let him come too close.*

Four

After weeks spent figuratively biting her tongue, Miss Lena did so literally one morning. All morning she had been thinking about how quickly B.J. had become her customers' pet, and blaming herself for not getting rid of him. The thought made her so angry she bit right into her tongue while biting off a piece of thread.

Miss Allinson, a December bride in more ways than one who was so unsure of her taste she needed B.J.'s approval of every stitch in her trousseau, had started it. Though she was the first to spoil B.J., the other ladies quickly fell into line. If he was not there, they'd ask disappointedly, "Where's B.J.?" Then they would usually hand Miss Lena some money and say, "Give him this for me." Sometimes they would also bring pieces of candy or homemade cake, and some of the more ignorant ladies would ask, "Where's your son?"

Miss Lena's response never varied. She always replied, "You mean B.J.?" without correcting them, then placed their contributions in his mayonnaise jar without comment. Outwardly she remained cool, but inside she was boiling with resentment.

Her pride stung more than her mouth did now that B.J. was the star attraction of her salon. Her customers no longer came to her for clever designing, precise tailoring, or elegant little touches like bound buttonholes and these hemstitches, so small you'd need a microscope to see them. No, they came for B.J.'s brash charm. She might as well put their hems in with a staple gun now, she thought bitterly, for all they'd care. Pride was the only thing that kept her turning out work that was up to her usual standard. She told herself for the thousandth time that it was silly to be jealous of a child, so jealous she had injured herself.

But the situation was serious. If she got rid of B.J., the business she had built up all by herself might fall off to nothing. If she kept him around, the same thing might happen, unless he learned to restrain his bold tongue. Sooner or later his fresh mouth would get them both in trouble. It had happened once already.

Except for that one time, however, B.J. had been able to get away with saying things to Miss Lena's customers that she would never dare say to them. They'd gone away loving it and come back for more.

Take last Friday, for instance. B.J. had asked Mrs. Roderick Lewis, a starched old dame whose family owned half the city, "Why you got blue hair? Was you born with it? It looks funny. I ain't never seen nobody with blue hair before." Instead of scolding him, Mrs. Lewis had thanked him and announced that she planned to scold her hairdresser instead.

Later that day, after Mrs. Reverend Johnson had invited him to her church, he asked her, "You got any daughters?"

"Listen to the little man," Mrs. Johnson said with a snicker. "Hardly hatched, and already he wants to scratch around the hen-house. Yes, I have a daughter, but she's a little old for you. She's eighteen. But there are dozens of lovely younger girls at our church."

"I don't wanna meet no girls," B.J. declared with all the distaste of someone who had been invited to become intimate with a nest of snakes. "I just wanna know, is your daughter big like you?"

"B.J.!" Miss Lena had screamed.

"It's all right, Lena," Mrs. Johnson said graciously. "I guess I oughta know what I look like by now, and if I don't, shame on me. She's big this way," she said, touching the top of her head, then moving her hands to her waist, "but not *this* way, thank God. At least, not yet. So far she doesn't take after me in weight. Only in height."

"That's good," said B.J. " 'Cause what I was gonna say was, why don't you give her that fur coat? It's such a *fat* fur. It's for a skinny lady."

While Miss Lena silently tried to convince herself she was not having a heart attack, Mrs. Johnson hefted the mass of horizontally worked opossum she'd arrived in. After studying it, she said, "You know, Lena, he's right. Can you cut this down for Monica?"

"He's only a child, Mrs. Johnson. Please try to forgive—"

The Hippo cut her off. "Nothing to forgive, Lena. He's right. I'm sick and tired of it anyhow. I'll just tell Henry he's giving me a broadtail for Christmas."

"What's a broadtail?" B.J. asked.

"It's a *flat* fur. For fat ladies," Mrs. Johnson said with a wink. "Now you can come to our church this Sunday, you hear? Tabernacle Baptist. Lena, you bring him. Maybe he can sing in our Junior Choir."

"I can't sing. My voice is changing," B.J. croaked convincingly.

"Well, you can pray, can't you?"

And you'll need to, Miss Lena thought after the next lady's visit. For both of us.

Dr. Dorothy Wells Norman was one of the city's haughtiest black ladies, not a salt-of-the-earth sister like Mrs. Reverend Johnson. Mrs. Johnson had never forgotten her humble past on a North Carolina farm. Dr. Norman never let anyone forget her proud present. She had a five-figure salary about which she was always boasting, and a five-by-five figure about which she was forever complaining. She was always, vainly, on a diet. To hear her tell it, she never touched anything but filets mignons and green salads. But Miss Lena suspected her of midnight refrigerator raids from which she emerged, reeling, with glazed eyes and a greasy mouth. She pretended to believe in the diet, though, and never echoed Dr. Norman's complaints about her figure. Her role, she knew, was to contradict them.

"It's too tight," Dr. Norman complained as Miss Lena tried to zip her into a new wool challis print. "I don't know what I'm going to do, Lena. I starve myself constantly, but I can't even wear an 18½ any more."

"This pattern tends to run small," Miss Lena lied discreetly. "I'll just ease the side seams and lower the armholes. It won't take long. You just relax for a few minutes." She dropped one of her sky-blue smocks over Dr. Norman's head so her customer could undress modestly.

"Well, I could use a break, Lena," Dr. Norman admitted. "I'm starved. This diet is killing me. Do you mind if I eat my lunch?"

"Go right ahead," said Miss Lena, ripping and snipping with an averted head. B.J., meanwhile, was staring straight at the roly-poly lady as she whipped out her sandwich.

"I brought a lobster sandwich, Lena," Dr. Norman said.

"My, that sounds like a real treat."

"Well, it's expensive, but it's non-fattening. Seafood is pure protein."

"You got mayonnaise on it, though," observed B.J., whose bright eyes never missed anything except Miss Lena's stare, which was on him now like a searchlight.

"Well, of course," Dr. Norman said. "No one eats dry lobster. If it's hot, it's served with melted butter or a cream sauce. And cold lobster is eaten with mayonnaise. That's pronounced *'myonnaise'*, little boy. 'Lobster myonnaise.' "

"Maybe I don't know how people say it, but I do know it's fattening. Ain't that right, Miss Lena?"

"Mind your business, B.J.," Miss Lena ordered.

"Well, am I right or not?"

"I *said,* mind your business."

"Well, *she* said she wanted to lose weight," he muttered. "Mayonnaise ain't nothin' but grease, no matter what you call it. Grease makes people fat. I know *that* much."

Dr. Norman stopped eating. She squeezed her sandwich, pushing out gobs of mayonnaise in all directions like toothpaste from a punctured tube. It was her turn to give B.J. a hard, brilliant, terrifying stare.

"Boy, come here and let me look at you. How old are you, anyhow?"

"Thirteen."

"Well, school is open today. What are you doing here?"

"Minyabusiness," he muttered defiantly, running the words together so she wouldn't understand.

But Dr. Norman had had too many years of experience with surly children not to understand. "School-age children *are* my business, young man. I think you'd better give me your name and address. When I leave here I'll be in touch with the truant officers."

B.J.'s diction suddenly became clear, and his tone

apologetic. "Uh, ma'am, excuse me, but it ain't my fault I'm not in school. They put me out."

"Is that so? Well, I have the authority to put you back in."

When wondering about B.J.'s school situation, Miss Lena had forgotten that she knew Dr. Norman. Here was an opportunity for him, if he had not hopelessly muffed it. She did her best to smooth things over. "Apologize to the lady, B.J. Then offer her some coffee to go with her sandwich."

He did both. After saying, "I'm sorry, ma'am," he did not utter another word to Dr. Norman. He served her, but there were no comments on how many heaping teaspoonsful of sugar she put in her coffee, or how liberally she helped herself to Miss Lena's non-diet cookies. Even after she was gone, he seemed afraid to talk.

"What that lady do?" he whispered. "She a teacher?"

"No. She used to be, I believe, but now she has a bigger job."

"Is she a principal?"

"No. She *bosses* principals. She's the superintendent of all the schools in this part of the city. In other words, B.J., she's nobody to mess with."

"Whooee," he more whistled than said. "I guess maybe I oughta find out who I'm talkin' to before I open my big mouth."

"Just what *I* was about to say," Miss Lena informed him. "I'm glad you figured it out for yourself. Dr. Norman is the kind of lady you have to treat with respect. You ought to show more respect for *all* my customers, B.J., but especially for her. Act like a gentleman, and she might do you a favor."

"What kind of favor?" she asked suspiciously.

"She can get you into the right school."

His face was closed. "I don't wanta go to school. I learn more from hangin' around you."

"Yes, but I don't have time to teach you all the things you need to know."

"Like what?"

"Like the difference between three yards of sixty-inch fabric and three yards of forty-five-inch."

Yesterday B.J. had gone to the store with a swatch, but without Mrs. Johnson's pattern, insisting that he didn't need it. After all, any fool could remember to ask for "three yards." But he had come back with a piece of crushed velvet far too skimpy to cover that expansive lady. No matter how Miss Lena turned the pattern pieces, she would never be able to get a dress for Mrs. Johnson out of the velvet, especially since the pile had to be matched perfectly. She was too meticulous to cut it the wrong way—her reputation depended on such details—but there was not even enough fabric to do it that way, not even enough for a tunic. At seven ninety-five a yard, it had been an expensive mistake.

Her point had hit home; there was no need to hammer it further. B.J.'s head dropped like a wilted weed. "I guess I ain't nothin' but trouble to you, Miss Lena."

"No, now, that isn't true, B.J. You've been a big help to me in lots of ways. I couldn't get over how easily you got hold of Mrs. Weinberg for me the other day. I wondered how you even knew she had an appointment at four o'clock."

"Shoot, that was easy," he said, pointing to the wall. "You write down all your appointments on your big calendar."

"Yes, but how did you find out her phone number?"

"You must think I'm *really* stupid. I looked it up in your phone book, of course."

"Well, I was impressed. Really, you amaze me constantly with how smart you are and how much you know."

"So why do I have to go to school?"

"I think I just pointed out to you that you still have a few things to learn."

B.J. developed a bad case of the "jaws", his cheeks puffed out like sails in a stiff wind. "Yeah, O.K., but why do I have to learn 'em in school?"

"Because that's where they're taught." Unconsciously Miss Lena had adopted the end-game tactic that was the last resort of all desperate parents: *"Because I say so."*

It ended the argument.

"Besides," she went on, now that B.J. was silenced, "I don't want Dr. Norman to lose weight yet."

"Why not?"

"If she gains five more pounds, she won't be able to wear any of her clothes. I'll have to make her a whole new closetful. And I *do* mean a closetful, because she has to look good every day."

" 'Cause she's a big shot."

"Right. And big shots don't keep clothes they can't wear; they give them to charity or throw them away. So next spring, when she starts thinking about bathing suits, I'll start talking to her about cottage cheese and low-cal sodas. *That's* when I want her to lose weight."

"So she'll need you to make her a whole bunch of new clothes all over again."

"Now you're getting smart, B.J.," Miss Lena said. "She goes up and down the scale like an opera singer. Her size changes every six months. You almost lost me my best customer."

B.J. was so subdued by shame after that, speaking

only when spoken to, and then only in monosyllables, while he swept and dusted and did other menial chores, that she began to feel sorry for him.

"How do you feel, B.J.?"

"O.K.," he said listlessly.

"I don't like that cough. A minute ago you sounded like you were going to spit up your insides."

"It's just the dust in here. It makes me sneeze," he said, and continued to push the mop.

"Then stop dusting and listen. You know you caught a cold the other day when you went out of here with your head wet. And you know I know it."

"Yes, ma'am."

After all their intimate chatter, that "ma'am" marked his retreat from closeness to a servant's distance. Or was he fencing off their generation gap? Whatever it meant, it disturbed Miss Lena even more than the cough. When he coughed again, she pressed forward.

"That could turn into pneumonia. You've done enough work today, B.J. What you need is rest. Rest and liquids. Did you have any orange juice today?"

"No ma'am. But I can get some at Foot-Long's."

An old, contradictory jealousy flared up; why was Foot-Long's greasy counter a more attractive place to eat lunch than her clean work room? "No," she said sharply. "That stuff he sells isn't real orange juice. It's just colored water. Get a quart of *real* orange juice at the market. Get some chicken noodle soup, too, and a jar of honey."

"What's the honey for?"

"Your cough. Later on I might run out and get a little whiskey, to make you a hot toddy."

B.J.'s eyes showed more white than usual. "Uh-*uh*, Miss Lena. I'm scared of whiskey."

"Why?"

"I don't want to get like my father. Once he starts drinkin' that stuff he can't stop. He's the main reason I bank my money with you. It ain't just the boys in the street who take money off me."

If she had been a man, Miss Lena would have removed her hat; if a Catholic, she would have crossed herself. Instead, like a witness to a fatal accident, she paused in silent awe. She had come to respect B.J. as a survivor with skills equal to hers, but now she realized that he was the master. At least she hadn't been forced to outwit her own parents in order to survive.

Of course, there *had* been the problem of getting to school. Her mother always wanted her to stay home and look after her younger brothers. Miss Lena's distaste for children probably dated from that time, when she had been forced to sneak out to school every morning and take a beating every afternoon when she got home.

It had all been worth it. At school, majoring in Home Economics and Business, she had learned the basics of her seamstress trade, as well as the dietary information she now passed on to B.J.

His evening meal should include green or yellow vegetables as well as meat. Brown bread was better than white. A piece of fresh fruit every day was important, and better than sugary sweets. The Muslim restaurant was better than Foot-Long's, but both were preferable to Bubba's Bar-B-Q and the Chili Bowl, which had dirty kitchens. Go to church often, there's always food there, good home-cooked food cheap. Even free, if you picked out the kindest woman (usually the fattest one) and told her you were broke and hungry. (Miss Lena knew, from hard experience.)

B.J. had soaked it all up raptly and followed her instructions, always feeding himself with his own money, carefully budgeted from his bank. Really, he was a good pupil, and had the makings of a fine, upstanding young man. If only she could teach him to zipper his lip!

Miss Allinson had come in that afternoon, wanting a dusty pink negligee for her trousseau. B.J., reeking of camphor, pillowed like a pasha and sipping hot tea with honey and lemon, had told her the color made him think of musty-smelling old ladies' underwear. That no one wore that color who hadn't been on Social Security for at least ten years.

"Now, you see, B.J.," she said to the air, as she'd done all weekend, "you have to stop being so frank. Ladies don't always like to be told what does not become them. You've got to learn diplomacy. What does that mean? It means finesse. It means tact. It means telling people things they want to hear—or, if you have to tell them something they don't like, telling it in a way that *makes* them like it."

"Yes," she could hear him answer, "but Miss Allinson didn't mind." True enough. She'd taken it as a compliment; he was right, she was "too young" for dusty pink lingerie.

"How 'bout light green?"

"Oh, *thank* you, B.J.!" On her wedding night she would wear the color of spring's first delicate shoots and buds.

"Yes," Miss Lena replied aloud to his imaginary rebuttal, "but Dr. Norman minded, and others will too. Your fresh talk has got to stop right now, B.J. Otherwise I'll have to put you out of here."

The sound of her own voice startled Miss Lena into some unpleasant realizations. She had been talking to herself again, and her latest threat to evict B.J. was as empty as all the others she had uttered. She had allowed him to keep hanging around until he had become a fixture in the shop and in her life.

What was worse, she had arrived at her shop an hour ahead of time because she had a million things to do, and none of the million things, which were really only eight, had been done. All she had done was make a list of them:

> *(1) Buy separating zipper for Miss Allinson's mink lining; (2) Buy interfacing for Mrs. Weinberg's suit jacket; (3) Find pattern to make Mrs. Johnson look good in church; (4) Finish Miss Allinson's coat to be picked up at two; (5) Cut and stitch muslin patterns for Mrs. Cosgrove's cruise clothes; (6) Cut and stitch muslin pattern for Mrs. Weinberg's suit; (7) Be ready for Mrs. Cosgrove's first fitting at four; and (8) Finish and press Mrs. Lewis's suit.*

When Miss Lena looked at her watch, she couldn't believe she had wasted two hours after writing the list. She tapped her pencil on it. Why couldn't she get started? What was she waiting for?

Coffee, that was it. It was time for coffee. She wasn't wide awake yet. Coffee would get her moving.

"And what makes you think," she said out loud, "that your coffee is going to get here all by itself? *Fool!* You have to go out and get it. *After* you get those other things!"

Miss Lena put the list in her purse and snapped its gold clasp shut angrily. Then she stamped out of her shop and headed toward Ninth Street, the heel plates on her boots striking the sidewalk like hammers. She had turned the corner and gone two blocks north before it occurred to her that she had forgotten to lock her front door. Was it safe to leave it unlocked until she got back?

"Of course not, fool!" she said aloud, causing several heads to turn in her direction. Miss Lena pivoted away from them on one heel and hurried south again. If she didn't stop talking to herself out loud they'd send the men in white coats for her. And maybe they needed to, soft as her head was getting these days. Talking to herself was not so bad. All people who lived alone did it. (Who else was there to talk to?) But walking out and leaving her shop unlocked was *really* insane. Especially with Miss Allinson's mink lining still there, after her insurance agent had told her nobody would insure her again if she put in another robbery claim this year.

"Hurry back, fool! Lock those locks. Hurry out again. Get that zipper. And get right back and finish that coat, if you don't do another thing today. Once she's picked it up, it'll take the biggest load off your mind."

Yanking the door open, going in still talking, she collided with B.J. coming out. He fell backward and sideways down her cement steps and lay there on his back with one leg crumpled under him.

"Where have you been?" Miss Lena shouted in a tone that made it clear what she was really angry about, and who was the biggest load on her mind.

As she stood over him, her thoughts were like the old blues:

I sent for you yesterday,
Here you come today.

And B.J., like the song, had his mouth wide open and didn't know what to say.

Five

Miss Lena held out her hand. "Can you get up?"

Giving her most of his weight, B.J. got to his feet slowly and limped inside, still hanging onto her hand. When she let go of him, he slumped against a wall. He looked afraid. Of her, judging by the way he was avoiding her eyes.

But Miss Lena did not have time to waste on questions about B.J.'s fears. "You think you can get up to the two hundred block of North Ninth Street and back in half an hour?"

B.J. seemed to relax as he considered this. "Maybe. What you want?"

Miss Lena was still angry. "I don't want a maybe, I want a yes or a no."

"I don't know," he said, bending and gripping his right knee. "See, I fell on my worst leg. It won't hold me up so good no more."

Oh Lord. His face was always so wrinkled, she hadn't noticed the extra lines etched by pain. And, intent on her bossy demands, she'd failed to see the blood soaking through the ripped knee of his pants. But she spoke as crisply as ever. "Well, then, do you think you can make it back to my sewing chair?"

"I'll try," he said, wincing as he put weight on his right foot. With the help of a hand on her shoulder, he succeeded, though.

Miss Lena reached for her first-aid kit, then knelt in front of him and gently rolled up the pants leg.

"Don't cry," she said.

"I ain't," he answered.

"I wasn't talking to you!" she shouted, pouring peroxide over the wound. "I'm a crazy old lady who talks to herself."

B.J.'s eyes were squinched tight against the pain that never came. When he opened them, the peroxide was still bubbling. The cut was not deep. Just a large scrape over the scars of many other scrapes. It looked, she thought with relief, exactly like the knee of every other boy his age in the world.

"Why do you call yourself old, Miss Lena? You ain't old."

"Yes, I am. I'm an old fool." She rummaged around in her first-aid kit. Oh, why didn't she have any large Band-Aids? Because Miss Lena only took care of Miss Lena. And Miss Lena never suffered any injury but an occasional needle-prick or a finger-burn from touching a hot iron.

"You don't *look* old."

"That," she said fiercely, "is because I've never lived."

"What you mean?"

"Never mind," she said. "It's not a bad cut. It's stopped bleeding."

"It's stopped hurting, too," he said, and wriggled forward to get out of the chair.

"Stay still," she said sharply. "Let it dry."

"But I want to see can I walk. I want to go to the store for you."

Miss Lena had completely forgotten her all-important errands. "I don't know if I want you to go, now. Anyway, wait another minute. You need a bandage."

"Just wrap a clean rag around it," B.J. said practically.

"It'll be O.K. It ain't my knees, anyway. It's my hips."

"Your *what?*" she cried, looking up at him.

"*Now* you look old. Just like my Mom," B.J. said.

Oh, the horrible frankness of kids. Miss Lena didn't know why anybody in their right mind would have them. Worrying about them was what aged you, and then they had the nerve to turn around and tell you it showed. "What *about* your hips?" she asked, conscious that strain was still wrinkling her face.

"They wasn't connected right when I was born. I used to have to walk around on crutches. The doctor said I would need a whole lot of operations, one every year till I stopped growing. But my parents didn't have the money. So he said they could wait till I finished growing and get me *one* operation. But in the meantime I would have to be real careful not to make my hipbones come all the way loose. So, every time I fall, I get scared, until—"

"Until what?"

"Until I get up and start walking again."

Miss Lena understood his need to get rid of fear fast. It was like that time two years ago when she was having those weak spells and headaches from high blood pressure and was afraid she'd fall out on the street in a faint. She was even afraid to get out of bed most mornings. But she had to get up and go out, and keep going out every day, until she got over it.

"O.K.," she said, "I'll let you up in just a few seconds." Deciding to follow his sensible suggestion, she took the unbleached muslin she used for patterns and ripped off a long strip four inches wide.

B.J., meanwhile, had turned his head and was looking at the opened pattern book. "What was you looking for? A dress for the Hippo lady?"

"How'd you know?"

" 'Cause this is the fat lady section."

"Hold your leg still," she said, winding the muslin around his knee. She tied a double knot, clipped the ends with her scissors, and stood up.

"I found it for you," B.J. announced, pointing. "See?"

Looking over his shoulder, she saw, all right. In a few seconds he'd found the one design she'd overlooked in two hours of absentminded gazing. A simple two-piece dress with a V neckline, its vertical seams outlined in white piping. The book showed it in yellow, but Miss Lena would make it up in navy. And fill in that low neckline with an edging of white lace. It was practically guaranteed to make a size 46 look like an 18. Or at least a 20.

"B.J.," she said, "you have a very good eye."

"My leg ain't so bad, neither."

While she was bending over the book, he had slipped out of the chair. Now he was hobbling around the room.

Lightly, covering a wave of fear, she asked, "The backbone's still connected to the hipbone?"

"Yep," he said, moving about experimentally. "And the hipbone's connected to the—"

"Thighbone," she supplied with a clap of her hands.

"Thighbone's connected to the—"

"Knee bone," she sang. *"Now hear the word of the Lord."*

He was almost, but not quite, dancing. Hobbling and hopping, in time to her hymn singing, at more than his usual speed.

She applauded his performance, then warned, "That's enough, now. And don't let anybody but me see you dancing like that."

"Why not?"

"Because I have a plan in mind."

"What is it?"

"I can't tell you till I know for sure."

He had fallen on her front steps. Maybe, she was thinking, her insurance would pay for an operation. Maybe it would pay for a whole lot of operations, if that was what he needed. And maybe they wouldn't cancel her policy. At least it wouldn't be another *robbery* claim. It was risky, though. She would have to talk to her agent. And B.J. would have to go on acting as if his condition had been aggravated by the fall. She might have to let him in on her plan. But not yet.

"You'll just have to trust me, and do what I say. Take it easy. Don't go running around."

"I only got five years. That's why I have to bank all the money I can. I think I'll be finished growing by the time I'm eighteen. Don't you?"

"Are you reading my mind again?"

His eyes were as big and black and blank as two cups of coffee. "What you mean, Miss Lena?"

"Nothing," she said. "Never mind."

"And that's why I want to go to the store for you. To make money. Can I go now?"

"Yes, if you go in a taxi."

"I don't need no taxi," he said with a scowl. "*Told* you I can walk O.K. now."

"I need these things in a hurry."

"Oh."

"I want you to go to Katz's Sewitorium on Ninth Street. Ask for Sidney. Don't let anybody but Sidney wait on you. Tell him you want a heavy-duty separating zipper for a coat lining and two yards of canvas interfacing. And be sure to tell him it's for me."

"O.K.," he said, and stuffed her ten-dollar bill in his pocket.

"Don't you want me to write it down?"

"What for? Katz's on Ninth Street. Heavy-duty separating zipper for a coat lining. Two yards of canvas interfacing. Ask for Sidney. And tell him it's for you."

Miss Lena thought again, I don't know why that teacher thinks he's retarded. Maybe *she's* the retarded one. But all she said was "O.K., B.J., get going. Use any of the hack taxis on the corner. They'll take you up there and back for two dollars."

He looked at her sadly, shaking his head. "I sure got to school you, Miss Lena."

"About what?"

"Them hacks."

"What about them?" About a dozen unemployed black men used their cars to make a living supplying taxi service to the blacks in the neighborhood. It was illegal but necessary, since the white drivers of licensed taxis were seldom willing to pick up black passengers. Conveniently, the hack stand was on the corner of Ninth and Berkeley, a block away.

"First of all, the price is *one* dollar. If you want, you can tip a quarter, but you don't have to. Second thing, the only ones you should ride with are Pops and Nelson. Nelson is the evil one with the gold-rim dark glasses and the green Pontiac Le Mans. Pops is the skinny old guy with the black Eldorado."

Miss Lena seldom used taxis, but when she needed one in an emergency, she simply walked down to the corner and stepped into the first parked car she saw with a man at the wheel. Since she had never owned or driven a car, all makes and models looked alike to her, except for color. She could tell a blue car from a green one, but not a blue Pontiac from a blue Buick. For that matter, all men looked pretty much alike to Miss Lena, too. But she would listen carefully and learn to make distinctions. "Why them, B.J.?"

" 'Cause they won't get you killed. And if they do, they got insurance to pay for it."

Miss Lena stopped laughing at this comforting information when she noticed B.J.'s somber face. He looked like a mourner.

"It ain't funny," he said. "You gonna listen to me or not?"

She nodded respectfully.

"Nelson is mean, but he stays sober, and he takes care of his car. He got to. It belongs to his wife, and she's even meaner than he is. If he dents a fender she liable to put a bigger dent in his head. 'Sides, he's blind in one eye, so he *got* to drive careful, or the cops will find out and take his license."

Miss Lena was able to keep from laughing only because her horror outweighed her sense of humor. "How'd he lose the eye?"

"His wife threw lye on him after she caught him riding a chippie around in her car. Pops, now," B.J. continued, "he even *more* careful, 'cause he's over seventy, and if he has a wreck he got to give it up forever. He'd never get a license again or insurance either, unless they drive cars in Heaven.

"The rest of them guys done lost their licenses so many times, won't *nobody* give them insurance. Rabbit, the one with the red Corvette, he stays drunk. That's how come they call him Rabbit, 'cause his eyes are always pink. And bald-head Bob, he ain't got no brakes on that blue Bonneville. If he's goin' fast, only way he can stop is hit somebody. Specially since his tires is 'bout as bald as his head."

"Why doesn't he fix his car?" she wondered.

" 'Cause he ain't got the money," B.J. explained patiently, with the air of an adult instructing a child. "Ain't none of them dudes got enough money to fix their cars except Nelson and Pops, 'cause Nelson's wife has a good job and Pops has a pension. If you ride with anybody else, you liable to get smashed up. And if you do, you got to pay your own doctor bills."

Left with a choice between a one-eyed driver and one so old he was likely to drop dead behind the wheel, Miss Lena decided she would continue to rely on her seven-league boots without making any exceptions. "B.J.," she wondered, "is there *anything* you don't know?"

"I expect not, if it's about this neighborhood," he said, flashing an impish grin. It faded suddenly as he glanced at the street through her display window. "That's *one* thing I didn't know. I didn't know *she* was coming here today."

"Who?"

"Miss Marvel."

Miss Lena followed his eyes and saw the hip-swinging hostess of the Lorelei Lounge glide past her window. Sure enough, a knock followed.

"Listen, let me school you about her," B.J. said. "She's a stone deadbeat. Make her pay you in front. She owes everybody on this corner. Now I better get out of here." He ducked toward the basement door.

"Come back here," Miss Lena said. "The cellar door to the street is locked. How are you going to get out to go to the store?"

"I was—" He hesitated. "I was gonna hide down there till she left."

"Why?" she said. "I'm not ashamed of you."

B.J., looking down at himself, seemed unable to believe her. "But I look so *bad* with these torn-up pants on."

"We'll do something about that later," she promised,

contradicting all her firm resolve of the week before. "Right now I want you to stay up here. And go out like you came in. By the front door."

He shook his head uncomfortably. "No, Miss Lena. These pants looked bad enough before, but now they look *terrible.*"

Miss Lena finally took pity on his embarrassment and drew the green drapes. Then she walked calmly to the door to admit Miss Marvel Scott, whose knocking was becoming impatient.

Miss Marvel usually looked like a high-fashion model, and today was no exception. She wore purple and lime silk pajamas with a peek-a-boo hole cut out above the navel to reveal a circle of brown velvet skin, matching two-toned shoes, and at least a pound of sleek false hair piled atop her proud, pretty head.

Her voice was as soft and silky as her costume. "I was wondering," she said, "if I could get you to make something for me."

"That's what I'm here for," Miss Lena said pleasantly. "Come in."

Miss Marvel pulled a length of stiff gold brocade from a paper bag. Miss Lena did not care for it. Gaudy, she thought. But expensive.

"The problem is, I need it in a hurry. I'm going to a formal in New York Saturday night."

"A formal? That's nice," Miss Lena said.

"Yes, a very special friend has invited me to this big affair, and I want to look really nice, you understand? But I don't have a single formal. If you can make me a long dress out of this by Saturday, I'll run in town right now and get some gold shoes to go with it."

"I don't usually like to work in such a rush," Miss Lena said hesitantly. "But I suppose I *could* get it done for you if I used a very simple pattern. How about a mandarin dress?" She gestured at her throat to indicate a high collar. "The Chinese look is very in this year."

Miss Marvel frowned. "I don't usually wear high necklines."

Yes, I know, Miss Lena thought. You usually show as much of yourself as you can without getting arrested. But Miss Lena knew how to get around *that.* "Well, of course, there will be slits up the sides, for walking, and they can be as high as you want."

"Can I see the pattern, please?"

"Certainly." Miss Lena slipped between the drapes without opening them, and found B.J. cringing against a side wall like a mouse trying to find a hole into which to disappear. She smiled encouragingly, put a finger to her lips, and returned with a book.

"You see," she told Miss Marvel, "the Chinese look is very good for this stiff fabric. And they're wearing it a lot this year."

"How much do you charge?"

"Oh, for a dress like this, seventy-five dollars."

Marvel's large round eyes narrowed angrily. *"Seventy-five dollars?* Isn't that pretty steep?"

Miss Lena shrugged. Actually it was her bottom price, her "black" price, half what she would charge a white woman. "I can't afford to charge less," she said. "Of course, you're free to go to someone else, if you prefer."

Marvel shrugged in turn, as if money were the least important thing in the world to her, and threw the fabric on Miss Lena's table. "Oh, all right," she said. "I'll pick up the pattern in town when I get my shoes."

"Let me take your measurements first."

Miss Lena disapproved of wearing a lounging outfit

on the street, but she recognized this one. It was either an original by a well-known designer or an expensive exact copy. Normally she would not have hesitated to extend credit to such a well-dressed woman. But now, remembering B.J.'s warning, she said softly as she adjusted the tape measure around Marvel's waist, "How large a deposit would you care to leave?"

The girl jumped beneath her hands. "What do you mean, *deposit?* I'm leaving my fabric with you. Isn't that enough?"

"Yes. Upholstery fabric, isn't it?" Miss Lena said in the pleasant, impersonal tone she had used throughout their conversation. "It's lovely, but I'm afraid I wouldn't have any other use for it."

"Can't I pay you next week?" Long false eyelashes, framing large melting eyes, fluttered at Miss Lena. *"Please?"*

Oh, Miss Lena thought, I'm the wrong sex for you to be trying *that* on, sister. I'm sure it would work on a man. *Any* man. But not on me. And you underestimate Miss Lena Ricks if you think you can make her believe you'll pay for a dress after you've gotten it and gone.

"We would really like to accommodate you," she murmured, "but I'm afraid we can't make an exception in our policy."

Marvel's soft voice suddenly became loud and strident. "What old *we?*" she asked belligerently. "I thought you worked here by yourself."

"B.J.?" Miss Lena called. "Don't you think it's time you took care of that business?"

"My associate, B.J.," she murmured as he slipped out between the curtains. "Miss Scott, isn't it?"

B.J. straightened up and stood tall in his rags. He tugged his scruffy front hair in lieu of a cap and walked proudly to the door, his new status supporting him like a cane. "Be back in no time, Miss Lena," he said.

Miss Marvel hardly noticed him. She was too busy telling Miss Lena what color of female dog she was and what she could do with her policy. Her beautiful face became quite ugly as she spat out the horrid words.

Miss Lena was glad B.J. was no longer around to hear them. But then, she thought sadly as she locked the door firmly behind Miss Marvel, he had probably heard them all before. He seemed to know far more than he should for his age—more, even, than someone who was old enough to be his grandmother.

Six

Miss Lena knew a thing or two herself, though. She hadn't survived all these years in the white folks' world for nothing, as she told B.J. when he returned with her purchases and $5.75 in change.

In the meantime she'd cut out all her muslin patterns, then spread a remnant of tan cotton gabardine on her cutting table. It was smaller than she had thought, but perhaps it would do. She hadn't planned to sew for him, but she needed to bait a trap. Kindness might make him slip up and reveal his intentions. And since all ghetto kids were style-conscious, clothes would be sweeter, stickier flypaper than candy.

"If you need things," she told B.J., "the best way to get them is make them yourself. The more things you know how to do for yourself, the better off you are in this country."

"Why?" B.J. wanted to know.

"Because know-how is something nobody can take away from you. The white man can take your money, but he can't take away your smarts. And if you know how to do a lot of things, you can make more money and keep more of it, too. Now stand still so I can measure you."

She passed her tape measure rapidly around his waist, then down the inside and outside seams of his trousers. Lord but he was thin. And short. The remnant would be ample.

Cutting lining and pants together with her electric

scissors, she continued, "And if you need something and can't make it, never pay the full price for it."

"You mean get a discount, like you got from Sidney?"

"Maybe you weren't standing behind the door when they passed out the brains, after all. Yes, get a discount, or get it on sale, or get it secondhand. The best way of all is getting things free, though."

"You mean steal stuff."

"I do *not,*" Miss Lena said, pulling herself up until she was as straight as one of her pins. She wasn't going to try to convince him stealing was wrong, though. Such a lecture would sound phony, even to her own ears. Instead she said what she believed. "Stealing is stupid, unless you're white and rich and can steal a whole lot of money, at least fifty thousand dollars. Then it's legal, and you'll get away with it. Otherwise it's not worth the chance of getting caught. Besides, you don't have to steal to get things for nothing."

B.J.'s cynical expression resembled an experienced old street hustler's. "Oh, come on, Miss Lena. That's a lot of jive. Ain't nobody giving away nothing free."

Miss Lena sat down calmly at her machine. "You think not, huh?" she said above the buzz of the motor. "What do you think I paid for this chair?"

It was a sturdy, comfortable chair, a secretary's posture chair upholstered in imitation leather, that swiveled a full 360 degrees and glided on casters.

"That chair you're sitting on? You *had* to pay at least a hundred dollars."

"Guess again."

Like all youngsters and all poor people of any age, he was comfortable with small sums of money, but unsure of himself when trying to deal with large ones. "Fifty dollars? A hundred and fifty? Five hundred?"

"Not one penny."

"How'd you get it, then?"

"Guess."

"You stole it."

Miss Lena almost stitched her finger in her anger. "I told you, I never steal."

"Never?" he asked incredulously. "You mean you never even took a little can of tuna fish out of the supermarket, or a lipstick from the five and dime? Not even a newspaper off somebody's front porch?"

"No."

He shook his head in wonderment and expelled a whistling gust of air. "I ain't never heard of nobody who didn't never steal. You're weird."

Their worlds were as far apart as Alaska and Australia; no wonder each thought the other was looking at life upside down. She had better stop trying to change him and start trying to understand him. This was a chance to discover the dimensions of the danger she might be in. "O.K., so I'm weird," she said cheerfully. "Who's normal?"

"Everybody. I mean, I don't know anybody who don't steal *sometimes.*"

"Like who?"

"Well, like mothers who can't buy enough food for their children, so they steal cans of tuna fish and things. And the children steal, too, else they don't eat. Then there's bigger guys who steal big stuff."

"What for?"

"Because they *want* it!" he exploded at her apparent stupidity. "Or because they want to sell it and get money. Take junkies, they need a lot of money. Then there's other guys who just want to be rich. Like this friend of mine—he don't have no habits to support or nothing, but he can't stand to be poor, so he rips off stores."

"What's this friend's name?"

That was a mistake; his face closed like a spring-operated door. "I don't know."

"He must be pretty dumb," she commented, "running risks like that to keep from getting a job. He may find himself working for nothing pretty soon. Making license plates or washing prison uniforms."

"He's not dumb!" B.J. shouted. "He *works* for the cops. Why would they arrest him?"

This was a new angle to Miss Lena. "Works for the cops doing what?" she asked with genuine amazement.

"Collecting from the gamblers. The cops tell him where all the games are, and he goes by and takes their cut out of the pot. This same cop he pays makes sure nobody bothers my friend when he breaks in a store. If I was big and strong like him I'd do the same thing."

"What's your size got to do with it?"

"You heard of these P.A.L. clubs? Tall guys can go there and play basketball. That's where the crooked cops pick out the ones they want to work for 'em. But a little guy like me can't even get in."

"Maybe you're lucky," Miss Lena said. "You still haven't convinced me this friend of yours is so smart." She had no great liking for the police, but the pervasiveness of their corruption was a revelation, dazzling as an icy street and just as menacing. "Sounds like he's mixed up in something bigger than he is. It might turn on him sometime and swallow him up."

"I don't think so," B.J. responded. "Unless some honest cop happened to catch him. All the cops ain't crooked, that's the only problem."

"So maybe my way of getting things *is* better," she

ventured, knowing she would meet stiff opposition if she ever made a serious attempt to convert B.J. to her respect for the law. She also knew now that he had a thieving friend he admired. And that, she reflected nervously, was *all* she knew.

"Maybe," he said without much conviction. "What is it?"

"You're the one who was supposed to guess."

"You still want me to guess how you got that chair?"

"Yes."

B.J.'s imagination improved. "Well, you had this rich boyfriend, and he took you out one night, and you were real nice to him, you know, real sweet and all that stuff, and then you just happened to walk him past the store window and show it to him, and the next day he bought it for you."

B.J. could not see her face, because she was bent over her machine, putting on a waistband, but Miss Lena was frowning. He had put his finger on the one technique that was missing from her system of survival. That was the way most lone ladies managed to get what they wanted, but Miss Lena had never cared to use it. Whenever anyone reminded her of how easy it was to get things from men, she began to doubt herself and wonder whether she was really so smart, after all. But then she would remember how living alone in a cellar had been preferable to living with Mr. Ricks in a big house filled with fear and fine furniture, and she would decide again that she would rather do without things than lose her precious independence.

"Wrong," she said. "Some people I didn't even know gave it to me. They put it out in their trash."

"You *got* to be kidding, Miss Lena."

"I am perfectly serious," she said. "Whenever I need

something, I don't shop the stores till I have to. First I shop the trash in the rich white neighborhoods. I shop the night before the trash is collected, because the junk men do *their* shopping first thing in the morning.

"I always know exactly what I want before I go shopping. And this one time I had been saying to myself, 'Miss Lena, you need a good chair to work in. A comfortable chair that supports your back, and swivels, and glides.' So I went out on Tuesday, the night they put their trash out on Fremont Street. I only had to walk two blocks before I found it. The top part had come off the bottom, but it was the chair I wanted. So I just picked up one piece in each hand and brought it back here. Then all I had to do was screw it back together again."

B.J. whistled. "You really got that good chair for nothing?"

"Well," Miss Lena admitted, "I did have to pay twenty-nine cents for the screws."

B.J. was studying her elegant salon. "I *know* you didn't get your other furniture that way."

"Yes, I did. Most of it, anyway," Miss Lena said. "I called up City Hall and found out which days they collected trash on all the high-class streets. Then I would go out the night before and do my shopping. That's how I got that table, and that rug, and the lamp, and the chair, and the smoking stand."

"The sofa too?"

"No," she admitted. "I paid a junk man five dollars for it. I hated to do it, because I knew he'd found it that morning on some trash pile I'd missed the night before. But it was too big for me to carry anyway, and it's a good antique, worth about five hundred, so it was a good buy.

" 'Course," she continued, biting off a thread, "it

didn't look like that when I got it. It was a mess. I had to strip it down and put in new springs and reupholster it myself."

B.J. was properly impressed. "Where'd you learn to do all that stuff, Miss Lena?"

"I taught myself, mostly," she said. "But some of it I learned in school."

"They teach you to fix furniture in school?" B.J. was wide-eyed, as if the idea that school might offer useful knowledge was entirely new to him.

"Sure, if you go to the right school."

"They didn't teach it at *my* school. They just taught dumb stuff like Llama is the capital of Peru, because it's full of funny-looking animals called limas—"

"Lima. Llamas," she corrected.

"Whatever. Who cares? And the square root of four is two, and other dumb stuff like that."

"You never know when it might come in handy to know those things."

"Nah!" B.J. protested loudly. "Anybody who cares about dumb old square roots has to *be* some kind of a square. You ever see a square root? Ain't no such thing. Roots are *round.* Sweet potatoes are round, white potatoes are round, onions are—"

She had to smile at his understanding of the term. "That's a different kind of root," she said. "And maybe you should be in a different kind of school. What school were you going to?"

"I forget," he said.

She was catching on to his evasive tricks. "Well, remember," she said firmly.

"Hale. But it has bars on the windows, so we just called it 'Jail'." He changed the subject quickly. "Hey, did you get *all* the stuff in here free?"

"I already told you, most of it. All the lamps and chairs and tables you see out there. Even my worktable here. It's just an old door I found at a place where they were tearing a house down, and put some legs on."

B.J. gave her a knowing look. "I bet you didn't get your TV free, though."

"No," she admitted. "I paid for it with the money I saved getting other things for nothing."

"But you didn't pay the full price for it, right?"

"No. I told you, I never pay the full price for anything if I can help it."

"Did you get it hot?"

"No, no, *no,* B.J.," she said wearily. "Buying stolen things is just as dumb as stealing."

"You sure are weird, Miss Lena," B.J. said frankly. "I never knew anybody like you."

"Maybe it's time you did."

"But what's wrong with buying stuff hot? Just about everybody I know does it. Some people I know make a good living selling hot things, too."

"What people?"

That had been too direct; his eyes were wary. "Oh, just some people I know. Grown people. They say it's big business, the only big business black people can get into. So what's wrong with buying things from 'em?"

The specious argument reminded her of someone. But who? Unable to jog her memory, she replied, "It's twice as risky as stealing, that's what's wrong.

"Number one, the cops can arrest you right along with the thief. Number two, if you buy something from a thief, he's liable to steal it right back from you along with all your other stuff."

"Was your TV on sale, then, Miss Lena?"

"No. I made the man *put* it on sale." Her dismay

dissolved in the memory of how she had contrived to get her television set for half price. She began to giggle like a girl B.J.'s age.

"See, I had been in this store before, looking the way I always look, to pick out the set I wanted. It was priced at three hundred dollars. The man tried to sell it to me that day, but I wouldn't buy it. I went back to his store the next day dressed like a country woman. I had on a red head scarf and a raggedy cotton print dress and a pair of backless house slippers. And I tucked in my lips so they looked like I had no teeth behind my top one and a pinch of snuff in my bottom one. 'Ike ish."

B.J. was giggling too, violently, as if someone were tickling him. "Did the man know you?"

"O' cour' not. With my lips sucked in, I told him, 'Ah'm jush up heah on a visit. Ah done promish to take a colo' Tee Hee home to my chirren. Ah wan' *dat* one. An ah ha' to catch de bus back Down Home t'*day.*"

B.J., doubled up in a fit of laughter, managed to ask, "What did the man say?"

"He said, 'How much money you got, Auntie?'

"So I untied this dirty handkerchief I was carrying and said, 'Ah shink Ah got a hunner fitty dollars heah. Yeah, da' what Ah got. A hunner fitty. Ah hope ish enough. Ah'd sho hate to dishappoin' dem chirren.' "

"Didn't he know you were putting him on?"

"Of course not. White folks are easy to trick; they think we're all alike anyway. When they see one of us acting like an ignorant fool, it makes them so happy they'll do anything we want. Besides, when he saw that cash money, that man's eyes got so big and greedy he couldn't see anything else. He took it, and I took my set right out of his store. And almost laughed myself to death all the way home."

"You smart, Miss Lena," B.J. said respectfully. "Almost smart as me."

"I guess you thought you were the only tricky devil on this street. Well, you know better now." She handed him the finished trousers. "Here. Run downstairs and try these on."

He disappeared in an instant, obviously excited. Soon Miss Lena heard water running down there, a lot of water. He would be a long time returning.

She took the fur lining and the coat it was meant for from their hangers and set to work. Though she was usually so skilled with zippers she could practically put them in blindfolded, for some strange reason she made a mistake on this one and had to rip it out and start over.

At first she blamed it on her nerves. Then she realized she had not been paying attention to her work. She had been thinking instead that there was something wrong with a world in which some people thought so little of money they could wear mink on the insides of their clothes, while others were thrilled at getting a single pair of cotton trousers. But that was still no excuse, in her opinion, for the deprived ones to steal from the comfortable ones. She wished she could remember who had argued that point of view. Someone so unpleasant, obviously, that she had made herself forget them.

Whatever was wrong with the world, she reminded herself, it was not the fault of Miss Allinson. As far as she knew, Miss Allinson had never done anything wrong except be the orphaned only child of rich parents. She seemed to be a nice woman, and such a lonely one that Miss Lena even felt sorry for her sometimes. In spite of these deliberately charitable thoughts, Miss Lena made a second mistake. On the third try she inserted the zipper perfectly, though.

B.J. came back in time to see her putting the finished coat back on her garment rack. "Hey! Is that mink? *Real* mink? Can I touch it?"

"Yes," she said to all three questions, for all she could see of him was shining clean—with a number of wet spots, however. Anyway, it was a definite improvement. Though he had made skimpy use of the towel, he had been thorough with the soap and water this time.

He stroked the fur with closed eyes. "Feels soft. Soft as Willie," he said to himself in a whisper.

"Who's Willie?"

"I didn't say nothing about no Willie!" he said angrily, snatching his hand away and putting on a new, tough personality that frightened her. "Hey listen, Miss Lena, you want to make a whole lot of money? I know some guys will rob you for nothing if I tell 'em you got a mink coat in here. Then you can get a whole lot of money from your insurance company. Maybe a hundred thousand dollars."

"Are they the same ones who robbed me last May?" He didn't answer.

Miss Lena heard the warning ringing in her ears that signaled a rise in her blood pressure and the start of a headache. Sure enough, her head tightened painfully almost immediately. She began to shake it from side to side. Whatever had made her want to get involved with a kid like this? The street had gotten to him first, and she could never undo its indoctrination. He was hopeless. Hopeless.

The pain and the dizziness that went along with it did not go away. They got worse. Her head drooped over her cutting table, then sank down of its own weight on her folded arms.

"Hey, Miss Lena, what's the matter? You sick?"

"No," she lied. "I'm fine."

"Did I make you sick, Miss Lena?"

"Yes," she said angrily, lifting her head only to feel a new wave of dizziness, and a more intense pain, like a row of steel bands clamping down on her forehead. She lowered her head again and spoke in a whisper. When it hurt like this she could not stand any noise. "You and your smart ideas. You know a lot, all right. But everything you know is wrong."

"But I was gonna help you get robbed *free,* Miss Lena! A lot of people in business *pay* guys to rob 'em, so they can collect on their insurance!" He was loud, excited. Iron spikes dug into her eyebrows.

"Yes, I know," she said tiredly.

"You said it was O.K. to steal if you got a lot of money."

"I also said only rich white people could get away with it. Do I look white to you?"

"No, but you're rich. And—well, what about the way you got your TV? Wasn't that stealing?"

"No, because a man like that is a thief himself. He robs poor people all the time, selling them stuff on credit, then taking it back when they can't keep up the payments and selling it to somebody else. And you better believe he was making a profit on that set at a hundred fifty dollars, or he wouldn't have let me have it, not even if I was one-legged, cross-eyed, deaf, and dumb. Maybe somebody stole it for *him.* I don't know." In her exhaustion, she felt less sure of herself. "Maybe it *was* stealing. I don't know. I'm tired. I can't talk any more. I don't know what to say to you, anyway."

"You ain't had your lunch, Miss Lena. Maybe that's what's wrong. You want me to go out and get it for you?"

"No."

"You want me to go away and leave you alone?"

She turned her head without lifting it and looked at him. The hard, swaggering manner was gone. He looked very small and very worried, his newly washed face wetter than before, shining with sweat as well as water. In her entire life, no one else had ever worried about Miss Lena.

"No," she said. "I want you to get me my handbag and a glass of water."

In her haste to get to the shop this morning, she had forgotten to take her pressure pills. Fortunately she always carried a supply in her purse. She took two of them now with a big swallow of water and followed them with a relaxer pill. Then she rose slowly and shakily, feeling herself in imminent danger of falling. Which, of course, made it all the more necessary for her to stay on her feet and walk.

"Lean on me, Miss Lena," B.J. said.

Keep your independence. Keep your pride. Do for yourself. Walk alone. It was her way.

"Please," he urged.

Never lean on people. They will turn into puffs of smoke every time, and blow away with the wind, and let you fall. It was her experience.

"I'm strong, Miss Lena. Let me help you."

The way you wanted to help me a minute ago? That wouldn't help me at all, Miss Lena wanted to say. But instead she placed a hand on each of his surprisingly broad shoulders and let them support her as she tottered to the green love seat and lay down.

It was the hardest thing she had ever done.

Seven

She lay there with her eyes closed for several minutes. When she opened them, B.J. was still standing over her with the same worried look.

Miss Lena managed a smile. "How do the pants fit?"

"Fine," he said, holding them up with his hands. "I just need some buttons or something in the front here."

"Of course you do. My button box is on the shelf right beside the pattern books. Find me four tan buttons to fit the holes, and bring them here with a needle and some thread."

His face was still screwed up with worry. "You're sick. You sure you ought to be workin', Miss Lena?"

"I'm not sick. I just forgot to take my medicine this morning, that's all. Besides, sewing on buttons isn't work. I can do it while I'm lying here waiting for my medicine to take effect. When it does, I'll be fine."

Actually, she knew better. It might well be a day, two days, a week, or a month before she felt like herself again. But she had to pretend otherwise, for her own sake more than his. She couldn't afford to stop going. It would be too hard to get started again.

B.J. tied the flowered fabric around himself this time.

"You're small below," she said, studying his odd figure, "but I never noticed before how big you are on top."

B.J. preened and flexed his arms, showing off his muscles like a model for a body-building ad. He had the barrel chest, broad shoulders, and husky arms of a well-developed fifteen-year-old. "Yeah, and I'm strong, too," he boasted. "I figure by the time I'm eighteen, I'll be a big guy. Only—"

"Only what, B.J.?"

"I never seem to get any taller."

"Don't worry about it," she said. "Lots of boys shoot up all of a sudden in their teens. As much as a foot in a year."

His face was sad, with an ancient, African sadness; he looked as old as the Sphinx. "I don't think *I* will. My legs are too messed up. This is all the growing I'll ever do."

Miss Lena decided not to lie to him again. Instead she admitted, "I don't know whether you're right or not, B.J. I just don't know." She added by way of consolation. "Your legs are small, yes. You wear a small boy's trousers. But your arms and shoulders have developed so much to compensate for your legs, you need a man's shirt. I'd say, about a fifteen."

"What's 'compensate', Miss Lena?"

"Later on today, why don't you go to the library and look it up in the dictionary?"

"How can I look it up if I don't know how to spell it?"

This logic was unanswerable. "Hmmm," she said. "I guess that *would* be a problem. Didn't they teach you spelling in school?"

B.J. became distractingly animated. "Hey, you sure made that Hippo lady look good in that long green dress. She didn't look fat any more. Just *big.*"

Miss Lena stared at him without speaking.

He became even more vivacious, hopping about as he talked. "I don't like big people, though. They always getting in my way, bumping into me and knocking me down. I only like little people. You nice and little, Miss Lena. That's why you look so young."

Miss Lena was feeling every bit of her age at the moment. Flattery will get you somewhere sometimes, she thought. This time it'll get you off one hook and onto another. "How," she asked, "did you get to see Mrs. Johnson in that dress?"

He banged his hands together nervously. "I don't care if I don't never get to be a big guy. I think I want to be little all my life, just like you."

"B.J.?" she asked in her sternest tone, the one that would not permit further evasion.

"I sneaked back and peeked through your front window," he admitted.

"It's not nice to peek, B.J."

"But the ladies never get undressed in front. Only in back behind the curtain," he pleaded. "I wouldn't peek at them without their clothes on. You know I wouldn't, don't you, Miss Lena?"

First flattery, then tears. He would try anything to get his way with her.

"I hope not," Miss Lena said, though for once he was not as accurate as he thought about what went on on her premises. Some of those "ladies" she sewed for would strip anywhere, even on a street corner. Mrs. Cosgrove, for instance, for whom Miss Lena was making a whole suitcaseful of bareback halters and bare-leg shorts and bare-everything bikinis, always "forgot" to step behind the velvet curtain before undressing, forcing Miss Lena to close all of her front shutters. Probably Mrs. Cosgrove wanted a sidewalk audience, though. One day Miss Lena might just let her attract one. She decided not to scold B.J.

Instead she tossed the finished trousers to him. "Here. Put these on, and we'll go shopping."

"You gonna buy me a shirt?"

Miss Lena thought about his pride, and phrased her answer carefully. "No. You're going to buy yourself a shirt at this place I'm going to take you."

"But I ain't got enough money."

"Yes, you do. You have thirty cents in your bank. Besides, you went to the store for me this morning. I've decided to pay you ten percent of everything you buy for me. What's ten percent of four dollars and twenty-five cents?"

He furrowed his brow. "Uh . . . forty cents?"

"That's close, but not quite. It's a little more than that."

"Well, forty cents is O.K. Forty cents is fine, Miss Lena."

"You're never going to have much money in your bank that way," she told him. "You're cheating yourself. Don't you know how to do percents?"

"Sure I do," he said with not-quite-convincing bravado.

"Bring me a pencil and paper and show me."

He brought the pencil and paper. After writing $4.25, he obviously did not know what to do next.

Miss Lena took the pencil from him, crossed out the dollar sign, and drew a little arrow under the numbers. "Look. To take ten percent, all you do is move the decimal point one place to the left."

"What's a dismal point?"

"They may be dismal, but you still have to learn how to use them. So you won't cheat yourself, and so nobody can cheat you.

"This dot is a decimal point. It divides money into dollars and cents. When it was in front of the two, you had four dollars and a quarter. Now that I've moved it one place to the left, what do you have?"

"Forty-two—" He hesitated.

She helped him. "And a half cents. Because the last number is always a fraction of ten. And five is half of what?"

"Ten."

"Good. You always round off a figure of five or more to the next highest number. So what do I owe you for going to the store?"

"Nothing, Miss Lena."

"What?"

He looked troubled. "I mean, I know ten percent of four dollars and twenty-five cents is forty-three cents. But you still don't owe me nothing."

"Why not?"

He was hedging. "Well, for one thing, you already made these nice pants for me."

"B.J.?" she queried in her warning tone of voice. "What were you going to say *first?*"

"I . . . uh . . . I didn't take no taxi."

"Why not? Didn't you see your favorite drivers?" And why was she offering him this easy way out? Perhaps to see whether he would take it.

He refused, thank goodness. "No. I was hungry. I kept your dollar and bought me two big baloney sandwiches with all the stuff on them and a big grape drink."

Miss Lena stifled her anger, which was less at his trickery than at his insistence on drinking colored water and eating factory floor-sweepings, because the headache would return if she let it explode.

"Well," she said, "at least you were big enough to own up to your mistake."

"But I shouldn't have done it, Miss Lena. Not to you. You been good to me. You made me these pants—"

Miss Lena dismissed the pants with a wave of her

hand. "The pants didn't cost me anything. I made them out of scraps. Consider them a gift." She put a hand on his head. It was wet; he had really washed all over. "Besides, if you're going to be my associate, you've got to have some decent clothes."

"How can you still let me be your 'sociate after I stole from you?"

Lord knows, thought Miss Lena. He was clearly a hardened liar and thief and, what was perhaps worse, a confirmed consumer of junk food. All she knew was that she hadn't quite given up on him yet, and did not know why.

"You won't do it again," she said with a confidence she did not feel.

"No," he muttered, avoiding her eyes in a way that did not increase her confidence.

"Only one thing bothers me," Miss Lena said. "Why did you insist on eating baloney, after what I told you about it yesterday?"

"Because I *like* it. That milk and cheese I had yesterday made me sick. I threw up on the street right after I left here. Last night I still couldn't eat nothing."

Miss Lena didn't ask whether there had been anything on the table at home last night had he felt like eating. She knew, somehow, that there hadn't been.

She also began to question her standards. Some of them, anyway. Maybe she'd been reading too many white women's magazines, with all that stuff about the Seven Basic Foods. In some black publication, though, she seemed to remember reading that 75 percent of all black children were unable to digest cow's milk and its products. Come to think of it, she had never liked milk or cheese herself, and ice cream had always been the easiest thing to cut out when she was on a diet.

"I'm sorry, B.J."

Astonishment dilated his eyes. "*You* sorry? What for?"

"I was wrong to tell you to eat something you didn't like, something that probably wasn't good for you."

"*I'm* the one who's s'posed to be sorry."

"O.K., we're even, then." She raised herself decisively and swung her feet to the floor. The wave of weakness she was expecting did not come. She felt as strong as ever. Triumphantly, she said, "Let's go shopping."

"Awww, what can I get for seventy-three cents?"

"A whole lot, at this place I'm going to take you. Besides, you have more money than that."

His eyebrows were exclamation points. "I do?"

"Yes. You saved me seventy-five dollars this morning. I would have made that Marvel Scott a dress on credit if you hadn't warned me about her."

"Aw, I won't charge you for that, Miss Lena."

"But I want to pay you. You saved me a lot of money. What's ten percent of seventy-five dollars?"

She wrote $75.00 on the paper and handed it to him. After studying it for several minutes with his forehead pleated like an accordion, he said, "Seven whole dollars and fifty cents?"

"That's right."

He whistled. "I ain't never had that much money in my whole life!"

"Don't worry about it. I'll bank it for you," she said, conscious of the dangers of sudden wealth. "You just decide how much you want to save and how much you want to spend. Now, how much is seven-fifty plus seventy-three cents?"

"Eight twenty-three," he replied after performing a

finger ballet in the air. "And I don't want to spend more than half."

"Good. How much is half?"

"Four dollars?"

Miss Lena was suddenly weary of the arithmetic lessons. Let somebody else teach B.J. to divide, someone whose job it was. Someone whose salary was paid by Miss Lena's high taxes.

"It's more than that," she said, "but that's close. We won't spend more than four dollars. Put your shirt on so we can go."

"I can't. I threw it away."

"Why?"

"I didn't want to wear that tired old shirt with my new pants."

"But you have a cold."

"Not any more. I'm fine."

He still had a suspicious sniffle, but what could Miss Lena do except let him walk outside half-naked?

"Where we going, Miss Lena?" he asked, bobbing along the sidewalk beside her, his stickle-burr head rising and falling as he shifted from his best foot to his worst one.

"To a thrift store."

"You mean, where they sell secondhand stuff?"

"That's right."

"Awww, why should we buy secondhand stuff when we can get new stuff free?"

"Where?" she asked him with a penetrating look.

His voice trailed off into a mumbled "Never mind. . . ."

"I don't think you've found any trash piles I've missed. So you must be talking about getting yourself free room and board at the penitentiary."

"You don't have to get locked up!" he shouted defiantly. "Some friends of mine get everything they want, and they *never* get caught!"

"I'd like to meet some of those friends of yours."

"No, you wouldn't," he said decisively, and seemingly made a rapid turnabout to her way of acquiring things. "I know where a thrift shop is. Over on Fairview Street. Only thing is, it smells bad in there." His face was wrinkled in distaste. "I don't think their stuff is so clean."

"We're not going to that one."

"There's one! Over there, across the street!"

He pointed to one of the Rummage Sale signs that were forever popping up in the black section of the neighborhood, only to vanish as quickly as they appeared. Someone would rent an abandoned storefront for a day or a week, fill it with junk from cellars and burnt-out houses, and plaster the window with signs like this one's: "Ladies Shoes 25¢"; "Men's Shirts 5 for $1.00." But the shoes and the shirts were seldom worth picking over, let alone buying.

"No, B.J." Miss Lena said. "That one's no good either. I'll tell you something I've found out. The best thrift stores are always in rich white neighborhoods. Just like the best trash."

"You mean white folks buy secondhand stuff?" He stopped on the sidewalk to consider this shocking idea.

"Sure," she said. "They only buy the best, though, same as they get the best *new* stuff. That's why we have to go out of our neighborhoods to shop." She prodded his shoulder gently to get him moving again. "Come on."

B.J. seemed nervous as they began to walk out of

familiar territory, past a school that occupied an entire block. He caught her arm just as she prepared to enter an alley that was too narrow for cars. "Not that way, Miss Lena!"

This was a very old city with many such lanes and alleys, built before the days of the automobile. They were one reason why her seven-league boots provided faster transportation than cars. Miss Lena was grateful for the short cuts they afforded, especially on a day like today, when she had less than two hours in which to shop for him and get back to admit Miss Allinson.

"Why not, B.J.?"

"You cut through that alley, you subject to get your pocketbook snatched. A bad gang of guys hang out in there."

"Friends of yours?" she asked, not bothering to conceal the scorn in her voice.

"It was winos I was thinking of," he answered, his eyes darting in every direction except her face. "You always got to be extra careful when you walk near a liquor store."

Since Miss Lena seldom patronized liquor stores, they were not among the landmarks she noticed. This one was only a few doors away, but B.J. had to point it out to her.

"Them winos get to needing a taste, they liable to hit on anybody. They always hang around near a liquor store and wait for ladies with pocketbooks. And if there's an alley nearby, that's where they hide. Once they get their wine, they go back in there and drink it. Don't never go through an alley if it's near a liquor store. It's best if you don't walk past one, neither. When you see a liquor store, you better off if you cross to the other side of the street."

Though it took her several steps in the wrong direction, Miss Lena followed his advice.

"See all them guys out front?" B.J. said.

She looked from the safe distance of the other side of the street and observed a dozen loiterers accosting people who went into the store.

"They trying to get their wine money together by begging it off people," B.J. explained. "If you walked by and didn't give them any money, they might snatch your pocketbook."

"And if I did?"

"They might snatch it anyway. It ain't exactly their fault. Winos can't help themselves; they need that wine. It's people's fault for going around them."

They walked on in companionable silence while Miss Lena tried to digest this philosophy, with which she did not agree any more than she agreed with his other values, until they reached a wide street lined with large department stores and small shops with fanciful names like Plum Nelly and Lalapalooza.

"Four dollars won't buy nothin' around here," he complained. "Won't even pay for the paper they wrap your stuff in."

"Yes, it will. Just wait and see," she said, and steered him toward a small shop tucked inconspicuously between glittering Kustom Kitchens and sleek Fashion Furs. Its sign was unobtrusive—"thrift shop", in lowercase script—and only a few choice items of merchandise were in the window: a dress, a hat, a string of almost-real pearls. Miss Lena approved of this restraint. It reminded her of her own sparse display window.

"A person would never even know this place was here," B.J. observed.

"White folks don't want us to know," she told him.

"They want us to go on buying high-priced trash, so we'll stay poor and they'll stay rich. They want to keep this place to themselves, because it has the real bargains."

A half hour later, when they emerged with a warmly zip-lined coat that had cost $1.50, a thick sweater (75¢), three sets of underwear (15¢ apiece), three shirts (25¢ each), and a pair of stylishly faded blue jeans (half a dollar), he had to admit she was right.

"I never saw so much good stuff in one place before!" he cried. "Some of it looked new."

"Some of it *is* new. Your shirts are new. So is your underwear."

"How can they sell new stuff so cheap?" he wondered.

"I think it's because the clothing business is so risky," she told him. "People who make clothes are always making styles they can't sell, or going out of business. They have to get rid of their stuff the best way they can."

B.J. gave her a puzzled look. "Why did *you* decide to make clothes for a living, then?"

She didn't have to think about her answer. "Because I like doing it," she said serenely, "and it's what I do best."

B.J. considered this gravely. "That's a good reason," he finally said.

"It's the *only* reason for choosing a line of work," she replied. "What do you want to do when you grow up, B.J.?"

"Oh, I don't know. Be a big-time thief, I guess."

"By that, I suppose you mean someone who does big time in prison."

"Naw!" he protested loudly. "I won't get caught! I won't steal nothing myself. I'll be the boss, the brains behind the operation. I'll have a bunch of other guys to do the stealing for me."

"Till they start stealing *from* you," she murmured. "Is that the best career you can think of?"

"Well, what else can I do? I'm too ugly to be a pimp. No girl's gonna work for me. And I don't want to work for *nobody.*"

"Not even me?"

"That's different. I mean I don't want to work for no man. Specially not no white man. I don't want to have to call some dude what's no better than I am 'Boss' or 'Sir'. If anybody gone be the boss it's gonna be *me.*"

The intensity of his statement jogged her memory, brought the distant past into sharp focus.

"I don't plan to steal forever, anyhow. Only till I get a whole lot of money. Then I'll buy me a regular business. A restaurant or a store. Don't you think that's a good plan?"

Now she recalled which demon's dreams his resembled. In the last years of their marriage, James Ricks had given up working for dreaming and drinking. The more he drank the more grandiose he became. Grandiose until comatose. He would be the greatest black capitalist the world had ever seen, richer than Carnegie or Rockefeller. And he would get his capital the only way a black man could—by stealing it. After that he would buy legitimate businesses—sometimes it was restaurants, sometimes gas stations, sometimes merchant ships, sometimes stores. Always plural. A fleet of ships, a chain of stores.

Until she learned to stop debating a madman, she was accused of small-mindedness which was somehow linked to her femininity. She had no vision, women never did; they could not see beyond the narrow confines of a job. No one ever got rich on a job. The only freedom, especially for a black man, lay in working for oneself. Dreaming his big dreams, glorying in his plans, he scorned her plugging away at the pitiful little job which paid their bills.

Time and distance had cooled and depersonalized her anger; she knew now that most black men felt the same way, whether they worked or not. Jobs were just another form of slavery; to call a white man Boss felt the same as calling him Massa. Pride and ignorance, a dangerous combination, made them easy marks for franchise promoters, fast-buck swindlers, cheap books and magazines that fed their dreams, Be Your Own Boss ads on matchbook covers, anything that promised independence. There would always be another woman to cushion their defeats until all the schemes failed and the fantasies had to be supported with chemicals instead.

Would he be jealous if he knew she had achieved for herself the independence he dreamed? No, she decided, her business was too small to satisfy his hunger for the spectacular. She had no need to be Number One at anything. Maybe that was an exclusively masculine need; maybe he had been right about her. If so, she thanked God for making her small-minded and female. It had been her salvation.

"I think," she told B.J., "it's the worst plan I ever heard."

"Then maybe I'll learn the business from you, and be a dress designer." His smile was so patently false, his speech so clearly intended to flatter, she turned away, sickened.

"I don't think about it too much, though," he went on. "Mostly I think I'll wait and see *do* I grow up first. The doctors didn't expect me to live this long."

Miss Lena pretended to toss off this information lightly. "Well, they were wrong, weren't they?"

"Yeah," B.J. said. "I'm tough, I guess. Why couldn't I get that red sweater, Miss Lena? I liked it better than the gray one."

"I told you, it had a flaw in it. I showed it to you."

"Yeah, I saw it. But I didn't mind."

"You would have later on, when it got to be a great big hole."

"I sure wish I could have got them boots, then."

The boots had been a good fit, with both soles and uppers of real leather, and only very slightly worn. They had been a good buy, too. But the price was four dollars.

"Think about all the other nice things you got for your money." She showed him the sales slip. "And look. You even have a nickel left over."

"Aww. You can't buy nothin' for a nickel. I wanted them boots. I *needed* them boots."

She was getting weary of his whining. Miss Lena detested whining, whether in children or adults. But she tried to imagine how she would feel if she expected to die young, decided that maybe she, too, would want everything all at once, and was gentle. "You'll earn more money this week. Then you can get them. Always have something to look forward to."

"Yeah, but they might be gone by then. Or *I* might be."

He was wearing Miss Lena down. He planned to die before the week was out, but she felt as if she might precede him to the grave. "Do you want to go back and leave a dollar deposit on them, B.J.?"

"How much money would I have left then?"

"You tell me."

"Uh—four dollars from eight twenty-three leaves four twenty-three. Plus a nickel. That's four twenty-eight. Take away a dollar, and—awww, *no.*"

"What's the matter?"

"I'll be done spent more'n half my money."

Miss Lena smiled at his frugality, so much like hers, and at its implication, that he had decided to postpone dying for awhile. She pushed open a massive oak door.

"Why we going in here?"

"So I can get some lunch." And some rest, because she had been feeling weak again out there on the sidewalk, much too weak to argue with him.

It was a dark, cool, tea-roomy sort of place with paper lace place mats and vases of real flowers blooming on all its polished tables. There were very few such restaurants left in the city, but Miss Lena knew the locations of all of them. She would starve before she would go into one of those ugly new plastic places that sold cardboard hamburgers on absorbent-cotton buns and instant fried chicken that turned to petrified wood in five minutes.

But B.J. preferred them, of course. "Awww, why can't we eat at Dino's or O'Donnell's?"

"They serve slop for hogs, that's why."

"What's wrong with Foot-Long's?"

"Everything but the coffee. Come on here."

He continued to whine. "Aww, no, Miss Lena. I don't look right to be in here."

Lord knew it was the truth; in the sort of place that required coats and ties on gentlemen, he was naked above the waist.

Miss Lena touched the bag containing his shirts and whispered, "The men's room is right over there. Go in and put a shirt on. Nobody'll see you."

When he came back, she was already attacking a fruit salad with cottage cheese and a cup of hot tea. She was not ready to admit that she might be ill. All she needed, she told herself, was nourishment.

"You look nice," she told him. The new plaid shirt fitted him perfectly. It was, as her practiced eye had predicted, a man's.

"I know," he acknowledged without false modesty. "I need that nickel for something, though."

"What?"

"A comb."

He had a point. His efforts with fingers and water had only succeeded in making peaks and tunnels in the thatch that covered his head.

"That's a good idea," she said. "You know, I just thought of something, B.J. There's one thing you never told me."

"What?"

"Your last name."

Suspicion covered his face like a veil. "Why you need to know?"

"I don't need to know," she said pleasantly. "I'd just *like* to. After all, we're friends, and we haven't even been introduced."

He scowled. "The trouble is, I got two last names."

Miss Lena almost dropped her fork, but she kept her hold on it, and kept her poise, too. "How come?"

"Oh, *you* know, Miss Lena."

"No, I don't."

"Well—" He squirmed uncomfortably. "My mom and pop wasn't married. Not to each other, anyway."

Miss Lena did not ask to whom they *were* married. She wished she had never asked him the first question.

"I saw my birth certificate once," he continued. "It says my name is Brown. That was my mother's name.

But around our way everybody called her Mrs. Riggs, so that's what I mostly went by."

"Which name do you like best, B.J.?"

He looked at her angrily. "I don't like neither one. I don't like Brown, 'cause that lets folks know my parents wasn't married, and I don't like Riggs, 'cause that's my father's name, and I don't like my father. If he *is* my father. Some people say—"

"Hush. Never mind," Miss Lena said. She didn't want to know what some people said. Besides, the waitress was approaching their table, and she didn't want her to know, either.

The waitress quietly deposited the check in front of B.J., startling both of them, and disappeared.

"You see what she did?" he cried. "She thinks I'm your man."

After her initial shock, Miss Lena could understand the woman's mistake. B.J.'s face was adult. So was his shirt and the torso beneath it, and the chairs equalized their heights. In the dimly lit dining room, it had been natural for her to assume that B.J. was not a child.

As, in so many ways, he was not. Right now he was reading the check like an experienced man of the world.

Miss Lena extended her hand. "Give it to me, B.J."

"Oh, no," he said. "Gimme a dollar of *my* money."

"What about the boots?" she reminded him.

"This is better," he said. "This is better than anything ever happened to me. Besides, I owe it to you." He walked over to the cashier and paid the check, came back with the dime change in his palm, and asked gravely, "How much must I leave for a tip?"

"That will be fine," said Miss Lena, quietly slipping a nickel under her plate.

He pulled out her chair for her. "Where did you learn to do *that?*" she marveled.

"Movies, TV, all over. Oh, I know how to act proper. I know how to put on airs. Ladies first. Hold open doors for them," he said, doing it. "Light their cigarettes. I wish you smoked, Miss Lena, so I could light your cigarettes for you. You ain't never gonna catch me kissing no hands, though. Not *me.* Yechhh!" Turning a cartwheel in her path, he was a child again.

Miss Lena wished he would not exhibit such winning behavior immediately after revealing his shocking lack of morals. He was no good, that was clear. But he was, just as clearly, a child with personality in his favor.

Heading south in the direction of her shop, they again reached the paved playground and the massive dirty brick building with barred windows and "Nathan J. Hale School" engraved in stone above its front door. Miss Lena was reminded of something she had resolved to do that morning. She glanced at her watch. Yes, there was time, just enough time.

"What we stoppin' here for, Miss Lena?"

"Oh," she said casually, "I thought we might go in and have a little talk with your teacher."

Emotions passed rapidly over his face like the lights of passing cars in a dark room: shock, fear, resentment, rage.

"You tricked me!" he screamed. "You had it in mind to bring me here all the time!"

"I did not trick you, B.J. We just happened to be passing this way, and I thought—"

But she never got a chance to tell him what she had thought. B.J. took off like an arrow. It was amazing to see how that crippled child could run when he wanted to. His sprint was jerky and erratic, but it quickly carried him out of earshot and down the street. Miss Lena watched his bobbing form grow smaller, wondering what could be inside the building that he wanted to avoid so badly. Then she became aware of a counterforce that attracted him.

A remarkably rich apparition emerged from the very alley she had been warned against. She stared as a tall, sooty boy glided brilliantly into view dressed entirely in pale leather: vest, jacket, and pants all tailored of creamy kid. Somehow, on his long, insolent frame, the effect was not excessive.

"Yo, Bobo! Wait up!" B.J. called to him.

The taller boy's walk was loose and graceful, like an athlete's, and his hair, flowing like ink, was either chemically or naturally straight. He paused, turned, flashed a smile that would have melted a glacier, and permitted B.J. to catch up with him.

Miss Lena strained, but she heard no more of their conversation, and saw nothing more except their ill-matched backs receding. Soon even those were dots in the distance. With a shrug, she turned and firmly placed her right foot on the first tread of a long flight of concrete stairs.

Eight

"What's happenin', little nigger?"

His hero's eyes were opaque, but there had been a moment when they flickered and recognized him. That was something, at least. He'd been away from the scene a long time. Call me anything but *little,* he wanted to say, but clamped his teeth shut on his anger.

"That what I wanta ask you. What's goin' down?"

"Just come from a business conference."

"With Jayjay?"

"Who else?"

Hatred pressured his chest, constricted his breathing, did something funny to his eyes so the street was bathed in red. Angry white bullets swam through the red haze. That old garbage bag. If I only had me a gun I'd shoot him.

"Well, what he plannin'?"

"Big things, little brother, big things."

"Yeah, yeah, yeah, but *what?*"

"Too big for little niggers like you."

"How come I got too little all of a sudden? I didn't used to be too little to work with you."

"Told you the last time. Jayjay don't want his precious son mixed up in his business. Not till it gets to be all nice and clean and legitimate." Bobo's mocking laugh indicated when he thought that would happen: sometime around B.J.'s ninety-second birthday.

Dirty old stinking wino. Messin' up all the good times he and Bobo'd had together. Copping things, stashing them, selling them, always having plenty money and whatever they wanted it could buy. Not that the things or the money mattered. What mattered was being with Bobo and feeling, for a little while, like him—tall, strong, invincible, cool, like a king. Some king. His king was nothin' now but a puppet with funky old Rotten Wine Guts jerking the strings.

"You don't need him," B.J. muttered. "What he do for you anyway? What he *ever* do but lay around soakin' up wine?"

"He don't *do* much, that's true," Bobo admitted. "But he knows plenty. Sometimes I think he knows everything. Like which door in a warehouse can be jimmied open easy. What time a truck gone come rollin' up to a platform. What gone be *in* that truck. What the night watchman's favorite taste, and what time he drinks it." He tapped his high forehead. "He studies all the time. Even when you think ain't nothin' happenin' up here, even when you think he sleepin', that Jayjay be steady studyin'."

"I tell you, you don't need him. Ain't nothin' wrong with your head. Why can't you study on your own?"

"I ain't got time," the taller boy said, and quickened his stride.

Doggedly, though pain shot through his hip, his small companion kept pace with him. "You better make time. Cause he gonna mess you up pretty soon. Tell you to go to Jamaica when what he means is Westchester. Tell you Monday midnight when he means Saturday noon. Maybe, when he knows he gonna see you, he gets hisself together. But the rest of the time he so drunk he—"

Bobo cut him off with, "All I know is, he takes care of business."

"How can he? He stays so drunk he don't know his behind from a tree stump. I know. You don't live with him. I do."

The sun bounced off gleaming teeth. "That ain't what I heard."

"What you heard?"

"I heard you ain't been home in a long time. Months. And what's waitin' for you when you get back is one sore behind."

"I kept one anyway when I stayed there. I couldn't stand no more of him beatin' up on me. That's why I moved out."

"Where you stayin' now?" Bobo's cool was momentarily thawed by curiosity. He paused, giving B.J. a chance to catch his breath and the beginning of an idea.

"I got a nice place to stay. I'm makin' out fine. I don't need him and his jive-ass plans. Neither do you, Bobo. Why can't it be like it used to be? Just you and me?"

In his eagerness, he clawed the suave leather.

"Turn loose my vines, you little ape. What 'you and me' gonna do? Rob the monkey house at the zoo and take all the bananas?"

"I ain't no ape," he muttered, but without much feeling. Bobo could call him anything if only he wouldn't laugh at him. If only he would let things again be the way they used to be, just the two of them, before the old man jumped in it and cut him out. But the other's strides were quickening again, lengthening, as if he were determined to shake B.J. His bad leg would not hold out long at that pace.

Desperate, he found he had a hole card, and played it. "Listen," he said, "I know a place where there's a color TV, a radio, and lots of dress goods. Leather too. Even fur. Mink."

"Yeah?" Bobo said without expression. But his slackened pace betrayed interest.

B.J.'s lips were dry. He hadn't meant to do this, not at all. But this tall, handsome figure was his god, in whose image he hopelessly dreamed of being made, and nothing he felt for anyone else was as strong as the need to win him back.

"It—it belongs to this lady I know. She ain't there at night, only in the daytime. And not always in the daytime either; she ain't there now. Gettin' in is easy as candy. I know how."

"Tell me."

"We gone do it together, Bobo? Just you and me? We gone be partners again and cut him out?"

"Sure, sure, tell me."

"We gone do *everything* together after this? Like we used to?"

"I *said* yeah. Now tell me about it."

For a full five minutes he had his hero's rapt attention. He basked in it as long as he could, padding out his narrative with many details of where things were kept and how the burglar alarm was connected. He left the crucial part, the easy way he had found of getting in, till last. But finally he had said it all. Inside him was a dry, hollow feeling, as if his insides had burned to ashes and even those had blown away.

"Well, thanks. See you around, chimp."

"What you mean?"

"I said 'later, chump'."

"Hey, wait up. Don't walk so fast. I can't keep up with you."

"You never will," came the answer, borne back on a crest of laughter.

B.J. was left with a mouthful of his own ashes; left to

swallow the burnt offering that had been rejected by his god.

The gray, windowless halls of Hale did remind Miss Lena of a jail. They also made her feel like Gulliver: in imminent danger of being surrounded, captured, and stomped to death by hordes of midgets. Classes were changing, bells were ringing, and the heavy tramp of a thousand feet echoed from the concrete floors and the iron treads of the stairs at the ends of the corridor. She was swept along by a wave of pygmies to a door that was marked, simply, "Office". It didn't say what kind of office or whose, but Miss Lena went in gratefully, wiggling her painful stepped-on toes in a vain attempt to restore circulation. This had better be the right place, because she was not going out there again until it was safe.

Inside the office, it was restfully quiet. A row of chairs was occupied by small, still offenders who seemed afraid to breathe. Behind a waist-high partition sat a prettily plump secretary, nicely dressed for work in crisp gray flannel.

"What you want?" she demanded in a belligerent tone.

Not "May I help you?" Not even a bored "Yes?"

Miss Lena reflected on what she already knew, that clothes did not make the woman, after all. But she approached the partition without fear.

"I want," she said clearly, "to speak to the teacher of one of your former students."

The girl seemed shocked. "*Former* student? We don't keep no files on no former students. Them files all go to the Central Office after a year."

"This boy was here *this* year. Last term, I believe."

"Oh," the girl said, clearly disappointed. "He might still be in my files, then. But you'll have to wait a few minutes."

Looking over the partition, Miss Lena saw why. An opened bottle of silver nail polish sat on the desk, and the girl was fanning the air with her aluminized fingertips. Miss Lena thought about her school taxes, which had doubled again this year, and said, "I don't have much time, young lady. This boy's last name is Riggs or Brown. His initials are B.J."

"What you mean, Riggs or Brown?"

"What I said," Miss Lena replied in her most civil tone, which had a patronizing note that could only be detected by the most sensitive ears. "I'm sure you can understand. There must be someone in your family who goes by two names. Your mother, perhaps."

"You puttin' me in the dozens?" The girl leaped to her feet and sprang toward the partition as if to leap over it and attack Miss Lena. Meeting a hard, level stare that conflicted with the sweetest, most patient of smiles, she turned away in confusion and flounced over to a row of file cabinets, muttering. "Got to be crazy, walkin' in here talkin' about my mama. Never saw me before in her life. Who she think she is? Ain't got no B.J. Riggs."

"Try Brown, then," Miss Lena said as if she had not heard anything else.

"Here it is," the girl said. She returned to the partition very slowly, as if reluctant to face Miss Lena again. "He was in Miss Echols' room. Room three-oh-eight.

"Wait," the girl called as Miss Lena started to leave. "You'll need a pass." She wrote out a pink slip and said, "Give this to one of the monitors."

"What's a monitor?"

"A hall guard. They wear red belts. Ain't no other kids got no business in them halls now the third bell's rung."

What kind of place is this? Miss Lena wondered, taking the slip from the girl. Bells, passes, guards. It reminded her of stories she had read about South Africa. Miss Lena nervously handed her slip to the nearest monitor, a curly-haired, olive-skinned goddess, about ten years old, in a starched white dress.

"You s'posed to have an appointment," the child said self-importantly. "Do you got an appointment?"

"No. But it's *very* important," Miss Lena said.

"Well, maybe Miss Echols will see you," the little girl said doubtfully. "She don't have class now. Just study period. Follow me."

At the door of Room 308, the arrogant child said, "Wait here," and went inside, rudely closing the door in Miss Lena's face.

In a minute she returned, though, saying, "Miss Echols will see you. But only for five minutes."

Miss Lena felt as privileged as if she had just obtained an audience with the Queen of England. And, indeed, Miss Echols did have a regal air, with a crownlike arrangement of gray curls atop a proud head. Her profile was hook-nosed and impressive, and she wore a lot of jewelry with a royal purple dress which did not really become her low-yellow skin.

When she turned bright black eyes that were more birdlike than human on her visitor, Miss Lena decided to take the initiative. "You think one of those big boys back there could fetch me a chair?"

Miss Echols beckoned with a jeweled fingertip instead of a sceptre, and said simply, "Alvin." The chair was brought and placed beside her desk by a husky boy who looked as if he belonged in the Army instead of in grade school. While he was bringing it, Miss Lena had time to observe the seating arrangement of the class. Up front were the little ladies and gentlemen, all super-clean, with hair ribbons and even a sprinkling of neckties, and all diligently writing in workbooks. The children increased in sizes and sloppiness as her eye moved toward the back, where sat a dozen Alvins, overgrown, unkempt, and clearly not expected to learn anything, since none of them were supplied with books. Instead they spent their time wriggling, whispering, and making strange noises to which Miss Echols paid no attention.

"I hope this won't take too long," the teacher began. "I have a lot of paperwork to do. Tests, records, lesson plans. You understand."

Miss Lena understood, all right. She could see the cover of that women's magazine that printed pictures of naked men in the half-closed center drawer of Miss Echols' desk. "Sure," she said pleasantly. "I'm a working woman, myself."

Like the girl in the office, Miss Echols considered taking offense at the remark, met Miss Lena's level stare, and changed her mind.

"Yes. Well, how may I help you?"

That's better, thought Miss Lena, remembering the clerk downstairs. "I want to find out all I can about a boy who was in your class last term, B.J. Riggs. I want to know why he isn't in school now."

"Riggs? Excuse me, but I can't seem to place the name. You understand, I had so many children last year, with this terrible overcrowding, and we're already well into a new term."

"He's small for his age. He limps."

A bit of life flickered in the blank black eyes. They blinked, and Miss Lena thought she heard a metallic click, like the sound of a computer retrieving information. "Oh. You must mean B.J. *Brown.*" Miss Lena heard the click again, and realized it was the teacher's loose upper plate.

"That's him."

"I always require honesty from my students. And honesty begins at home. Like charity." Miss Echols flashed a brief, false smile that was more alarming than her normal frozen expression. Fortunately the smile vanished as quickly as it had appeared. "Therefore I always insist *above all* that they be honest about themselves. His name *is* Brown, is it not? Bond J. Brown?"

"That's what his birth certificate says," replied Miss Lena.

"Exactly," said the teacher triumphantly. "Well, Mrs. Brown, I must say it's a little late to be coming here asking about your son. Where were you last spring, when he was in so much trouble?"

Miss Lena neither confirmed nor denied the appellation. She simply asked, "What kind of trouble?"

"Poor attendance, for one thing. You *must* be aware of that."

Miss Lena's blank stare was improving with practice. "Go on."

"Well, after Christmas recess, he was out of school more days than he was in. I don't have the attendance records any more, of course, but I don't believe he was here more than two days out of any week, or ten days out of any month."

Miss Lena pounced. "Did you ever try to find out why he stayed out so much?"

Miss Echols waved her arms in a gesture of futility, setting off a cacophony of jangling brass. "Really, I don't think you can begin to appreciate the multitude of problems I have to deal with here. I had thirty-eight children to teach. I couldn't be out in the streets looking for one. That's the attendance officer's job, after all. Besides, Bond didn't have the capacity to do fifth-grade work."

"Are you sure about that?"

"Positive. As you know, he had already been left back twice, once in the fourth grade and once in the fifth. He scored in the low seventies on his I.Q. test."

"Where did he sit when he was here?"

"Back there," said Miss Echols, waving at the rejects in the rear.

"Mm-hmmm," Miss Lena said.

"It was very sad, but what could I do? I couldn't raise his intelligence quotient, after all. Maybe if he'd had more stimulation in the home—"

"Like what?"

"Well, if you read books to him. If he even saw *you* reading books and magazines. If you talked to him more, told him interesting things, took him to interesting places. A number of authorities say the I.Q. score is as much a function of environment as it is of innate capacity."

"You don't say," was Miss Lena's non-comment. She was not ready to correct the teacher's mistaken assumption that she was B.J.'s mother. She wanted to learn all she could first. One of the most interesting things she was learning was how it felt to be a reject, and to be treated by this royal personage like a cockroach that had crawled onto her shoe.

"Well, that is all speculation, of course. As it was, I had to think of the other children, the ones who wanted to learn and were able to."

The little ladies and gentlemen, thought Miss Lena,

who soaked up information like computers, and would grow up into big computers like this one.

"Your boy," Miss Echols continued, "was never here enough to catch up with them. But when he *was* in class, his behavior was terribly disruptive."

Miss Lena continued to pretend ignorance. "Meaning?"

"Mischief. Pranks. Throwing paper. Making noise."

"Maybe he was bored," Miss Lena suggested. "They say bright kids get bored the easiest."

The teacher gave her a pitying smile. "Oh, I doubt that, Mrs. Brown. Really, I doubt it. I know all parents like to believe their children are bright. But in Bond's case, all the evidence pointed to the contrary. Believe me, I put up with his behavior as long as I could. I was sympathetic to his special problems."

"Which were?"

"His physical and mental handicaps, of course. I kept him on the roll most of the year, as you know. But I finally had to ask the principal to suspend him."

"What for?"

Miss Echols bent her majestic head close to Miss Lena's and whispered, "Stealing," as if she were whispering "sodomy." "I caught him in the cloakroom, taking the other children's lunch money."

"Did you ever think maybe he took it because he was hungry?"

The brilliant black eyes, which seemed to have no lashes, gave Miss Lena a piercing glance. "Of course. But I am not supposed to feed these children, only to teach them. As it is, I do more than that. I don't just teach them to read and write; I try to give them some of the standards which may be lacking at home. That is why I will not tolerate dishonesty. Naturally, I thought Bond might be undernourished. I could guess that from the terrible state of his clothing."

Miss Echols' bright eyes moved from Miss Lena's polished black kid boots to her matching purse and her finely tailored dress of double-knit yellow wool. Miss Lena was aware of an adding machine behind the eyes, clicking off the cost of each item.

When she had added up the grand total, the teacher said, "Really, I find it hard to be sympathetic with the selfishness of some parents. From Bond's appearance, I assumed that poverty was a problem in his home situation."

"If you knew anything at all about his 'home situation'," Miss Lena replied, "you'd know you was talking to a dead woman."

"I beg your pardon?" said the startled teacher.

"I won't take up any more of your time," Miss Lena said, making a swift, smooth exit. "Thank you very much for talking to me. I've learned a great deal."

The main thing I've learned, she thought as her heel plates clattered down the iron steps and the cement ones, is that B.J. doesn't belong in that woman's classroom. Neither does any other human child. I wouldn't send a *dog* there.

Miss Echols was the retarded one; unable to learn anything new since her graduation forty years ago from some Abnormal School. Somewhere else in the city there might be a school that would hold B.J.'s interest, with a teacher who would understand that he deserved to be treated as an equal. A man teacher, hopefully, who would know about things like carpentry and machinery that provided sensible reasons for learning long division and decimals. If her strength held out, Miss Lena would try to find such a teacher. But first she had to find B.J., and she had less than ten minutes in which to get back to her shop and admit Miss Allinson.

Nine

When Miss Lena reached her shop, what greeted her eyes was a scene so hideous her brain at first refused to register it.

Her window had a jagged hole so large it appeared to have been smashed by a charging rhinoceros. Behind the hole the denuded mannequin lay on its side like a decapitated war victim. When she finally forced her numbed legs to carry her to the door, it was as thoroughly locked as she had left it. So much for her efforts at security. Out of habit, she started to relock all three locks behind her, then abandoned the useless effort and left the door open.

A stiff breeze blew through the hole in the window, lecherously lifting empty skirts and riffling magazines. Her shop, on superficial inspection, looked as if a hurricane had struck it. But a quick check made it clear that Miss Lena had been the victim of a human hurricane.

It or they had made a mess of everything, but had selectively removed only those things that could readily be sold. Her thousand-dollar inventory of piece goods: velvets, leathers, silks, wools, tapestries, tweeds. Her color television and her AM-FM radio.

Her antique furniture, unpopular in style, was untouched. So were the unfinished garments in her work room. Missing only were the completed items: the mannequin's new yellow silk dress; a long beaded gown, padded to transform a transvestite into a voluptuous woman; a misty mauve lace dress that belonged to her richest customer, Mrs. Roderick Lewis; a signature print shirtdress painstakingly tailored for Miss Van Wyck. Also most distressingly missing were Miss Allinson's coat and the mink that was to have lined it.

Who had done this to her? Who? Suspicions crossed her mind, and one suspicion in particular kept recrossing, but she had no time for speculation now. First she took the folding screen she had used to protect her customers' privacy before she made the velvet curtain and placed it to block off that chilling breeze. Then she made three phone calls. First to the police. Then to her insurance agent, who said, "I guess you know what this means."

"Yes," she answered quietly. No more insurance. Nothing to replace her lost stock or her customers' garments if it happened again. No operations for B.J., either, though his problems were the least of her worries right now.

She was persuading the reluctant carpenter to come board up her broken window when that unfortunate boy sidled around the door and into her devastated salon, looking, in spite of his new clothes, as bedraggled and ashy as a veteran ragpicker.

"You talk to my teacher?" he asked.

Motioning him to be quiet, she raised her voice to a pitch of hysteria and threatened everything but suicide, a bravura performance that moved the carpenter to promise to be there before five o'clock. Miss Lena hung up and thrust a broom into B.J.'s hands.

"Help me clean up this mess. I'm expecting a customer in ten minutes. Move!"

He was eyeing her strangely, but she didn't have time to decipher his expression. "You talk to my teacher?" he asked again.

"Yes."

"What you find out?"

"What you told me. You can't go back to that school. For God's sake, get a move on, B.J. Help me get this place looking decent before Miss Allinson gets here."

"What happened?"

"What does it look like happened?" she asked irritably. "Use your eyes. Some hoodlums broke in here and robbed me."

B.J. was still motionless. "I'm sorry."

"Why? It's not your fault."

"Yes, it is."

"What do you mean?" she asked sharply. A picture flashed into her mind, of him talking to that smoothly dressed older boy.

"Uh . . . if you hadn't taken me out shopping, it wouldn't have happened."

Briefly, she considered this notion, and decided she was lucky. If she'd been there when the thieves came, she might be lying on the floor now, helpless and broken as that mannequin. "You don't know that," she told him.

He started to say something else, then looked down at his arms, seemed surprised to find a broom at the end of them, and went into furious motion. She worked briskly beside him, gathering his sweepings into a large trash can. Working was good; it kept her from thinking about her misfortune. They worked so well together they had the salon looking neat again by the time there was a knocking at the door, too gentle to be the police. Miss Lena drew the green curtain on the back room's disorder, B.J. ducked behind it, and Miss Allinson practically fell inside.

Miss Lena would never stop marveling at the extreme self-centeredness of most people. Miss Allinson had not noticed anything unusual about the condition of the shop. Nor—relieving Miss Lena's most pressing worry—did she ask to try on her coat. She only wanted to talk, it seemed. Flopping down on the love seat like a bag of laundry, she complained, "That awful Mr. Porter at my bank is driving me crazy. He thinks Raymond is only after my money." She gestured downward over her plump body, which was clothed, as usual, in a loose, matronly dress of no particular color. Miss Lena had made it, and a dozen others indistinguishable from it. Much as she would have liked to brighten up Miss Allinson, give her a little zip, she firmly believed in giving her customers what they wanted. Especially her steady customers.

"Oh, I know I'm not much to look at," Miss Allinson continued, "and I'm no spring chicken either. And of course Raymond is younger than I am. But, really, ten years—is it such a terrible difference these days? Why can't people believe somebody could want me just for myself?"

Her eyes, as red-mottled as her complexion, looked piteously at Miss Lena. "I feel like I'm being persecuted," she said. "I know it sounds crazy, but those awful people at the bank are persecuting me. Mr. Porter has had Mr. Major calling me every day. And now one of those young lawyers in Mr. Major's office is calling me *three and four times* a day. He's a terrible young man, that Mr. Schneider. Like a bloodhound. He never gives up." She dabbed at her eyes with a bit of lace-edged linen. "This morning I couldn't stand it any longer. I walked out and left the phone ringing."

"What do they want?" Miss Lena asked with more interest than she felt. She knew that listening to her customers, and never repeating what they said, was as important a part of her business as dressing them. If she ever stopped providing a sympathetic ear for women's troubles she might as well take down her sign.

"They want me to make Raymond sign a lot of horrible papers they've drawn up. Signing away all his rights to my money before I marry him."

And they're right, thought Miss Lena. "If he loves you, he'll sign them," she said practically.

"That's what Mr. Porter said." Miss Allinson's eyes begged for understanding. "But I *can't* ask him, don't you see? It would hurt his pride. Raymond doesn't make much money, driving a cab, but he's terribly proud and sensitive. Maybe it's because he's always been so poor."

"I see," Miss Lena said. Oh, I see, all right, she thought. You're afraid you might lose him if he can't get his hands on your money. You don't believe somebody could want you just for yourself, either. She felt pity for the unhappy woman slumped before her, then checked her emotions. Didn't she have enough to worry about without taking on rich white folks' problems? The days when mammies worried about Miss Ann's headaches while their children were dying of starvation in the cabins had been over since slavery.

"I don't think you do," Miss Allinson said, and drew herself up on the love seat with touching dignity, her stout neck rising turtlelike out of her high collar. "I wanted to give him a small sum of money as an engagement present. Just a thousand dollars. But he wouldn't take it. He intends to support me." She waved a miniscule engagement ring under Miss Lena's nose. "This was all he could afford. But it was a real sacrifice for him. It means more to me than the Kohinoor." She began to cry again.

B.J., who had disappeared into the work room when

Miss Allinson arrived and had been discreetly busying himself back there ever since, came out with a box of Kleenex.

He delicately offered it to Miss Allinson. "Don't cry no more, ma'am. Brides shouldn't cry. Would you take off your hat, please?"

He seemed to have a hypnotic power over Miss Allinson, who dutifully removed the colorless cloche she always wore. Her hair sprang free like flames shooting up in dry tinder.

"Excuse the way it looks, please," she apologized. "I left the house in such a hurry, I didn't even take time to pin it up."

"Why pin it up? It's beautiful!" B.J. said, and darted back to the work room again.

"Raymond thinks so," Miss Allinson said shyly.

"Raymond is right," said Miss Lena, who had never seen Miss Allinson's magnificent hair before. It was such an unbelievable shade of bronze-red it had to be real. No chemist could duplicate that color.

"Green," B.J. declared, returning with a piece of grass-colored silk the thieves had overlooked. "Don't you think so, Miss Lena?"

"Definitely. With that hair, yes, definitely, green."

"But won't it be a bit . . . gay?" Miss Allinson asked hesitantly.

B.J. said firmly, "Brides are *s'posed* to be gay."

As if in response to his command, Miss Allinson produced a smile. Miss Lena had never seen *that* before, either. It was a nice smile, with very white, very even teeth, causing a dimple to dent one cheek. Miss Allinson was growing better-looking every minute, in spite of her dowdy clothes. It really didn't matter what rich folks wore, thought Miss Lena; with all that good dental care from childhood on, you could always see their money in their mouths, right up front where it counted. Sometimes she wanted to cry for the working women who came to her, especially the black ones. By the time they could afford to dress well, any effect she could create for them was invariably spoiled by gaps in their teeth. Often she wanted to tell them, "Forget about clothes till you've bought some bridgework." But of course she never did.

"I don't know," Miss Allinson said doubtfully. "I never wear colors."

"Why not?" B.J. asked boldly.

She had no answer but, "Mummy always said . . ."

B.J. challenged her. "That was a long time ago, right?"

"Yes, and bright colors at *my* age . . ."

"You're younger than me," said Miss Lena, who wore, today, a knit dress in brilliant golden yellow. "Let me make it up for you as a wedding present." Since B.J. had opened the door on an opportunity, she was going to walk right through it. From one wedding-present dress could grow an order for an entire trousseau.

"Where did you get this wonderful elf?" Miss Allinson asked.

Miss Lena laughed. "I found him on my doorstep one morning."

"Keep him. He'll bring you luck."

"I think he already has," Miss Lena said, though a contrary idea, only half-formed, was tugging at her mind.

Miss Allinson flashed her perfect smile again and said, "Oh, Lena, I'm so glad I came here today. I was so confused this morning I was almost crazy, but now I know what to do. I'm going to marry Raymond at

Christmas just as we planned, and I'm going to invite you to my wedding. Please bring this wonderful little boy. He's done so much for me, I wish I could do something for him."

"Well," said Miss Lena, pointing to a mayonnaise jar with a slot in its lid that had recently appeared on her counter, "this is his bank. He was saving up for the future till someone broke in here and took his money."

"Oh, Lena, what a shame. Did they take anything else?"

"A few things," she said drily.

"Lena, why didn't you tell me? I'm ashamed. I was so wrapped up in my own problems, I didn't even think to ask about you."

You're not unusual, Miss Lena thought. Very few people do. Aloud she said, "That's all right. How could you know?"

"Anybody who looked at that window could know," B.J. pointed out.

"B.J.!" Miss Lena rebuked him.

"Could I help somehow?" Miss Allinson offered eagerly. "Could you use a loan?"

Independence was such a deeply ingrained habit with Miss Lena she did not even consider the offer. "Oh, no, I have insurance. I'll manage."

"But those companies never pay the full value of what you've lost. And some things are impossible to replace."

"True," Miss Lena said, thinking of a certain lining that had been custom-made to fit a one-of-a-kind coat.

Miraculously, Miss Allinson was not thinking about the same thing. "Lena, if you have any trouble getting insured again, please let me know. My brokers will do a favor like that for me, I'm sure."

That was the kind of help she could accept. "I will," Miss Lena said gladly.

"Now, I mustn't forget this little boy's bank. How much did you have in it, dear?"

"Four or five dollars," B.J. muttered.

"Well, now you've got it back."

Only Miss Lena noticed that his eyes filled with tears when Miss Allinson put a five-dollar bill in the bank. And her only reaction at the time was to think, *Kids are strange.*

Miss Allinson, preparing to leave, was chattering happily to herself. "I suppose we can't have much of a honeymoon; Raymond only has a week off. Where can you go in a week? Oh, how silly of me. Jets go anywhere in a few hours. I've always wanted to see Rome, but it's up to Raymond. In any case, I'll need clothes. Dresses and coats and skirts and blouses and—*I* know what I'm going to do this afternoon. I'm going to walk through all the stores and look at everything, and not buy a single thing. I'm just going to decide what I want and come back here and have it made."

"B.J.," Miss Lena said after her customer had floated out of the shop, "I don't think you should have talked to that lady like that."

He shrugged as if to say, "Why not?"

"Look," said the expert eavesdropper, "I know them bank guys are right. This young dude gonna spend up her money. Sure. But she got plenty, and she gonna have a good time while he spending it. And we, we gonna be busy making clothes for her. Clothes, clothes, and more clothes, so she can keep looking good for him. So *everybody* gone be happy. What's wrong with that?"

"I don't know," Miss Lena said, unable to attack this fortress of logic, yet feeling that it stood on slippery moral ground. She sighed. Everything in her life had changed since B.J. entered it, even her firmest business principles, such as leaving her customers' lives strictly alone. Her own life was in danger of being taken over by this brash brat. She had better put him in his place right now.

"Now, this next lady's different," she warned as a silver Cadillac hit the curb at an angle, mounted it arrogantly, and parked on the sidewalk. "You just leave her to me."

She hadn't needed to warn him, though. Mrs. Cosgrove's perfumed, jangling presence was too much for B.J. He kept edging toward the door while she paraded around the salon in the muslin pattern for one of her costumes, a halter bra and a brief sarong. "Marvelous!" she shrieked. "I must have three of these! No, four!" The air was further shattered by the stamping of her platform-soled shoes and the clatter of the four pounds of junk metal she wore on her wrists.

Miss Lena, who did not lie, except by omission, commented on the only item she could honestly admire, a new mound of iridescent stones that rose from Mrs. Cosgrove's right hand.

"Oh, do you like it? Edward gave it to me for our anniversary," her customer said with distaste. "I have to wear it for awhile, or he'll be hurt. But I don't think it suits me, really. So *pale.* Besides, I've heard opals are supposed to be unlucky."

"Some people say they are, unless they're your birthstone. But I wouldn't pay any attention to that. It's a beautiful ring."

"My birthday's in July."

"Then," Miss Lena said, "you should wear rubies."

"Rubies. Yes, *they* would suit me. I must tell Edward," said her customer, strutting and posing in front of the mirror. For five minutes she was too absorbed in her reflection to notice either Miss Lena, patiently waiting to insert some pins, or "the darling little boy" with his back to the door. When she finally saw B.J., she shrieked and swooped to embrace him. He ducked, wriggled, and got away with a mere head-rubbing.

Mrs. Cosgrove was almost too much for Miss Lena today, too. There were six costumes to be fitted, and by the time she was finished, all that chatter, all that overpowering *ego*, had given her a severe headache. But she was not going to get any relief from her headache that afternoon.

Ten

As soon as Mrs. Cosgrove left, the carpenter and the police arrived in a big clumsy cluster. They crowded awkwardly into her little salon, which was arranged to a woman's proportions, and a dainty woman's at that, stamping and pacing and snorting like caged animals.

"I'll come back later, Miz Ricks," offered the carpenter, whose name was Mr. Bumby.

"Oh, no," said Miss Lena, who knew how many weeks away "later" might be. Mr. Bumby, a tall, flabby man with a drooping moustache that matched his sad expression, was a pensioner twenty years her senior. He never did a job without complaining that he didn't know why, since he was retired on full pension and didn't need the money. "These police officers won't take long, I'm sure, Mr. Bumby. In the meantime, why don't you help yourself to some coffee?"

"Uh . . . don't you have anything stronger?"

"No."

"Well, if you'd pay me a little something in advance, I could just nip around the corner for a few minutes and . . ."

And come back staggering. Or never. Miss Lena had learned about paying him in advance the hard way. "I'll pay you *after* you do the work," she said firmly.

"But I need money to buy plywood," Mr. Bumby whined.

Miss Lena knew how to get around that problem. She wrote out a check to the Hance Brothers Lumber Company and handed it to the carpenter, who waddled out, grumbling about how these womens were so evil these days they didn't trust nobody.

"When did this happen?" the tallest and broadest officer asked. She had already jotted down his name, Oliveri, and his number for the insurance company.

"It had to be sometime between eleven-thirty, when I left the shop, and a quarter of two, when I got back."

"How did they get in?"

The question reinforced the impression of stupidity she'd gleaned from a moon face set with eyes blank as pale gray stones. "You can see for yourself, Officer." She pointed to the shattered window.

"Yes," said the younger, slimmer cop, who must have barely met the height requirements for the force, and whose dark restless eyes focused sharply wherever he looked, "but it looks like it was broken from the *inside.*" He probed the floor in small circles with the toe of his boot. "Notice, Joe? No glass on the floor."

"We swept," she explained.

"Shouldn't have done that, lady," said Oliveri.

"But I was expecting a customer. If you'd arrived sooner, you'd have found plenty of glass on that floor, I assure you."

"Should have waited for us before you cleaned up, lady," the big cop repeated like a robot.

"Doesn't matter, Joe," said the younger one, whose name was Ramirez, and who clearly outranked him. "There's a bushel of glass on the sidewalk. They had to break it from the inside." Focusing those dark eyes intently on Miss Lena, he asked, "Anybody got a key to this place besides you?"

"No one, Officer."

"Well, then, can you explain how the thieves got in?"

"I believe that's your job," she said haughtily, then regretted it. Her high tax bills had given her the bad habit of treating all civil servants like personal servants. To seem more cooperative, she added quickly, "My front door was tightly locked when I got back. As you can see, it has three locks, including one on a short chain that can only be opened with my key after both the other locks have been unlocked and the door has been opened a few inches."

"And they were all locked when you got back?"

"Yes," she said, worried about her insurance, feeling suddenly stupid. She should have lied and said the door was open. She should have told B.J. to sweep the sidewalk, not the room.

But how could she have thought of so many things so quickly? And how could she be sure it would have fooled that smart young officer, anyway?

"Any other way to get in this place?" Oliveri asked.

"Cellar door, Joe. I already checked. Padlock is on tight. Doesn't look tampered with. Unless somebody besides her knew the combination—"

Miss Lena shook her head.

"You got insurance, madam?" the big officer asked.

Suddenly indignant, she shot back, "Yes, and if you think I arranged this robbery myself just to collect it, you must think I'm insane. I lost almost everything I need to carry on my business, and there's no chance I'll get enough money back to replace it. I'll be lucky if I get half, and some of the things can't be replaced for any amount of money."

"You don't plan on closing up your business?"

"Of course not. How would I live?" she snapped, her anger getting out of control.

"Calm down, lady," the young Puerto Rican policeman said. "Nobody's accusing you of anything. There's just a small mystery here that has to be cleared up, that's all. Looks like somebody got in here the easy way, then smashed the window to make it look like they did it the hard way. Maybe you can help us find out who that might have been. Got any ideas?"

Yes, vague ideas, repulsive ones, but none that made sense as yet. Miss Lena shook her head and remained mute.

Ramirez pressed on. "When I noticed the floor in here was clean, you said, '*We* swept.' Who was here besides yourself?"

"A boy who helps me. Here he comes now."

B.J., looking as if he had come to the wrong place and was about to leave abruptly, was back from the fictitious errand he had invented to escape Mrs. Cosgrove.

"You know anything about this robbery, boy?" Oliveri asked roughly.

B.J. shook his head.

The big cop shook him by the shoulder. "Speak up, boy! Answer me."

"He couldn't have done it, Officer. He was with me while I was out."

"The entire time?" Ramirez asked.

Miss Lena paused to reflect. B.J. had run off and left her at the school. She had gone inside alone and come out alone. She had spent an hour, or at least forty-five minutes, without him. Miss Lena did not like the turn her thoughts were taking. But she saw the mute pleading in his eyes, which were white as golf balls, and said, "Yes."

"He didn't have to do it himself," the young Latin cop said thoughtfully. "He could have tipped someone off."

Miss Lena recalled that arresting figure gliding out of the alley. Why had B.J. been so anxious to see him? What could he and that tall, elegant boy possibly have to talk about?

Another question broke in on her reverie. "Does he have a key to this place?"

"Who? B.J.? No, Officer, I told you, no one has access to this building except me. And the landlord, of course."

The big cop jerked a thumb at B.J. "But he hangs around here a lot, right?"

Miss Lena nodded yes.

"Do you know the combination to that cellar door lock, boy?"

"No *sir,*" B.J. answered quickly.

"Well," Oliveri summed up briskly, "we'll write up our report. *'Theft by person or persons unknown.'* Give us a list of everything you lost, ma'am, so we can O.K. your insurance claim."

Miss Lena was relieved. Apparently Oliveri was the ranking officer, after all, and he was impatient with the younger one's clever detective work. There only remained to hand over the list of missing items, which she was afraid to pad because the circumstances of the theft were so suspicious.

"We'll come back from time to time to check on you till you get reimbursed," Oliveri said, and left with his companion.

Miss Lena had not expected any extra police protection, but why was it promised only until she got paid? Why not afterward, as well?

B.J. translated the policeman's parting remark for her. "He gonna make sure you give him some of it."

"Why? What for?"

"For making it look good to your insurance company, of course!" he shouted as if at an idiot.

"I hate crooked cops," Miss Lena said vehemently.

"I hate *honest* cops, myself," B.J. said.

"Why? Because they might catch some of your friends?"

"They mess up *all* my friends. Even you. That little Spanish cop almost kept you from collecting on your insurance." He added darkly, "He'll change, though. He'll have to. Most *cops* hate honest cops too."

While she pondered this, he made a cautious tour of the shop, looking suspiciously in every corner. "She gone?"

"Who? Oh, you mean Mrs. Cosgrove. Yes, thank God."

"You need to put some more clothes on that lady. She too old to be running around half-dressed like that."

"I know. But I have to give my customers what they want, B.J."

"I know you got to do it sometimes, Miss Lena. But do you got to do it *all* the time? That lady got a razor back with a hump in it. You could take a hammer and play a tune on her ribs. Her jugs got wrinkles. Her legs look like road maps, and she so bowlegged you could drive a bus between her knees. If I was her husband I wouldn't let her out the house. And if I was you—"

"Yes?"

"I'd cover all that stuff up with cloth before she scares somebody and gives 'em a heart attack."

"I was afraid you might say something like that, B.J. That's why I asked you to stay out of it."

"Oh, you didn't have to worry 'bout me sayin nothin' to *her*, Miss Lena. I didn't want her huggin' and kissin' on me. I might catch whatever it is she got."

"Stop it before you make me laugh, B.J. I have a headache." Miss Lena had always wondered why ugly people got such glee from poking fun at other people's looks. B.J. was no Prince Charming himself, and never would be, unless the witch who had messed him up came along to change him back. But she did not remind him of that.

He looked at her with eyes so narrow they disappeared into wrinkled pouches. "Where she gonna wear them clothes? On a beach?"

"Yes."

"She better hope they ain't no buzzards hangin' around."

Miss Lena was choking on her own laughter. "Buzzards only attack dead people, B.J."

"That's too bad," he said. "People like her don't never die. They just ugly away."

Miss Lena tried to move him to repentance. "She liked you, B.J. She said she was sorry you had to leave. She even put a quarter in your bank."

"She got to give me a lot more than a quarter to let her hug me. I want more than that just for looking at her. I want fifty dollars just for letting her rub my hair. Hey, Miss Lena, why white folks always got to be messing in our hair? They think they gonna find some money in it?"

"Maybe," Miss Lena said. "Maybe they think it brings them luck."

"I think so, too. A lady around our way paid five dollars for a money-drawing lodestone, but her number ain't come out yet. Would that ring be bad luck for you?"

"I told you, I don't believe in unlucky stones."

"She oughta give it to you, then. She don't like it nohow. When's your birthday?"

The question triggered the annual depression that always sent Miss Lena running off on a trip to somewhere—anywhere—in late December. Her headache had been lifted by laughter, but now it was replaced by the dull pain around and behind her eyes that meant she needed and wanted to cry. She was unable to, though. Years of self-discipline had made it impossible for Miss Lena to cry for herself. She could not even feel self-pity any more; all she could feel was this general sadness and pain. She tried to stave it off by saying lightly, "Oh, I never think about my birthday. I have too many other things to think about."

"You mean you don't like to think about getting older?"

That too, she thought, resenting his bluntness because it was so accurate, but refusing to admit he was right. "No, it's just that nobody else ever remembered my birthday, so I got in the habit of forgetting it too."

B.J. looked astonished. "Nobody ever remembered *your* birthday? Why not, Miss Lena?"

The gloom was thickening, but she spoke lightly. "Oh, I guess because it comes at a time when people have too many other things on their minds."

B.J.'s forehead was knotted in puzzlement. "When's that, Miss Lena?"

"I was born on Christmas. December twenty-fifth."

"God's birthday!" he exclaimed. "No wonder everybody forgot about you."

"I was outclassed by the competition," she said drily.

"Well, this year somebody's gonna remember, Miss Lena."

"Now, don't you be planning something foolish, B.J. I told you, my birthday doesn't mean anything to me."

"Well, it means something to me, because nobody ever remembered mine either. Until this year."

"What happened this year?"

"You made me a new pair of pants."

"You mean today's your birthday?"

"Yep. I'm fourteen today, but I feel like I'm only one, cause this was my first *real* birthday. You made me a new pair of pants, and took me shopping for a whole lot of other good stuff, and took me to a restaurant, and everything."

"But I didn't know it was your birthday, B.J."

"It don't matter. You *acted* like you knew it."

"Well, happy birthday, B.J."

"You already made it happy."

"I'm glad. But I didn't buy you those things, remember? You bought them yourself, with money you earned. So don't think you have to pay me back."

"I don't think that," he said. "I'll tell you what I do think, though. I think you like jewelry."

"*Some* jewelry," she said. "Not costume jewelry."

"What's that?"

"Imitation stones. Junk. I only like the real thing."

"Was that ring real?"

"Yes. It was the only real thing she had on."

"Like I said before, she oughta give it to you. She too ugly to wear it anyhow."

"I won't hold my breath waiting," Miss Lena said cynically, for Mrs. Cosgrove was as stingy as her behavior was extravagant. "Besides, I wouldn't wear it."

"Why not?"

"Because it was a great big clump of stones. Look." Miss Lena held out her small, bare hands. "I wouldn't put a lump like that on these little fingers. It would weigh them down. I would only wear a very small ring, because I'm a small woman."

"But you don't wear no jewelry at all, Miss Lena.

How come? Didn't your husband give you a diamond like that other lady's?"

"Yes," Miss Lena said. *"Exactly* like that other lady's. The smallest one in the store."

"Where is it?"

"I sold it."

"Why? Didn't you like diamonds?"

I didn't like *him,* she thought. I got so I didn't want any parts of him and his big ugly self, or his big ugly house, or his stingy little jewelry either. None of it was worth having to listen to his lying schemes and his nasty talk every night and then go wash out his stinking socks in disinfectant. She had thought that old anger was long extinguished, buried under years of ashes, but it still had the power to leap up and sear her. She squelched it and said simply, "I needed the money."

"Wouldn't you like to have your diamond back?" he wanted to know.

"No."

He clearly disbelieved her. "If *I* was a lady, and my birthday came on Christmas, so I only had one day to get presents, *I'd* want a diamond."

"Oh," she said, "I'd be happy if someone gave me a stone like that, B.J. But who would?"

"I might."

"You'd better not."

"But you got to let me get you something now!"

"Why now?" she asked sharply. "What's so special about now?"

"Well, you just got robbed and everything. . . ." His voice trailed off.

"B.J., who was that boy you were talking to outside the school?"

"A friend of mine."

She tried a wild shot. "Well, you can tell your friend for me he's an amateur."

"What you mean?"

"Whoever robbed me didn't have sense enough to break that window from the outside. All the glass is out on the sidewalk. So it's clear they got in here another way. Have you any idea what way that was, B.J.?"

"No, ma'am," he mumbled. But his eyes had performed a wild ballet while she questioned him. Miss Lena was remembering the first day she'd seen him. Her trash was out on the street before she arrived. And the inside of her locked shop had been cleaned. She was putting two and two together, adding another two, and getting an unpleasant sum that seemed less improbable each time she rechecked her calculations.

"Where are you going, B.J.?"

"Out to sweep up your sidewalk."

She would have detained him to question him further if the carpenter had not come clumping back then with his plywood. She had decided that she wanted a pair of hinged doors behind her window, to be closed from inside with a heavy iron bolt that would turn the window into a sealed box.

Of course, if the police were right, the thieves had not entered through the window. What should she do, then? Buy fierce dogs, to pollute her salon with foul odors? Hire armed guards, to frighten her few remaining customers away? Oh, it was a trek across the desert in pursuit of an ever-receding mirage, this quest for "security" in a predatory world. Nevertheless, Mr. Bumby was standing there awaiting her instructions, so she gave them.

"You should've told me right off," he complained. "I didn't buy materials for all that. All I can do today is board it up."

"Board it up, then," she told him wearily. "But I don't want it left like that for more than a couple of days."

"You gonna pay me today?"

"I'll pay you when you're *finished,*" she said firmly.

She ignored Mr. Bumby's whining—if somebody gave him a thousand dollars with no strings attached, he would complain because it was not more—and tried to ignore his banging and hammering as well. But that was not easy. He was the sort of man who could not do a job without calling constant attention to himself.

The carpenter's hammer was driving more nails into her forehead than into her window frame, and his accompanying complaints made her want to scream. Instead, she took a tranquilizer and lay down to wait until he was finished. Only when Mr. Bumby was gone did she rouse herself to go outside and look for B.J.

There was no sign of him, only a broom leaning against the boarded-up window, and the neatly swept pile of glass waiting in the gutter to destroy someone's tires. Maybe it was her fatigue, or her headache, or the pill she had taken to relieve it, but she made no effort to remove the broken glass. In her present mood, she didn't care if Mrs. Cosgrove's Cadillac ran over it. Nor did she care to search for B.J.

She could easily put off questioning him until another day. After all, the worst she had feared had already happened. He could do her no further harm. He would pop up again shortly, like weeds and pimples and all other perennial nuisances. In the meantime she would do better to be quiet and add what she had learned to what she already knew.

Eleven

Pop Earl Boggs, a fat cigar in his fat mouth, grunted in disgust. "We can't sell this thing."

"What's wrong with it?" asked Bobo.

"No black woman's gonna hide mink *inside* her coat, fool," Pop said around his cigar.

"What we gonna do with it, then?" his big scar-faced son Earl Junior asked. "You want it, Marvel?"

Earl Junior's main girlfriend, Marvel Scott, was wearing a long silver thing with nothing under it. B.J. could tell because it was cut down almost to her waist in front, and when she shrugged, she rippled all over like water. "Like your old man said, I want my good stuff to show," she said.

"Too much of it shows, if you ask me," Earl Junior complained.

"It's mine to show."

"The hell it is," Earl Junior said, grabbing at her rear as she swayed past him.

Marvel gave his possessive hand a sharp slap. "I ain't your property, nigger," she told him, and walked over to the sofa to nestle beside Bobo.

From the corner, where he had seemed to be sleeping, Jayjay rumbled, "Put her out of here. She ain't got nothing to do with our business."

"Take it easy, Jayjay," Earl Junior said to him. "Marvel's the smoothest professional east of Chicago. Put her in a maternity dress, and she'll walk out a store with half the stock on her stomach."

"And that's the only way you'll ever get me in a maternity dress," she informed Earl Junior.

Then she took Bobo's hand and placed it on her knee, cutting her eyes at Earl Junior to see if she could make him mad. Bobo began to stroke the thin covering of silver stuff. It looked like Reynolds Wrap. B.J. was surprised it didn't crackle. B.J. didn't like Marvel Scott. She had silver fingernails, too. He was glad he had put Miss Lena wise to her. At least he had saved his friend from being cheated that one time. He didn't want to think about the other thing he'd done that had caused her to lose much more. He couldn't stand to see Bobo petting that nasty woman, either. Especially with Earl Junior reaching inside his jacket to where he always kept a knife.

B.J. walked over to the sofa. "You tricked me," he accused. "You went on ahead without me and did it by yourself."

Bobo opened eyes that had been blissfully closed and said, "Not quite."

"Who was with you?"

"A couple of my boys. You don't know them."

"Well, you should of took me instead. They messed up."

"What's your complaint, Short Boy? We broke the window, didn't we? Ain't no way they can blame it on you."

B.J. had learned some painful things lately. His hero had several flaws. He was attracted to a nasty old thing like Marvel Scott, he was deceitful, and, worst of all, he was dumb. "I thought you had brains, Bobo, but you're dumb. Dumb, dumb, dumb! Breaking that window was the dumbest thing you ever did. The sidewalk was covered with glass. Any fool could see you broke it from the inside. You should have broke down the door instead. Now you got the cops interested."

"I got the cops covered," Bobo said, closing his eyes again and sliding his hand higher up the silver column.

"Not this one, you ain't. He's a new one. A smart little spic you ain't never seen before."

Bobo opened his eyes and frowned. "What's his name?"

"Frank Ramirez."

"I'll get him taken care of," Bobo said with assurance. But he was not touching Marvel Scott any more; his fingers were nervously twining and untwining around each other instead.

"Yeah? Well, who's gonna take care of *you?* You need a keeper or something. Here I thought you were smart, and come to find out all you got is bean soup for brains. . . ." To his shame, B.J. found he was crying.

"SHADDAP!" a voice roared from the corner. "I give the orders around here. Tall Boy, if you'd stick to what I tell you, you'd never have any trouble. Now, what's Short Boy got to do with this?"

"Nothing," Bobo lied. "Nothing at all, Jayjay."

"He better not. I told you to leave him strictly alone. Short Boy, you run along and let us get finished with our business. And you leave too, girl."

Marvel bristled and got suddenly ugly the way she always did when she was mad. "Ain't that some nerve? Asking me to leave my own apartment. You hear that, Junior? I'm staying."

"Hon," Earl Junior coaxed, "ain't you got a little shopping or something to do downtown today?"

"I like it where I am," she replied, and moved closer to Bobo on the long white plastic couch, pressing her silver leg against his long leather one.

Earl Junior said, "If you're gonna rob the cradle, why stop there? Short Boy, here, is even younger."

"He's so short I can't even see him," she said arrogantly.

B.J. stung with the truth of this. That day at Miss Lena's, he'd ducked into the back room because he was afraid Marvel might recognize him and tell all his business. But, then and now, her eyes slid over him with as little recognition as if he were an ant. No, less: she would at least notice an ant long enough to step on it.

He was too absorbed in these humiliating thoughts to notice exactly when the flash of steel appeared in Earl Junior's hand. Marvel had provoked the trouble she wanted.

"Well, Ima fix that one there so he's too short for you too. Ima cut off his legs and leave him some stumps to walk around on. Then, just to make sure you ain't interested, Ima cut off that other thing too."

B.J. wished fervently that Earl Junior would cut Marvel instead. Slash her face and make her *permanently* ugly. But it was Bobo he was after; poor stupid Bobo who, suddenly alert, had risen from the couch and was circling around behind it, his arms held out pleadingly-protectively in front of him. "Hey, man, take it easy. I'm sorry. You my ace, you know that. I didn't know she was your woman."

"You wouldn't know your face from your shadow, either. Both of 'em so black they blot out the sunlight. I wish you'd get out of here so I could see."

"Hey, hey, man, I'm sorry, O.K.?"

Marvel Scott was not worth getting cut over, but B.J. did not like to see Bobo back down. "Why don't you fight him, Bobo? He's an old man. You can beat him easy."

But that "old man," Earl Junior, was powerfully built, armed, and agile. Instead of challenging him, Bobo swung a hand against B.J.'s mouth so hard it knocked him to the floor.

He scrambled to his feet and hammered Bobo's chest and stomach with his small fists. *"I'll* fight you then, dammit," he screamed through tears dyed red with rage.

He was flung backward against the wall. As he slid to the floor, something came crashing down on top of him.

"My new lamp!" Marvel screamed. Yes, it was a lamp, a plaster African that had held up a bulb instead of a spear. Now he was headless and bulbless as well as spearless. B.J.'s own head ached as if it were going to break off next.

"Earl," rumbled Jayjay, addressing the elder Boggs, Earl Senior, "we can't have a meeting if you can't keep your women and children under control."

"They're not all *my* children," Pop Earl informed him pointedly. "Marvel, honey, you got any wine in the kitchen?"

"Who's gonna pay for my lamp?" she demanded.

"Don't worry," he soothed. "You can buy yourself a dozen new lamps after we get through with what we got here. Now go get us some wine, that's a good girl."

Muttering something under her breath about crazy niggers, Marvel went out to the kitchen and returned with a bottle of wine which she poured into glasses for the two men and Bobo. She did not bother to give Jayjay a glass; just took him the rest of the bottle.

He drank half its contents, wiped his lips, and spoke. "The point is, I don't care what you got, I don't like Tall Boy running around pulling capers on his own."

Pop Earl said in his warm, slow, molasses voice, "But

it was a good job, Jayjay. We'll get at least fifteen hundred for this merchandise, and we can sell most of it easy."

"I don't care if it's worth a million," Jayjay said, banging his fist on the floor to emphasize his words, "he works for me, and he's supposed to obey my orders. You all heard Short Boy say he made some dangerous mistakes."

"Yeah." Earl Junior had not yet put his knife away. "And he still makin' em. Next time they might be *fatal* mistakes."

"That's my first point." Jayjay banged his fist on the floor again. He always lounged on the floor, probably so he wouldn't have so far to fall when he passed out. Already his words were becoming slurred. "No more jobs unless I plan 'em."

"But—" Earl Senior began.

"No buts. Unless you want *your* butts put out in the cold. You and Junior are strictly in charge of the selling end. *Getting* the merchandise for you to sell is strictly up to me.

"Which brings me to my second point. Seems to me everybody's forgotten our long-term plan. You, Tall Boy, wearing five-hundred-dollar suits. You, Junior, keeping company with this high-priced hussy. How we gonna go into a *real* business if we don't build up our reserves?"

The two Earls, father and son, exchanged disgusted looks that to B.J. meant clearly, "Oh, now we got to listen to him talk his bidniss doo-doo again, and we got to pretend to believe it."

"Finish the wine, Jayjay," Pop Earl offered genially, clearly hoping B.J.'s old man would pass out soon.

But Jayjay seemed likely to stay conscious awhile. "*I*

don't waste money. You've seen how I live."

They exchanged looks again which meant, "Yeah, like a rat in a hole."

"Like the Jews. Like the Chinks. They don't mind sacrificing to make a point, and neither do I. That's because I have a dream. You see some Jew living behind his store, some family of Chinks living above their restaurant, and you wonder how can they stand it. Then all of a sudden they got five stores, ten restaurants, and you wonder how they did it. Simple. Sacrifice! Discipline! They were willing to sacrifice for a dream. Well, I have a dream too."

"So did Martin Luther King," Bobo said in a sinister tone, "and he dead."

Jayjay did not seem to hear him. "I don't plan to be a two-bit thief forever. I understand this country. This country was built on stealing. It doesn't mind if you steal as long as you don't get caught, and as long as you use the profits to go in a legitimate business and get respectable. Once you do that, you get respect. You don't have to bow down to any man. You can be a king. King of your own business empire."

Jayjay drained the bottle of the juice that crowned him king, and continued, "Now, I've got my eye on some nice properties not far from here. I'm thinking about nursing homes. Have you any idea how much money can be made on nursing homes? Old people are living longer, and most of them got no place to go. The government pays plenty to look after 'em. Why shouldn't they be paying us?"

Last time it had been fast-food restaurants, and the time before that, a chain of car washes. B.J. didn't want to hear the details of his father's latest dream. The others had to listen, maybe, but he didn't. Hoping Jayjay's eyes would close soon, he began sliding along the wall toward the door. . . .

"Now, your overhead on each patient should be fifteen dollars a week. Less if you run a really big operation and save on food. It's best to keep 'em healthy, though, else you run into all kinds of hassles about nurses and doctors. The government pays you twice your overhead. Four times as much if your patients got Social Security and not just welfare." B.J. could hear the effect of the wine in the way his old man was beginning to repeat himself. "People are living longer. Most of these old folks got no place to go. Big volume, and no turnover but death! No turnover till they stop turning over. Hah! If we could buy that big old mansion down the street, we could handle the funeral business too. All we need is a little more capital and one licensed mortician. I know one. I know a nurse, too. Registered. I make it my business to look up the right people, cause I've got vision. There's a great future waiting out there for men with vision. But do you have vision? No. You smalltime crooks have small minds. You can't see any farther than the next highball, the next prizefight, the next costume change, the next joy ride, the next piece of tail. . . . Come back here, boy!"

James J. Riggs' red eyes were glazing, but they could still see.

"You told me to leave, sir," B.J., at the door, said meekly.

"I changed my mind, Short Boy. I just remembered I ain't had time to discipline you for running away from home and not telling me where you been. Not properly, I ain't. So you just stay right there till I'm finished. . . . Now, where was I?"

Bobo's hateful grin looked like an entire piano keyboard. That was when B.J. knew he had to run.

"Oh, yeah. Now, to buy these buildings and turn 'em into nursing homes, we need capital. Investment capital *and* working capital. I'd say, at least forty-five thousand dollars. I've got my fifteen thousand; have you each got yours? No, don't bother to tell me, Earl, you've both been spending it fast as you get it, and neither one of you got two quarters to rub together. You better change your way of living, or I'll have to look for some new partners."

Jayjay was nodding now. B.J. made his run for it. Even if he was going back into a possible trap, it was better than the certain danger he was running from.

Twelve

Seven days gone by, and still no sign of B.J. The headache was constant now. The thing that sat on her shoulders had become a solid block of cement rigidly bolted to the granite column that was her neck. She could not turn it in either direction, and bending it forward produced a blinding stab of pain. Also, there was a rhythmic beating in her ears, deep and slow, like a bass drum. With each *boom,* the cement shattered into fragments, only to solidify in the ensuing silence. Miss Lena, who had never heard the sound before, went to the window to see if there happened to be a parade passing by. But of course there was no parade. The noise was her own pulsebeat, amplified.

Thoroughly frightened now, she thought: My pressure must be way up. Call the doctor. No; lie down and calm yourself. Put that pesky kid out of your mind. Put *everything* out of your mind.

Ten minutes of rest on the love seat had reduced the boom to a roaring like the sea when there was a rapping at her door. For a wild moment she both hoped and feared it was B.J. with her coffee.

But it was only LaReine, née Leroy, Harris, for whom Miss Lena had refused to make an evening gown last week. Her excuse had been the short notice and her busy schedule. Her real reason had been a wish not to expose B.J., who had already been exposed to too much else, to this particular side of her business.

But now there was no reason not to admit LaReine.

She was kind and amusing; she would distract Miss Lena and might even make her feel better.

LaReine was wearing what was, for her, drag: a man's black raincoat over gray trousers and a black saddle-stitched blazer, with a white shirt and a conservative tie. The effect was disturbing: a masquerade. Leroy's real personality, as he always said, was only expressed by the things Miss Lena made him.

Taking her cue from the clothing, Miss Lena said, "Well, Leroy. How are you?"

"Never been better, Miss Lena"—his standard reply. One of the things she liked about Leroy was his cheerful refusal to make others suffer with him; he would say that even if he were coming down with pneumonia, and once had. "I just dropped by to tell you how it went Saturday night."

Saturday night had been Hallowe'en. It had also been "Boys Will Be Girls Night," a transvestite beauty contest, at the Basin Street South Club: the social event of the year for all LaReines. Miss Lena would never understand why this underground event, which was held secretly and never made the newspapers, was so important to people like Leroy, but she knew it was the biggest thing in his life. So she asked, as if it mattered to her, "Did you win?"

He pouted, unfurling thick lips that were usually minimized by makeup. "I would have, but some prejudiced judge disqualified me. They gave the prize to a stumpy little white thing that looked like a fireplug."

"That's a shame."

"Shame ain't the word for it, Miss Lena. She hadn't even bothered to *shave.* I don't mean her face, I mean her arms and legs and chest. They were covered all over with hair. And then she had the nerve to let it all hang out in a two-piece outfit."

Miss Lena chuckled. "Like a gorilla in a bikini, huh?"

"Exactly, Miss Lena. You took the words right out of my mouth. It was out and out discrimination. There I was in my gorgeous black satin gown, the one you made me last year, with the fabulous figure built in and the coq feathers all around the hem. I had rhinestone earrings down to *here,* and an eight-foot coq feather boa I found at the Broadway Costumers. And when I slung that girl over my shoulder and let it drag on the runway, they were whistling, stomping, cheering, even throwing flowers at me! Nobody else got a reception like that. I mean your mother was into her *thing!* And then they turned around and gave the prize to Queen Kong."

"How could they do that?"

"Oh, that old saggy-butt judge was just jealous 'cause I looked better than any of the white contestants. Or maybe the fireplug was her nephew, I don't know. Anyway, the judge recognized my gown from last year and disqualified me because you can't wear the same drag two years in a row."

The drum was pounding again; he had made her feel slightly guilty. "I'm sorry, Leroy."

His eyes, naked without false eyelashes, were wide with dismay. "Oh, please, Miss Lena, don't say that. I didn't tell you about it to make you feel bad. It wasn't your fault. It was mine, 'cause I didn't give you enough time to help me get my thing together. You know your girl has to have the best, a five-hundred-dollar gown or nothing, and I wanted to make sure I had the bread before I asked you to make it. I didn't get the money till the beginning of last week."

"Well, at least you've still got it," she consoled him.

"Yes, and I'm not going to waste it on any more bigoted affairs in this small town. Next time your mother steps out, it'll be in New York or Hollywood. This is a hick town, and the people here are strictly smalltime and low-class. That's what offended me, Miss Lena. The vulgarity! I told you that number who walked off with first prize had on a two-piece outfit. Well, not only could you see the hair on her stomach. When she bent over, you could see the Jockey label on her underwear!"

Miss Lena applied pressure to her throbbing temples. "Don't make me laugh, Leroy. It hurts."

"She was probably a cop," he said darkly. "That's why she won. The cops have taken over everything in this town, and an honest girl doesn't stand a chance. I haven't told you the worst. Here I was, Van Raalted from the skin out, with my fine custom-padded frame, and all she'd done was stick some more of that old Jockey underwear up front. I was ashamed to even be seen competing with something like that."

"Better luck next year, Leroy."

"Told you, I'm not casting my pearls in front of those swine any more. If I go at all next year, I'm going straight. Black tie and tails. You be my date, and we'll sit back and laugh at the pigs on parade. Is it a date?"

"Why not?" It would be amusing, she thought. And what a relief not to have to spend all of next October padding Leroy into the shape Nature had not given him. He was fussy, even more of a perfectionist than Miss Lena. But he paid well. All the boys who would be girls did.

"I thought I might take that money and blow myself to some silicone treatments. What do you think about them?"

What would he come up with next? But she remained cool. "I hear they're dangerous."

"Oh, your girl believes in living dangerously."

"Also, they slide down. The force of gravity, you know."

"And spoil my waistline? No thank you," Leroy said in horror, hands moving downward over his beautifully tapered body. What a waste, Miss Lena thought briefly: he was so clearly intended to be a man. Yet, when fitting him, running tape measure and hands over that sleek perfect body, she had never felt the slightest stirring of excitement. Was it because she had lived as an old maid for so long she had become one? No, she decided, it was not a lack in herself, but a lack of interest emanating from Leroy. He had thought of himself as a woman for so long that he was tuned in to the female wavelength, and she could only relate to him as to another woman.

"Besides," she said practically, "how would you keep your job?"

Leroy was a sanitarian for the city, checking on the observance of health codes in beauty parlors, food stores, and restaurants. On the side he peddled a line of cosmetics to all the beauty shops on his route. His commissions were more than his salary, but he spent both faster than he earned them. Recalling the amount he'd spent on evening gowns over the years, Miss Lena regretted her decision to sew only for real women. B.J.'s innocence, if he had any, was hardly worth that much money.

As if he'd read her thoughts, Leroy asked, "How's the little fella?"

"Oh, he had a cold. I sent him home." Inside her head, the surf pounded on sand.

"You don't look so good yourself. Been working too hard?"

"I guess so."

"Child, listen to your mother. It ain't worth it. You better take some time off and enjoy yourself. I think I'm going to take that money and treat myself to a week in the Virgin Islands. Why don't you come with me?"

She might, at that. People like Leroy were charming companions who made no demands, and that was all Miss Lena wanted now. At the beginning of her life alone, it had taken a massive effort of will to channel all of her urges into her business, but she had succeeded. With all her energy drained by creative work, she had not wanted a real physical man in years. And what for? Miss Lena had observed that many of the men who were not in jail seemed headed there by the fastest route possible, if they were not committing slow suicide with drink and drugs. She had decided long ago that she was better off without one, and it was too late to turn back now.

"The only reason I might not go," Leroy announced, "is if I decide to get those silicone treatments."

"What about your job, Leroy?" she reminded him again.

He made a grimace. "I guess you're right. I have to keep a steady gig to support my life-style, at least till I find a rich sponsor. Then I can be a lady of leisure." He looked at his watch, a complicated affair with a blue face and three silver dials. "Lord, I've got five beauty parlors to check out before lunchtime. And we've got a new office manager who watches the sign-out sheet like it's the family jewels. He uses the phone to spot-check, too. And if you ain't exactly where you're supposed to be when he calls—" He made the gesture of cutting his own throat. "So you know your girl can't goof off like she used to, popping in on her friends and cruising the boutiques. I've got to fly."

"It's always nice seeing you, Leroy. Come back soon."

"Listen, think about going on that vacation with me. You look like you could use it. And you get free room and board at the hotel if you can find one."

"One what?"

"A virgin, of course. Anywhere in the islands." With a giggle and a wink, he was gone, leaving Miss Lena smiling. She was able to close her eyes and imagine herself already at the beach. The surf still pounded inside her head, but not as strongly. It was low tide. Bathers in straw hats and bikinis waded in the shallows. On the shore, a colorful fashion parade swayed past in samba rhythm: tourists in Paris-made wrappings, natives in homemade ones. A soft breeze tickled the palm fronds, sent bright sailboats scooting across the horizon.

A sound like distant thunder interrupted her daydream. The trash trucks, like prehistoric monsters, were already rumbling up the street, pausing at each door to gobble their meal of discards. They sounded close. And her cans were not out on the sidewalk.

Miss Lena clattered down the cellar stairs without even taking time to switch on the light. She knew the arrangement of her basement so well she could find her way around it in the darkness that was barely lit by two small windows.

But at the foot of the stairs, she stumbled over something that had never been there before. It gave out a metallic clang as it struck the wall.

On her hands and knees where she had fallen, luckily without serious injury, she groped for and found the overturned object. It was the enameled pan she had used for washing out lingerie and stockings during her years of basement residence. But now it gave off an aroma very different from laundry. Miss Lena sniffed and choked back nausea. Someone had been using her washbasin as a cooking vessel. There was a slimy, stinking gravy spill mixed with the dust on her knees and her hands.

Disgust at the mess postponed her panic. Miss Lena got to her feet and headed straight for the lavatory. On her way there, she thought she heard a strange sound, but that did not deter her. She was still gagging, and her fastidiousness was too strong to let her vomit on the floor. Once she was standing in front of the toilet, her self-control prevailed, and her breakfast stayed down.

Here, too, there was evidence of an intruder. The seat was up, and the selfish male who had left it that way had aimed badly. Dirty towels and wads of paper littered the floor in the kind of piggish disorder that Miss Lena could not tolerate, along with stiff, balled socks. They reminded her of her husband. Was it possible that Ricks had pursued her here? For the first time she felt fear. Ignoring it, she turned to the filthy basin and scrubbed it before washing her hands and knees. Her skin was scraped, but she did not feel pain, only annoyance at her torn stockings. Nor was she frightened when she turned off the water and heard labored, wheezing breaths, interspersed with bubbling snores, coming from just outside the bathroom.

Even if he was down on his luck, Ricks wouldn't dare come back to her. She was one-third his size, but she had given him forty licks in return for his one the only time he had struck her. The beating had literally brought him to his knees, ending his domination over her and, with it, their marriage.

Remembering her strength back then, the last of her

terror abated. All she felt was fury. Whoever had been dirtying her basement was still sleeping here. Probably some low-life bum, so rum-soaked all that noise had not wakened him. Probably a dangerous character, too, but Miss Lena did not consider going for help. She wanted immediate action. The police would take too long to arrive and, once there, would be likely to leer at her and imply that the intruder had her permission to sleep on the premises. That was what had happened the last time she called to report a prowler. And if it *were* Ricks —in the dark, eerie basement, she could not totally reject that irrational possibility—they would say he had a perfect right to be there. At the beginning, when it seemed important, she had not had the money to buy a divorce; later, when she had the money, she had put him out of her mind so completely it no longer seemed as important as other things.

Nervous again, but fully alert, Miss Lena edged back toward the stairs on tiptoe. Her eyes had become accustomed to the dim light, and she did not stumble this time. There was a broom at the foot of the stairs, and she got a firm grip on it with her right hand before flicking the light switch with her left. Snores still came from the cot across the room, but their source was not visible. She only saw a mound of covers. Miss Lena advanced stealthily toward it.

The mound did not stir while she aimed the broom at the area which she judged to be its posterior. When the blow landed, the covers recoiled. Miss Lena struck again. First a stream of foul language, reminiscent of Ricks, emerged: "Muhfuh, I ain't messin' with you. Lemme the fuh alone." Then a head of long woolly hair, sticking up at wild, uneven angles, popped out. Miss Lena rapped it smartly with the handle of the broom.

"Ow! Cut it out, Miss Lena! It's me!"

The sleep-bleared eyes had recognized her before she could recognize B.J. Her own eyes were clouded by a red film of rage, and through the red mist her arms continued to rise and descend like pistons, striking not just B.J., but James Ricks, her lazy brother Lester, low-minded cops, all the no-goods who had tried to mess up her life.

"I don't care who you are, you got no business sleepin' down here without my permission. Git out of that bed before I kill you."

"I ain't got no clothes on."

"I don't care. *Git!*"

The broom descended again, and B.J. leaped naked from the cot, turning his back. His modesty only made it convenient for her to aim another blow at his rear.

"Ow! Let me get dressed, Miss Lena! It's cold down here!"

"Never mind. I'm gonna warm you up good and proper." She made good her promise, landing several more swats as she chased him around the cellar, until the naked imp got away from her and ducked into the bathroom. She heard the latch click.

She mounted guard outside the door. "Won't do you any good," she said, panting heavily. "You've got to come out sometime. I can wait all day."

"I'll come out now, Miss Lena. Just gimme my clothes."

As her breaths slowed down she felt her sanity returning. "First give me some answers, you tricky devil. How long you been living down here?"

He was sobbing. It did not move her. Too bad trickery and deceit were the basic weapons in B.J.'s arsenal of survival. She could not stand trickery, especially when she was its object; it always turned her to stone.

Sniffle, wheeze, cough, sob.

"Well?"

"A long time."

"How long?"

"Since August."

She gasped. All that time, when she thought she was alone in her shop, this lying, sneaky kid had been living down there and eavesdropping. Learning her schedule, her secrets.

"How'd you get in?"

Sniffle, sob. "I—I hung around all summer. You never noticed me. I always hung on the corner and watched you open your lock. Didn't take me long to figure out the combination. It was easy. Four-three-two-one."

So he had been spying on her all summer, too. Humiliation fueled her anger. She thought she had been clever to pick a combination that she could remember easily and open quickly. It had never occurred to her that it would also be easy for a determined crook to figure out. And that was what B.J. was: a crook.

"Unlock that door and I'll give you your clothes."

The latch clicked and the door opened a crack. A brown claw emerged from the crack and snatched the clothes from her.

She waited thirty seconds, then asked, "You dressed yet?"

"Yes."

"Well then, come out of there."

"You gonna beat me some more, Miss Lena?"

"No."

Only his spiky head appeared cautiously around the edge of the door. B.J., wishing to grow a bushy natural, had never given in to her urgings to get a haircut.

"You gonna put me out, Miss Lena?"

"Yes."

"You want me to put the trash out first?"

"The only trash I want out of here is you."

"Please, Miss Lena. I been sick. We ain't got no heat at home. No hot water, neither."

He had tried tears first, then an offer of helpfulness, and finally a plea for pity. None of them worked on her. Not this time. She was stonily silent.

"We had heat and hot water for awhile, though, even after we couldn't pay for 'em. See, my father used to work for the gas company, and he knew how to go out to the curb and turn the gas on himself. All you need is this little tool to open a valve and get gas free. But the company found out he done it, and they came out and turned it off *permanent.*"

"Proud of him, ain't you? That's where you belong, at home with your tricky father. Till the cops come and put you both in jail where you *really* belong."

"Aw, Miss Lena, what law did I break?"

"Breaking and entering. Trespassing on private property. *Stealing* private property. And tricking your best friend. That's worst of all. I can't stand lying, tricking, deceitful . . . Now *git!*" she cried, because her own tears of hurt and rage were threatening to spill over. She brandished the broom at him.

He stood, hesitating, midway between the stairs to the street and the stairs to the work room.

"Which way you want me to leave, Miss Lena?"

"The fastest way. You want me to help you up them steps with a boot in your behind?"

He fled up the interior stairs, pausing halfway to call, "If you don't hurry, you'll miss the trash men."

"One thing sure," she said. "I won't miss *you.*"

Thirteen

B.J. heard the ragged baritone voice haranguing before he pushed open the door, and trembled until he saw that for once the old man wasn't talking to himself. Good. The presence of Bobo and those two smaller guys meant the postponement of Pop's wrath. It also meant some extra body heat to take the chill off the room.

Jayjay, his attention on the others, might not even have noticed his son if B.J.'s chest hadn't acted up again like it had been doing all week. It squeezed in, then exploded out in a loud hacking cough.

"Oh-oh. Here comes bad news," Bobo said.

"Boy," Jayjay thundered, "why you always show up at the wrong time? Get out of here. Can't you see I'm busy?"

"I'm too sick to go out," he said between two volleys of hacking.

His father made an indistinct angry noise, then said, "Get in the bed then. Cover up. Your head too. I can't stand the sight of you right now. Can't stand the sound of you either. Shut up that coughing!"

B.J. tried, muffling the cough with his covers, snuffling the cold up inside his head and keeping the poison inside his body like some precious essence. He wanted to seem asleep. He knew he wasn't supposed to hear what the old man was saying to the others, so he covered his head. But he parted the rags to leave himself a one-eyed view.

"Now," Jayjay said, "I'm gonna run through the plan again, and this time maybe something besides lint will stick in your nappy heads. Where you gonna meet?"

"Larson's main entrance on Clearview Street," said Bobo.

"What time, Pee Wee?"

"Eleven-thirty," the smallest boy answered.

"And what you gonna do first, Twinky?"

"Go up to the boys' department and buy some sweaters."

"*Buy* some sweaters?" the littlest one, Pee Wee, asked incredulously.

Jayjay gave him a head-cracking slap on the left ear that made B.J. jump. "Yeah, *buy* em, jackass. They don't like kids hanging around the store, so you got to spend some money, or they'll put you out. And no helping yourselves to anything else in the boys' department. Understand?" He emphasized his point by smacking the boy's other ear just as hard.

"Hey, cut it out! That hurt!" Pee Wee cried.

"I meant for it to hurt. I want you to remember."

"I'll see he does," Bobo promised.

"I wish I could count on that. Nobody's told me yet what you're supposed to do *first.*"

"Buy a shopping bag," said the boy who was about B.J.'s age.

"Thank you, Twinky," Jayjay said sarcastically. "Now see if you can remember the rest of this. There's a shopping bag machine just inside the main door. They sell small Larson's bags for a dime and big ones for a quarter. You get a big one. Now, you got to be out of the boys' department and back down on the main floor by what time?"

"Twelve o'clock," the hapless Pee Wee piped, then ducked to evade a third blow.

"No, dum-dum, twelve-fifteen. Maybe we better give

up and forget the whole thing," Jayjay said wearily.

"No, no, don't give up, Jayjay. They'll get it, I swear," Bobo pleaded.

Jayjay picked up his wine bottle, sucked on it a few seconds, then went on, "Twelve-fifteen is when you gotta be back downstairs. Twelve noon is when Earl Junior's woman gets there with her lover boy."

"Earl Junior gonna work with us on this?" Bobo asked. B.J. was surprised too; he knew the Boggses Junior and Senior never stole.

"No, jackass, this is some other dude she knows, someone she uses for her act. You don't need to know their part, but they're gonna ask to look at engagement rings. When you first get there, check out the jewelry counters and see where the diamond rings are. It should be the first counter on your right when you walk in the main entrance."

"But they're always *under* the counter!" the one called Twinky protested.

"Yeah, well, they won't be by half-past twelve. They should be right out on top, waiting for you to grab 'em." Jayjay grinned his hideous snaggletooth Dracula grin. "Marvel and her boyfriend gonna get the salesgirl to take out all the trays of rings. They're gonna have a little argument about size and price. First a lovey-dovey discussion, you understand, *then* an argument. By the time you're on the scene, they should be soundin' like they ready to kill each other instead of marry each other. Then Marvel gonna walk off mad in one direction, and her boyfriend gonna walk off in another direction. And that's when my friend Carmichael steps in."

"Who's Carmichael?" Bobo asked.

"The security guard I told you about, fool. Big, black,

about four feet wide, with gray hair and bad feet. Carmichael's gettin' tired of walking. He wants to pay down on a car, that's why he's workin' with us. Anyway, Carmichael's gonna grab Marvel for copping one of the rings. And that's when you slide up to the counter and do your number. Not till the salesgirl's down at the other end, though."

"How you know she gonna go down there?" Pee Wee wanted to know.

"Do I have to tell you kids everything? Marvel will swear she didn't do it, naturally. She gonna say the salesgirl must have been careless and dropped it. Then she gonna run behind the counter to look for it, and Carmichael gonna chase her and call the salesgirl to help him. It's gonna turn out the ring *is* on the floor, cause that's where Carmichael will pretend to find it after Marvel slips it in his hand. He and Marvel will both start blaming the salesgirl for being so careless. But by that time the three of you should be long gone. While they're into their hassle, you slide the trays into the shopping bag and put the sweaters you bought on top."

"And run like hell," Twinky added.

"No, take your time. Stroll out like you got all the time in the world and not a thing to worry about. 'Cause you ain't. You all got bicycles?"

"Bicycles!" they chorused in amazement. "What for?"

"I been thinkin' bicycles are the best thing to get away on. Cop cars can't chase a bicycle through all them little alleys and side streets downtown. You with the knobby head, what's your name?"

"Twinky."

"You stay out front and watch the bikes, Twinky, and

let Bobo and Pee Wee here go inside the store. That way I only got to pay for two sweaters."

Jayjay felt around under the stained mattress he was lying on and pulled out some money. He handed a ten and a twenty to Bobo. "For the sweaters." To Pee Wee he gave a quarter. "You know what this is for?"

"For the shopping bag," the boy answered him. "What about carfare?"

"We gonna ride our bikes downtown, fool!" Twinky answered him, arresting Jayjay's hand before it struck Pee Wee a third time.

B.J., seeing his old man produce money, decided to dispel the illusion that he was not awake. "Can you have them get me some medicine, Pop?"

"What you want medicine for, boy?" Jayjay growled.

"I got a bad cold. I need food too. And orange juice, and vitamins . . ."

"Orange juice? Vitamins? Who's been giving you all them big ideas? What you need is a good kick in the pants, but I'm too busy to give it to you now."

"But I'm really sick."

"Shut up and go to sleep. You ain't supposed to be listening to us right now. Now, you knuckleheads think you got it all straight?"

They each recited the plan back to Jayjay, one at a time, until he was satisfied that they had it memorized.

"Oh, one other thing. Don't go down there in them Hallowe'en costumes."

"What you mean, Hallowe'en costumes?" Bobo asked indignantly.

"Them velvet pants and shiny shirts you got on. Them purple sweaters. Them high-heeled shoes. I want you to dress neat and clean, but plain. Look like schoolboys."

The chorus of cynical laughs this produced indicated that none of them had been to school in a long time.

"I think maybe you all forgot what schoolboys look like. So I think you better get into your school clothes tomorrow and come back here for an inspection. Get out of here, now."

After they were gone, there were five minutes of silence before B.J. dared speak up again. Five minutes while he shivered under the covers and watched his old man polish off a large jug of wine. He supposed it kept Jayjay from feeling the cold in the room.

"Pop?" he ventured finally.

"Huh?" the old man replied with a jerk of his head, as if he'd forgotten B.J.'s presence and had already drifted into a warm dream.

"Pop, you really got fifteen thousand dollars?"

"That's for me to know and you to guess. Why you ask?"

"Well I was just thinkin', if you got that much money, maybe you could spend a little bit of it to get me a doctor."

"You don't need no doctor," Jayjay said, starting on another bottle. "I always say if it's your time to go, it's your time. If it's not your time, you'll live. Doctors is just racketeers." Jayjay pulled on the bottle, then sank back on the mattress, back into his world. "Besides, I can't spend what I got. It's my working capital. That's the only difference between niggers and white folks, boy, and don't you forget it. Niggers have money, but white folks have capital. You may think I'm mean and stingy now, but you'll thank me for it someday. You're a cripple; nobody's gonna give you a job. But nobody can fire the president of the company, either. When you take over the business, you'll say, 'I never gave my old man enough credit. He sure was thinking about my future.'

I may be dead and gone by then, but you'll thank me when you're sitting behind your desk and running the factory."

B.J. didn't bother to ask what kind of factory. The latest issue of *Opportunity Magazine* lay on the floor, with a headline on its cover that said, "Small Parts Are Big Business." Nor did he bother to ask again for medicine or for food to stop the cramps in his belly. Jayjay was in his wine world now, dreaming about small parts or whatever business he was going to invest in this time for B.J.'s future, and there was no way to reach him to say he did not believe in a future for himself any more.

The day seemed unusually hot for this late in the year, the kind of steaming, oppressive heat that could get a person bear-caught, the Southern expression for sunstroke. Breathing was difficult, and walking more so, as if the air were a solid mass that she had to displace in order to move. Miss Lena swam through it laboriously in the direction of the hardware store.

Faces, the same faces she saw every day, nodded to her through the broth that seemed to rise from the sidewalk. She nodded back. That was as far as Miss Lena's street conversations ever went. To keep people out of her business, she stayed out of theirs. If she encouraged them to become familiar, she would be inviting trouble. So she did not know the names of the newsstand owner with a blue film of age over his dark eyes, or the grocer arranging baskets of produce outside his store, or the short-order cook turning hamburgers on the grille in his window, the barber cutting hair in his, the two men repairing a car, or the fat woman who sat on her steps minding a crowd of small children so close in age they could not all be hers.

As a wave of dizziness assailed her, and the pounding

of the surf recommenced in her ears, Miss Lena had a frightening new thought:

If I felt myself fainting and hollered for help, what name would I call? If I fell out on this street right now, who would rescue me? Who would pick me up off the sidewalk; who would call for an ambulance?

She knew the chilling answer: No one. Miss Lena had remained a stranger in her own neighborhood, and city folks were reluctant to get involved with strangers. Especially black folks, for whom survival was such a desperate struggle most of them had something to hide. It might be a job to supplement welfare, drinks sold after hours, or a basement full of stolen goods for sale. Whatever the secret, a stranger was suspect until proven trustworthy. Even a petite lady past fifty might be a plainclothes detective, a probation officer, or an investigator for the Welfare Department. Until she was known, she would be shunned.

Miss Lena recalled the wistful tale of a pretty young customer: "I was going steady with a detective last year. I really liked him a lot, but I had to break off with him when the people in my neighborhood found out what he was. *Everybody* around my way's doing something wrong."

That "something wrong" might only be preying on the government, but when that failed to suffice, Miss Lena knew, poor black people preyed on each other. That was why she had kept her neighbors at arms' length. The truth was, she was more comfortable with white people than with low-class blacks. Not that she trusted whites, but she understood them thoroughly and knew how to handle them. Blacks were more unpredictable and more desperate, therefore more dangerous. Trusting neither group had left her very much alone.

A child scooted into the street, and the woman who was too heavy to chase him screamed, "Tyrone, come back here!" One of the men straightened from his task under the hood to loop a long arm around the boy and haul him back to safety. It occurred to Miss Lena that not all of these people might be hostile and dangerous. They seemed to look after one another. Perhaps, if they knew her, they would look after her.

But they didn't know her. "So that's that," she told herself fiercely. "You can't fall out on this street or anywhere else. You have to stand on your own feet till the day you die."

She did not realize she had been talking out loud until a bunch of fingers, big as bananas, closed firmly around her elbow. The large hand was attached to the same long, sinewy arm that had scooped up the child and carried him out of danger.

"Can I help you, ma'am?"

"I don't believe I know you," she said frostily.

"Probably not, ma'am. I know you, though. You're Miss Lena, the dressmaker. B.J. is always talking about you."

"Oh?"

"Sure. He says you're nice people. Can I walk you home?"

The eyes were kind, but the earth-brown face had so many scars and trenches in its surface it looked like a battlefield.

"I can manage fine by myself, thank you," she said, withdrawing ever so slightly from his hand.

"You sure?" he asked, his eyes shaded with doubt. "You been hugging that pole like it was your long-lost mamma."

Not till then did she realize that she had been "standing on her own two feet" only with the help of both arms tightly embracing a telephone pole. Her fingers, it seemed, had become locked together. She disentangled them with some difficulty.

"You sure you O.K.?" the man repeated.

"I'm fine, thank you," she said, sounding distant even to her own ears, which were ringing. The sidewalk looked distant, too, but if she stepped carefully, her feet would reach it. She experimented and stumbled; the pavement was higher than she had thought. He caught her arm again.

"It's nothing," she told him. "Just the heat. So unseasonable. I should have worn a hat, but I never expected it to be so hot this late in the year."

"I think you ought to let me take you home."

And let this dangerous-looking character, who might have stepped from a Most Wanted poster, find out where she lived? Break in, rob her, perhaps kill her in the middle of the night? Oh, no.

"I'm not going home, thank you," she said firmly. "I'm fine now. It was nothing. Just heat exhaustion. Perhaps a touch of sunstroke."

"A touch of something else, if you ask me," a woman's voice mocked as Miss Lena stumbled up the street, coping as best she could with the pavement that rose and fell perversely to confound her sense of balance. "You mean a *taste* of something else," a man's voice quipped.

They think I'm drunk, was her furious thought. Pride steadied her walk. She followed the lines in the paving to keep from reeling. It worked. It also stilled the laughter.

Curbs were the most difficult to navigate. The vast stretches between them were jungles inhabited by careening monsters with grinning radiators and shrieking horns. Still, impelled by single-minded determination, she made it to the hardware store, where she looked over an assortment of padlocks and finally selected the one she wanted. It was the most expensive lock in the store. A little brass pin, inserted in its side, allowed her to change the six-digit combination as many times as she wished. After the man showed her how, Miss Lena turned her back and set the lock to open at her birthdate: 12–25–19. She would remember the combination, but no one else would be able to guess it.

Thinking how shocked B.J. would be the next time he tried to get in kept her laughing exuberantly and dizzily all the way back to her shop. Just let that little monster and his thieving friends try to rob her again! She really ought to put in an electrified wire to give those little devils a foretaste of hell. But the sturdy new lock would frustrate them enough for awhile.

After she had switched the padlocks, Miss Lena could not think of any reason for staying at her shop. Her single urgent errand had drained both her energy and her memory; she could not remember anything else that needed to be done today. She headed for home.

The stairs to her third-floor apartment were unusually steep today, but there was a sturdy iron railing, and no one in the hall at this early hour to observe how heavily she leaned on it. Once the familiar, comforting interior enclosed her with its safety, Miss Lena was sure she did not need to see a doctor. She should never even have allowed her mind to dwell on illness. It had been the heat. Only that.

To counteract its effects, Miss Lena prescribed for herself a tepid bath and a large pitcher of lemonade. Also briny pickles and salted crackers to replace the salt lost by sweating, though she was supposed to be on a low-salt diet. Salt and fluids were exactly what she needed. She rejected her tranquilizers and pressure pills just as she had mentally rejected the doctor; all that sort of thing went along with illness, and Miss Lena definitely was not ill. A little dizzy from the heat, perhaps, but time would soon take care of that.

Her favorite hostess gown did not seem to be where she had left it last, so she settled for the nearest thing at hand, a terry cloth after-bath wrapper. She would never have allowed company to see her in it; but then, she was not expecting company. Only the people on TV.

Stretched out barefoot on her white sofa, careless of the wet spots her bare feet made on it, Miss Lena abandoned herself to the unaccustomed luxury of watching daytime TV. Oh, she often had it on in the shop, but only as a background to work; she never really watched or listened. The steady stream of arriving and departing customers made that impossible. Now she learned at last the names of the people on *Secret Heart* and the reasons why the beautiful young patient on *General Hospital* could not marry the handsome young resident: she had leukemia, and he had a spiteful wife who would not divorce him. The revelation did not make Miss Lena sad. Theirs would be the most beautiful sort of love, all hand-holding and poetry, and the perfection and the poetry would not end, as they usually did, with the white gown and the flowers and the organ music. The romance would go on forever in his and the viewers' memories.

Her favorite, an afternoon talk show, followed. The host was sleek and amiable; his guests, glittering. Their clothes, though, she noted critically, were not half as well designed as the ones she turned out in her work room. If she dressed that curvy red-haired movie star, she would definitely not put her in pink ruffles. Glancing down at her half-open wrapper, which was stained with lemonade and older, less identifiable stains, she was glad the TV people lived behind one-way glass and could not see her as well as she could see them.

That was not the only agreeable thing about them. They only came into her house when invited, and whenever she tired of them, they left instantly without hurt feelings. While they were there, she could be as rude or as attentive as she liked. They did not require her to join in their conversations and did not even notice if she failed to listen. If they became boring or offensive, she could turn off the sound.

She could not do the same with her customers' conversations, with Mrs. Cosgrove's strident boasting or Leroy's frothy chatter. Nor could she turn off B.J.'s endless, persistent questions, any more than she had been able, a dozen and a half years ago, to stop her husband's drunken ravings.

After all those years, she thought she had erased the vicious monologues that were vomited by his sick imagination from her memory as thoroughly as he always forgot them by the next day, but now they unreeled with the horrible fidelity of a tape: "You're the worst person I ever knew in my life. You don't deserve to be alive. You giving it away in the street, but you too good to sleep with me. And you giving away my money, too. . . . I oughta kill you, I oughta do the world a favor and strangle you, but I won't, I'm just gonna leave you. But first I'm gonna tell everybody about you. And then I'll leave you with nothing, not a dime, not a quarter, not a pot to pee in or a rag to cover your skinny behind. And nobody will want you, nobody will even speak to you, 'cause I'm gonna tell everybody about all the rotten things you did to me. . . ."

In the end it was she who had left, taking nothing,

and she had never regretted it. Not even in the bleakest, hungriest days in the basement.

Ah, it was good to be alone. In time she would stop thinking about B.J., even sooner than she had stopped thinking about her husband. Ricks was a hopeless loser, but B.J. was a survivor. He would make it, the same way she had made it; the only way a poor black person *could* make it in this city of villains and parasites—*alone.*

Fourteen

When the shrill ringing awakened Miss Lena, she reached for her alarm clock to silence it, but could not find the noisy little monster in its usual place at her bedside. The reason, she discovered on opening gritty eyes, was that she was not in bed. She was still on the couch, covered only with stained terry cloth, and the TV was still transmitting what seemed to be the same talk show. The jangling was intermittent, not continuous; not the alarm clock but the phone.

Picking it up, she heard cultivated indignation in the voice of Mrs. Roderick Lewis, who had come for her appointment at three and found no one there.

"What time is it now?" Miss Lena asked sleepily, with a thought of going back to the shop right away to meet the old girl. She seldom made mistakes like this, but when she did, she believed in rectifying them immediately.

"Eleven o'clock," was Mrs. Lewis' reply.

"Eleven o'clock at *night?*" Miss Lena asked incredulously. It was hard to believe she had slept that long.

"Yes. I would never have called this late, Lena, but I found myself worrying about you. It's not like you to just disappear without letting people know."

Lena had to agree that it was not like her. She explained that the heat that afternoon had been so exhausting she had gone straight home.

"Heat? It didn't seem hot to *me* today. I wore my tweed suit under a coat, and I was most comfortable. Are you sure you're all right?"

"I'm fine." Old ladies were always cold, Miss Lena reminded herself. Mrs. Lewis was pushing eighty.

"Yes, well, I'm glad to hear that. I was very surprised when I found you gone, and later I began to get worried. You know I'm depending on you, Lena." Mrs. Lewis was too well-bred to display anger, but there was a grating like sandpaper in her voice. "I *do* need that dress for the Humane Society party. It's a nuisance, of course, but one must look one's best at these things. And of course it's for a good cause. Do you know there are over ten thousand abused horses in this city?"

"I can see you first thing in the morning," Miss Lena said quickly, to avoid hearing more about the suffering horses.

"Let me look at my book. Yes, I'm free tomorrow morning. Roddy Junior is taking the car, so I suppose I can ride in with him and take the train home. Yes, that will be fine."

"Good," Miss Lena said, and hung up without bothering to apologize. But an uneasy feeling was spreading like a polluted mist in her mind. Her usually orderly schedule had suddenly turned topsy-turvy. She had slept all afternoon, so a long wakeful night probably lay ahead. A night with no supper, since she was not hungry. She seemed to remember stuffing herself with an odd meal of saltines and pickles before her nap. There would be nothing to do in the hours ahead but wonder and worry. How would she tell Mrs. Lewis tomorrow that her gown had been stolen? Had she told anyone else to come in first thing tomorrow morning? More important, had she forgotten anyone else's appointment today?

The phone, jingling again, soon confirmed that she had. It was her other Christmas bride, Miss Everett, who was not as easygoing as Miss Allinson or as well-bred as Mrs. Lewis. Nor was she as rich as either of them, which perhaps accounted for the differences, though she spent more on her clothes. She was a homely, hard-working black woman who was putting all of her savings into her wedding and wanted it to be exactly right. And she had been at Miss Lena's shop with her entire wedding party at five-thirty.

"Well," Miss Lena said reassuringly, "it's a long way till Christmas."

Miss Everett was not reassured. "Do you got any idea how hard it is to get five working women together in the same place at the same time? One bridesmaid lives all the way up in the country, and I had to go up and fetch her myself. Another one's car broke down, so I had to fetch her too. And my matron of honor has three children. She can't always get a baby-sitter."

"Just call me for another appointment as soon as you can get them together again."

"I don't know when that'll be. *Some* people can take afternoons off from work any time they want, but I can't."

Miss Lena ignored the sarcasm. "Whenever you can bring them will be fine, Miss Everett. I'll cancel my other appointments for you if I have to."

"You wasn't there today. How I know you gonna be there the next time? I can't afford no sometimy dress-maker. This is my *wedding.*" Unspoken but implied was the idea that Miss Everett expected her wedding day to be the high point of her life, with nothing but dreariness afterward, as before. She was probably right. Miss Lena did not blame for her hanging up without making any promises.

It was that kind of a week, the sort of week Miss Lena

had never lived through before and hoped never to live through again. Her little salon crowded with misscheduled appointments. Customers bumping into each other as they crossed the threshold, and sometimes turning around and walking out again, muttering vows never to return. Urgent work, work that was supposed to be finished immediately, lying untouched on her table, while garments that were not due for another two weeks hung finished and pressed on the rack.

Through it all Miss Lena maintained a curious detachment and calm that only infuriated her customers more. She offered no explanations or apologies. None of this was her fault, her serene attitude seemed to say; it was all an accident, the work of that elemental force, the spirit of disorder and chaos, that periodically appears on earth to unsettle the most carefully organized human enterprises. Miss Allinson had been patient and understanding, and so, in her reserved way, had Mrs. Lewis, but not so some of the others who had been forced to tap their toes on the floor while others were attended to, only to find their clothes had not even been cut for a scheduled fitting.

None of this upset Miss Lena, and she could not understand why it upset her customers. It all seemed to have nothing to do with her until Friday afternoon, when she found herself stitching the gray flannel sleeve of one dress onto the pink crepe body of another. She separated the two pieces and stared at them for a long time. Obviously they did not belong together. Where were the dresses they matched, and for whom was she making them?

Unable to come up with the answers, she decided that her head needed clearing. She prescribed a walk for herself. This was the perfect sort of day for the purpose: brisk, clear, and cool, a day that belonged in November. That other day when she had felt so ill had belonged nowhere but in July.

On the street, the voices she had managed not to hear all week long penetrated her consciousness at last and caused pain. The voices came from faces to which, for the first time, she was beginning to attach names. She knew Foot-Long, of course; her first stop today was his counter for a cup of mind-clearing coffee. But now, thanks to the friendliness of B.J., her unappointed ambassador of goodwill, she also knew that the newsstand proprietor with the cataracts and the creased face was called Bubba, and the barber King William (King of the Comb), and the ancient shoeshine "boy" who worked in his shop, Solomon. The overweight baby-sitter, who was childless, but had informally adopted all the preschool children of the neighborhood during the hours while their mothers worked, was Mom Boggs, and the two men who seemed to spend all their time fixing a car they never drove were her husband, Pop Earl, and his son by a previous arrangement, Earl Junior. Encouraged by B.J.'s reports that she was as good as everybody else and "real regular" besides, they had introduced themselves and asked politely about her health. But as the week wore on, all of them had a more urgent question, an irritating echo of the refrain she had been hearing constantly from her customers:

"Where's B.J.? Is the little fella O.K.? We ain't seen him all week. We missed him."

Each question was asked in a faintly accusing tone, as if B.J., by virtue of association, had become her responsibility. That, she perceived, was the way things were in this neighborhood. She also perceived that if she were going to go on living and working around here, polite evasions would not silence her questioners. She was now what she had so long sought to avoid becoming, a member of this community. In response to its pressure, she would have to get some real answers.

Asked about B.J. by her seventh questioner in two blocks, a ragpicker known as Sneaky Pete, probably because he had managed to sneak a fine porcelain lamp and two handsome ladder-backed chairs into his wheelbarrow along with piles of old newspapers, Miss Lena decided her mission could not wait. With this decision, the chronic pressure of her headache vanished. As she turned south on Ninth Street and approached the liquor store, she was not discouraged by the sullen stares of the winos who lounged around its precincts. She had a feeling of absolute rightness, as if her errand were divinely ordained and came under heaven's protection. The loungers sensed this, she imagined, from the assured buoyancy of her walk, for they slunk back into their holes without asking her for money, and none of them followed her when she turned into the alley B.J. had once warned her against. It was, she realized with a little shock, the only way of reaching Mole Street.

She had to walk carefully, picking her way over piles of broken glass and rusty wire and around heaps of garbage. Bordered with broken fences, the narrow refuse-filled alley gave out onto an only slightly wider canyon.

Mole Street hardly deserved the name, since it was merely five feet wide and half a block long and had only six houses. Five of them were boarded up, and a dozen rubble-strewn lots were all that were left of the others. Half a dozen cars had also been parked on Mole Street for the last time, in a condition that made Miss Lena wonder how they had been driven there. One rested on rims instead of tires; another, a convertible, had been stripped of its top and its seats; a third had been charred by fire. All of the cars were used as playground equipment by swarms of small, grubby children. Even on Mole Street, it seemed, people persisted in coming together and making more people. How many of the lives that began here would end here? A cloud crossed the sun, turning everything gray.

Miss Lena shivered as she approached the only unboarded house. When she opened the door, she was flooded with light. The house could not possibly be inhabited. It was a mere stage set—a front wall with windows and doors, but no back wall and no roof.

It should be torn down. It was unsafe. Those children! Thinking these indignant thoughts, she proceeded unhesitatingly to the boarded-up house next door.

This one, at least, had a roof and four walls, for the hallway she stepped into was impenetrably dark. And it was cold—a clammy, breath-stopping coldness, like a tomb. But it sheltered someone, for Miss Lena could detect the odors of recent cooking. She felt along the greasy wall for a light switch, found one, and pressed it before she remembered B.J. had told her they had no electricity at home. She knew that he and his father lived without the conveniences others took for granted, but she had not allowed herself to picture the stark details of what such a life would be like.

So she was not at all prepared for what she saw after she felt her way along the long black hall, tried all the locked doors, and finally opened the last one.

A cold, greasy stove and an old-fashioned sink on legs, its single basin piled high with empty cans and cartons, indicated that this back room had once been the kitchen of the house. It was now an all-purpose box for living, as grim and confining as a coffin. Under the single cracked window, which was curtained by a piece of ragged gray fabric, sat a littered table flanked by two rickety chairs. A length of wire was strung across one corner to serve as a clothes closet. On the floor were two bare mattresses without sheets or blankets. And that, except for the roaches and the flies and the nauseating odor, was all.

But not quite all. Two heaps of old clothes were piled on the mattresses. As Miss Lena's eyes began to adjust to the dimness, the smaller heap stirred and coughed. It was the kind of racking cough that was self-perpetuating; as soon as the victim survived one cycle of coughing, the irritated place in his throat automatically triggered a new one. B.J., rising from the mound of old coats and sweaters like a weed pushing through heaped-up earth, seemed to have lost a lot of weight. Or was it just that his mop of hair had grown, making his face smaller in contrast?

Certainly his eyes seemed larger, though they were sunken and dull. They regarded her solemnly, without surprise. "I knew you'd come," he said. The four words set off a new spasm of coughing. No wonder he still had that cold. It was chilly as an icebox in here.

"I don't know what for," Miss Lena said, for the balloon of her assurance had just collapsed under the weight of reality. What was she doing here in the midst of all this misery? What could she possibly do here, except cause herself a lot of worry? The situation was beyond her small powers to improve.

She could see better now, and found to her surprise that the room was a small, highly specialized library. Scattered around the floor, piled on the radiator, and stacked against the walls was enough hallucinogenic literature to feed the fantasies of all the would-be businessmen in America. Magazines like *Success, Opportunity, Independence,* and *Business World;* enough *Wall Street Journals* to paper a warehouse, and books with titles like *Go for Yourself, 101 Sure-Fire Small Businesses, Call No Man Boss, The Lazy Man's Way to Millions,* and *What Carnegie Knew.* The last title had been a favorite of her ex-husband's, along with an inspirational tract called *Find a New Need, and Succeed!* Find a new need, indeed! They had needed food, fuel, clothing, *everything* in the days when James had been mesmerized by that book. But those, of course, were old needs, old as the human race and its struggle for survival, and therefore uninteresting to a visionary. She was surprised to find it missing from this collection, and her orderly nature was gratified, along with the pleasure of finding an old enemy in reduced circumstances, when she spied its hated orange cover on the greasy kitchen table.

"Has he found a new need yet, I wonder?" she asked no one in particular.

B.J. touched a finger to his lips. "You better talk softer. You don't want to wake him up." He jerked his thumb at the larger heap on the other mattress.

Her eyes had grown accustomed to the permanent twilight of the room, and she saw now that the mound of rags rose and fell in a regular rhythm. As she watched, fascinated, a bare foot, large and horny as a turtle's shell, poked from beneath its coverings and began to twitch in rhythm with the breathing.

"Why not?" she said boldly. "I might want to talk to him." But what would I say, she wondered? Tell this man he's not taking good care of his son? Miss Lena knew how strong the law was that bound juveniles to their parents. He could tell her, quite properly, to mind her own business and go to hell. And he would be right.

"Ain't nobody can talk to him. *He* does all the talking. Specially when he's had a whole bottle of that."

Following his eyes with hers, Miss Lena saw an empty half-gallon bottle on the floor. It was labeled Sweet White Catawba Wine. Miss Lena felt an unreasonable clutch of panic. It was strange that the memory should assail her now, but Ricks had gone in for Sweet White Catawba during the last months she had spent with him, in a pathetic attempt to control his drinking. Wine was lower in alcoholic content than whiskey, he said. But since he drank four times as much of it, he got just as drunk.

"He liable to wake up mad," B.J. warned her. "He might do you like he did Willie."

She seemed to remember his mentioning the name before and refusing to say more. "Who was Willie, B.J.?"

Again his face closed like a fist on the memory, and he was silent.

"Who was Willie?" she persisted. "What happened to him?"

His voice was hoarse. Perhaps it was the cold. "Willie was my cat, that's all. Just a little old raggedy black kitten I found in the alley. He didn't want me to keep it. But I did anyway. I hid him inside my coat and carried him around with me. At night he slept with me under the bedclothes. I kept him hid for about two weeks. Then one night while I was sleep he sneaked out of the bed. Pop caught him and slammed him jam up against the wall."

Miss Lena did not dare ask her question, but B.J. answered it anyway. "Busted his little cat brains out. I saw 'em, running down the wall. He died so easy. He was such a little kitten, didn't take much to kill him."

Miss Lena was silent, thinking, and you are such a little boy.

"He said he'd do the same thing to me if I ever didn't mind him again."

"So you've minded him ever since."

"Yes. Except when he's drunk. Then I just get out of his way. When I come back he don't never remember what he said to me, anyhow. But I can't get away now."

"Why not?"

"I'm too sick." He coughed, as if to prove his point, but Miss Lena was convinced it was no act. No one could simulate such a prolonged, racking cough. She remembered that cold he had caught before she put him out. There was no way here for it to get anything but worse. No heat. No running water. Nothing she could see that even resembled food.

"Do you get enough to eat, B.J.?"

"No," he said. "I ain't had a meal in two days. I only get food when I go out for it, and now I'm too weak to go. *He* don't go out for food 'cause he don't want none. All he wants is wine. You come to take me with you, Miss Lena?"

"No," she said. "I just came to see how you were doing."

"I'm doin' bad," he said. I might die if I stay here. Please take me home with you, Miss Lena. I mean home to your basement. I won't be no trouble."

"I can't, B.J.," she said gently.

"Why not?"

She was choking on an undigestible lump of feeling for which she had no name. "Love" was not in Miss Lena's vocabulary; the word had been emptied of meaning by too many people who used it to describe the sort of behavior that produced children on Mole Street. But there *had* been a rush of tender feeling, opposed by a powerful conditioned reflex that, after twenty years of discipline, was as strong as the habit of breathing. To keep from being sucked down into the swamp of ghetto life, she had trained her heart to behave like a clam—to shut itself tight whenever a sea of sympathetic emotion threatened to rush in and drown her. This was what was happening to her now, but she was unable to express it.

Instead she fell back on the impersonal authority of the law. "You belong with your father. I can't take you away from him. It's against the law."

"Even if I'm liable to die if I stay with him?"

"Yes, unless I go to court." It was cruel, but it was the truth.

"I'll be dead by then. Don't wait, Miss Lena," B.J. urged. "Take me away with you. Now, before he wakes up."

"I can't," she repeated helplessly.

"Sure you can," a deep voice rumbled from across the room. Miss Lena flinched. Terror made her skin prickle as if it were covered with ants. That voice was an echo from the depths of her worst nightmares. And the large, shambling figure rising halfway from its pallet, shedding layers of old clothes and rich fur like so many reptilian skins, was the one that stalked her most hideous dreams.

But the fur was familiar too. When she saw whose piece of mink he had been sleeping under, fury drove out her fear.

"All you got to do," he said, "is take me too. Unless you'd rather stay here and keep house for us."

"Jail," she said, "is the only place I might take both of you." She picked up Miss Allinson's mink lining. "This was stolen from me. What you got to say about that?"

"You looking good, Lena," was all her husband said.

Ricks had lost weight; his skin hung in folds from his broad frame, which had once been well-muscled and powerful. The giant shape that had once been able to terrify her was now only a frail skeleton. But its height was still imposing, and its eyes were the same: deep-set, hypnotic, brimming with malevolence. And the laugh, the deep chuckle with an edge of malice, had not changed.

Standing up to him as always, she replied, "Sorry I can't say the same for you."

"That's all right," Ricks replied. "A few days of eating your good cooking and sleeping in your soft bed, and I'll be just fine."

"You got more nerve than I thought, if you'd fall asleep in my bed. I just might see to it you never woke up."

His chuckle was uglier this time. "See, boy? Watch out for little women. They just like banty chickens and feisty dogs, ten times meaner than the big ones. I ain't worried, though. She wouldn't kill nobody. She's a law-abiding woman, she just told you so herself. And the law says she's got to take care of me."

B.J. looked frightened and bewildered. His father seemed to take great pleasure in explaining. "Didn't she ever tell you, boy? This here is my legal wedded wife. If you don't believe me, I can prove it. I still got the papers around here somewhere. And I ain't never got no dee-vorce." He grinned, a terrifying vampirish effect. In the years since she'd seen him, he'd lost all his front teeth, leaving only two pairs of yellow fangs.

The shocking news made B.J. look more ill. "You married to him, Miss Lena?"

"I was," she admitted.

"You *is,*" the spectre corrected gleefully. "We ain't never got divorced, Lena. So we might's well let bygones go by."

There were just too many of those bygones to dismiss, she thought. The horrors he had put her through, and then her new life, and his second woman, and now this boy who completed the circuit, forming an uncomfortable new bond between them.

Ignoring Ricks, Miss Lena recited to B.J. as if she were intoning a eulogy for the dead, "James Ricks, who I married, was a fine upstanding man. A big, handsome black man with clean habits and nice, refined ways. A good-hearted gentleman who was kind to every living soul. He always respected himself, and treated me like a lady. He set me down in a nice house and saw to it I had everything I wanted. But that James Ricks is long gone. He left long before I left his house. He died. Drowned. Drowned in alcohol." She kicked the Sweet Catawba bottle so that it rolled, clinking, until it was stopped by the wall.

"I don't know who that is over there, but it's not James Ricks. Not my husband. It's just a container for wine, that's all. Some kind of old dried-up leather wine bag. James Ricks is gone."

"Lena," Ricks said hoarsely, "my drinking, it ain't a sin. It's a sickness."

"I know," she said. "But I can't cure it. I know. I tried."

"The law says, if your husband is sick, you got to take care of him." The crafty smile opened up like a cavern in his face, an abyss into which she might fall.

"Then," Miss Lena said, "they'll have to put me in jail."

The stubbornness of her refusal reduced him, for the first time, to pleading. "I quit while this boy's mother was living, Lena. As long as she lived I was sober."

"You was not," B.J. contradicted hotly. "You was drunk a whole month before she died. Nobody could even wake you to go to the funeral."

"Hush, boy," his father commanded. "Can't you see I'm tryin' to look out for your future?"

"You just messin' it up!" B.J. cried.

"Lena," his father declared, "I quit once. I can do it again. If you'll take me back, I'll quit for you."

"Don't do it for me," she said sharply. "Do it for yourself." She gestured at his library, sweeping some pamphlets to the floor. "What about all your big dreamin' about being a businessman? You gonna quit that too, and get a job?"

James covered his dismay with a hollow-sounding laugh that turned into a cough. "I expected you to be more understanding about that now, Lena. Aren't you in business yourself?"

"Yes, but my business is real, not just a big mixed-up mess in my head. I ain't got time for that kind of mess any more."

From somewhere, he summoned up some pride that made him almost convincing. "My mess, as you call it, will soon be real also. Then you'll see. And you'll be glad you took me back."

"Well, I ain't makin' you no promises. 'Cause I don't know who you are, and I don't believe I'll ever see James Ricks again."

"Turn me down if you want," he said with a new

humility. "I don't blame you, Lena. But what's gonna happen to the boy here? I'm in no shape to look after him, and he's too weak to look after hisself. Maybe you can't save me, maybe I ain't worth saving, but you can save him. You want to save him, don't you?"

"Not that bad," she said, and turned swiftly to shut out the sight of B.J.'s small, stricken face. She had planned to drag the fur lining with her, but relented and tossed it over him for whatever brief comfort it might provide. Then she started blindly back down the long dark hall toward the solitude which she now knew was a kind of death, but was still the only security she had ever found.

Fifteen

It was always a pleasure to eat a solitary meal in her kitchen. The kettle bubbling and singing for her tea, the crab cakes in the oven dispensing a steamy ocean of aroma, the pretty salad, raisins with raw carrots and cabbage shredded on her grater, all cheered her. So did the prospect of having to wash only one cup, one bowl, and one plate. Aloneness was a comfortable habit now, never a cause of pain. And if she ever wished for company, there was the television.

She turned it on while waiting for the crab cakes to heat through. They were a special treat, deliberately chosen from her freezer to coax herself into eating. Ever since Monday, when she had slept all afternoon and awakened near midnight, Miss Lena could not summon an appetite at suppertime. The pattern set that day had remained in force all week—a hasty snack on arriving home, an early nap, then wakefulness until morning. Miss Lena thought there might be a connection between her disrupted schedule at home and the chaos of jumbled appointments at her shop. If things returned to normal here, perhaps the rest would fall into place. In any case, it would not help anyone if she starved herself.

Refusing martyrdom, she firmly drew a chair up to the table and sat down. But the crab cakes she usually found so delectable did not tempt her. She pushed the plate away. Perhaps a sip of wine would put an edge on her appetite. There was a bottle of Moselle in the refrigerator which she had been saving—for what, she could not say. Miss Lena brought a cut-glass goblet from her dining room breakfront and made a ceremony out of pouring the wine. She raised the goblet to her lips. The bouquet brought back to her in full force the cheap wine stink of that crowded little back room and a vivid picture of its contents. Foolishly, she took a sip anyway. Her nausea could not be stifled this time.

Miss Lena clung to the edge of the sink like a seasick passenger at the ship's rail. She had the good sense to know when she was licked, though she promised herself it was only for a little while. Later she would reheat the crab cakes, force herself to eat them, and keep them down. Now, though, she would give in to the habitual urge for early sleep that was weighing down her eyelids. She turned the television off; it was time for the news, and the news always gave her a headache. But she could not blame this one, which was like a hot knife plunged into her temple, on the news. She had not paid attention to a word the announcer said. She fell awkwardly across her bed and slept.

Her nap was a light, fitful one. In her dream she was talking to B.J.—repeating, explaining, justifying the point she had made earlier, that the law would not permit her to do what he asked. He had answered, "Why don't you tell the truth, Miss Lena? You don't want me. You just using that for an excuse."

She awoke to the sound of her own voice shouting, "Well, suppose I don't want you, is that a sin?" and to the terrifying experience of feeling like a leaf caught in a tornado. A violent force threatened to fling her off the bed and toss her up to the ceiling. She clung to the mattress, flattening herself against it and digging into it with her fingernails, to keep from being thrown around the room. The horrible feeling lasted only a few seconds. Then she knew the bed would not eject her. Gravity was in charge of the world again, and she was safe. The large orange spot in front of her eyes took longer to fade, though. It had not been the setting sun after all. Soft daylight still filtered in through her dotted swiss curtains. She had only slept a short while.

The frightening bout had left Miss Lena panting for breath. She wished for a pillow to prop herself up and make breathing easier. There was one, used only when she had a cold, in the cedar chest against the wall. Miss Lena swung her feet down to the floor and started toward it.

But the walls receded from her, and a haze like the shimmering heat of summer came between her and objects in the room. The cedar chest that held her linens seemed to fly away from her as she approached it. She must get her eyes checked soon; she might need glasses. She was trying to think of the name of an eye doctor when her right leg gave under her and she landed face down on her soft, thick, white rug.

The rug was like a cloud. She was not hurt. But the time had come to face an unpleasant fact. She could no longer put off calling her doctor.

Miss Lena pulled herself up to a sitting position and reached for the phone. Misjudging its location on the table beside her bed, she missed it and caught the cord instead. That would do. One yank brought the instrument clattering down beside her. She picked up the receiver with her right hand, but dropped it. That hand seemed to have lost its strength. Miss Lena used her left hand instead, and was comforted to hear the dial tone. But what was her doctor's number?

A dozen numbers passed through her mind: Mrs.

Cosgrove's, Mrs. Lewis', the grocery store that delivered, the drug store, the dry cleaners, her Social Security number, her checking account number—every number that was important to her except Dr. Kloster's.

Miss Lena paused to decide whether she was ill enough to justify making a real fuss. She hated fusses, and had always taken good care of herself to avoid just such a contingency. If she called the police, they would come with heavy boots and threatening pistols, with flashing red lights and earsplitting sirens, as if to arrest her, not rescue her. It would alarm the whole neighborhood and set off a chain of gossip.

It could not be helped, she decided bravely when her right forefinger refused to spin the dial. Securing the receiver under her chin, she used her left hand to dial "O."

"Are you a person or a machine?" she asked the voice that answered. Her own voice sounded so mushy and thick she had to repeat the question.

"A person. May I help you?"

Miss Lena was grateful. These days, most voices—on phones, in elevators, in subways, everywhere she went—were machines. "I need an ambulance," she said.

"Are you the one who is sick?"

"Yes."

"Then I'll get it for you. May I have your name and address, please?"

Though the right side of her face felt stretched, as if pulled backward by invisible wires, she managed to impart the information.

The ambulance came much too fast. Miss Lena only had time to toss a nightgown and a comb into her bag. The police refused to wait while she packed more clothes and toiletries. And they insisted, despite her protest that she was perfectly able to walk now, on making her lie on a litter so they could carry her down the stairs. The neighbors would have plenty to talk about, Miss Lena thought as she was driven off in a blaze of lights and sirens.

She was still in charge of her life, though. She made that perfectly clear in the ambulance, sitting up and giving instructions. The clarity of her speech had returned suddenly, along with the strength in her right leg. "Take me to Cosmopolitan Hospital, please," she said.

"General's closer," said the attendant who sat beside her.

"My doctor is on the staff at Cosmopolitan," she said. "He'll know what to do for me."

"What do you think this is, lady, a taxi service?"

"No," she said crisply, "a *tax* service. For which I pay dearly."

The attendant groaned. "Hey, Harry," he called to the driver, "we got another taxpayer back here. The third one tonight. Better take her to Cosmopolitan."

The ambulance swerved on screeching tires and started off in a new direction.

"Does he always drive like that?" Miss Lena asked. "A lot of the patients must get killed before they even reach the hospital."

"That's the idea, lady. To get them there before they die."

"Well, I am in no danger of dying, I can assure you."

"You don't know that," the policeman said grimly. "That's for your doctor to say. What's his name?"

"Dr. Kloster. Dr. Arnold Kloster," she said.

"We'll ask for him. Now lie down, will you?"

"I breathe better sitting up," she informed him. "But I will lie down if you will promise to do something for me."

"Anything for a taxpayer," he said sourly. "What is it, lady?"

"As soon as you leave me off at the hospital, I want you to take this ambulance to the 900 block of South Mole Street. Only one of the houses there has people living in it. You will find a very sick boy in the back room on the first floor. He's fourteen years old, but small for his age. No matter what his father says, I want you to bring that child to the hospital. The *same* hospital."

"Is he likely to give us trouble? The father, I mean?"

"Yes," she admitted. "He is likely to be drunk."

"Well, how can we do that, lady? We can't take a kid to the hospital if his parents won't let us."

"Of course you can. You're the Law, aren't you?"

"The Law can't do everything. A lot of people think so, but we can't. What are you to this kid, anyway?"

"I am his father's wife."

"The kid's mother, you mean?"

The lie came easily to her lips. "Yes."

"O.K.," the officer said, "we'll do it, lady. Does that make you feel better? Will you lie down and keep quiet now?"

"Yes," she said to both questions, though lying flat made breathing so difficult he had to give her oxygen. How stupid, when all she needed was to be sitting up instead of reclining.

But that was only the first of the many stupidities she was to endure. The absurd performance with the stretcher was repeated at the emergency entrance of the hospital. Once inside, though she was perfectly able to walk, the police insisted on transferring her to a wheelchair. They also refused to leave until she was seen to, instead of taking off immediately for B.J.

Fortunately her wait was short. The benches of the waiting room were filled with desperate cases, most groaning, many bleeding, and Miss Lena expected to wait until they had been treated. But she was wheeled straight to the admissions desk, and there was only a brief delay when she could not come up with the name of a close relative.

"What about your husband?" the policeman who had brought her offered helpfully.

"I have no husband," she said automatically, then remembered and amended it. "I mean, we are estranged."

"Oh," the officer said. He shot a glance at his partner which clearly meant, "Trouble."

"Don't let that stop you from keeping your promise, Officer," Miss Lena admonished him. "Is a relative's name really necessary, Miss?"

"Well, it's hospital policy," the admissions clerk said. "Mainly it's for financial responsibility. And also in case we need someone to give us permission for special procedures. But that doesn't come up very often."

"I am responsible for myself," Miss Lena pronounced clearly, and produced the card she had been fumbling for in her purse. "And, as you can see, I have full coverage."

The card produced instantaneous results. "She has High Option," the receptionist told a nurse reverently, as if saying, "She has Holy Orders." Miss Lena was permitted to sign herself into the hospital. But that turned out to take more time than the rest of the nonsense. First she had to read the fine print of the long document which absolved the hospital of all responsibility if it accidentally maimed or killed her. Then she picked up the pen and dropped it. Another pen was offered, and she managed to hold that one in her shaky fingers, but was unable to exert enough pressure to sign her name. Finally, grasping her right wrist with her left hand to steady it, she managed to write her name. But the result was wavering and scrawled—not at all like her usual neat signature. Miss Lena panicked at the discovery that something had gone wrong with her working hand. She put all her faith in her doctor. He had better come soon.

So far he was nowhere in sight, but the insurance card was like a magic sword cutting through the rest of the red tape. Miss Lena was whisked past the moaners and bleeders and screamers, all the tormented people on the benches, into an examination cubicle. A nurse appeared to take her temperature, pulse, and blood pressure.

"What's my pressure?" Miss Lena asked when the grip of the constricting canvas on her arm relaxed.

"We're not allowed to tell."

More stupidity. "Why not? It's *my* pressure, isn't it?"

"Hospital policy," the nurse parroted. "But I can tell you it's low."

"Young woman, are you sure you know how to read that instrument?"

But the nurse was mute until a young doctor arrived. Then she told him in Miss Lena's hearing, "Her pressure is ninety-five over seventy, Doctor." So much for hospital policy, Miss Lena thought.

"That's ridiculous," she said. "My pressure is usually almost twice that high. I have pills for it in my purse. Why don't you give me one?"

He ignored her. Miss Lena decided there was no point in talking to this boy anyway. He looked too young to be drafted, let alone have an M.D. after his name. His smooth baby-pink cheeks came close as he listened to her chest and her neck, peered into her eyes and ears, tapped her right knee. It bounced.

"Good," he said. "Raise your right arm, please."

She concentrated grimly. Her arm rose a few inches, then fell.

"Can you raise it all the way over your head?"

Ashamed to admit she couldn't, she created a diversion. "I am Dr. Kloster's patient. Please send for him. I want to see him."

"You will, in the morning. In the meantime, nurse, admit her, and see that she gets another of these if she wakes up in four hours."

Another *what?* Miss Lena wondered. She had not been given any medicine. "The ambulance that brought me here will be coming back directly," she informed the intern. "They went to get my son. He is very ill. Oh!"

She had not noticed the nurse move silently to a position behind her. One swift movement, and her left arm was punctured.

"We'll take care of him," the intern promised. "Now, you take it easy."

Like most things the hospital staff said to patients, it was meaningless. Miss Lena had no choice except to take it easy. They wheeled her into an elevator with trays and cabinets and bottles and other helpless, inanimate objects. As the elevator began its slow, creaking ascent, she sank groggily downward. Before they wheeled her out of it, she was asleep.

Sixteen

Two identical pink balloons bobbed on strings at the foot of her bed.

"I didn't know you had a brother, Dr. Kloster," Miss Lena said.

The balloons wobbled, waved, moved toward one another, and merged into a single ruddy face, homely and pudgy as a cooking apple.

"Oh!" she said with a gasp. "I thought there were two of you."

"Were you seeing double, Mrs. Ricks?" the doctor inquired.

"I was just waking up," she grumbled. "A person might see anything when they're still half asleep. With all the needles and pills they put in me, it's a wonder I can see at all."

"It's a wonder," he agreed. Something about the grave expression on his usually jolly face scared her.

"You mean I was really very sick? So sick I might have—"

He spoke cautiously. "I wouldn't say that. Not about you. Someone else—maybe. But you have survived. Which proves there are no hard and fast rules in medicine, only individual patients."

"I'm stronger than most people," she concluded triumphantly. "It's because I've always taken care of myself."

"Probably," he agreed. "I've always told you you have the body of a much younger woman. Your weight has always been good, your heart good, your general condition excellent. Except for your hypertension, all your checkups have been fine. So I'm wondering, really, what brought this on. Any unusual emotional stress lately? Any worries?"

She laughed. "I have nobody but myself, Doctor. What would I have to worry about?"

"That's what I want you to tell *me*," he said.

She squinted in concentration, searching her memory. Recent days and weeks were hazy, but she found herself recalling things long forgotten. Her mother plaiting her hair in ugly corn rows because it was less trouble than curling it, plaiting it so tightly her face felt drawn, as it did now, but on both sides, not just one. Then forcing her to stay home from school and do all the dirty work: cleaning house, laundry, minding her little brothers. She remembered the rough hands pulling and twisting her hair, causing her first headaches. And Lester and Harold deliberately messing up the house after she'd cleaned it. Pouring Karo syrup and sand on her freshly scrubbed floor. Why she hated kids, especially boys. Why she'd married at eighteen. To get away from them.

She still had not answered the doctor's question. "Did you notice any symptoms before last night?" he prodded. "Headaches? Dizzy spells? Blurred vision, perhaps? Fatigue?"

Urge it as she would, her mind stubbornly skirted the recent past and delved instead into long ago. The first years with Ricks, living like a pampered queen adored by an awkward giant. He objected to nothing she did except her refusal to have children. Not that she refused *him* in those days. Oh, no. He was clean then, and decent, and good to love. It was only that she always placed the dead thing, the rubber barrier, between them. With him she felt safe, cherished, like a precious doll in his arms. Security. A dangerous dream. Then his mother's death, and her awakening. The drinking. The mean streak it revealed. The lies. Pretending to have a job long after he'd been fired. Borrowing money and telling her it was his pay. Then gambling to pay back the loans, and losing, and lying some more. Hating her going to work when it became obvious someone had to shovel away the snowdrift of bills. Stealing when borrowing and gambling left him owing more than before. Stealing and scheming, using his dreams of becoming a big businessman to justify his crimes. She kept hoping he would get caught, but the legendary luck of fools and drunks prevailed.

The lies, Miss Lena had thought at first, were the worst. Lies upset Miss Lena, always had, always would. But soon after the honesty vanished, the kindliness and the cleanliness went too. She lay beside a stranger whose mouth spoke filth, whose pores reeked like a distillery, whose unwashed feet could have sprouted mushrooms between the toes. Then alone in a separate room up a flight of stairs, terrified of his belligerence, her only peaceful hours the ones when he slept so deeply and drunkenly not even an earthquake would have roused him. In those hours she lay awake pondering various solutions, even considered having a child. It might pacify him, she thought; might wake him to his responsibility. Morning brought her back to reality. A child would only be an extra burden when she finally had to leave. That time came soon: the night he broke down the door and struck her after she refused to let him into her bed. The night she fought him back, and won. How long ago was that? It seemed like last week.

"Headaches, I think, Doctor," she said.

She had paused so long he guessed her problem. "Can't you remember?"

"I seem to have trouble remembering anything except—long ago. Things I thought I'd forgotten. Things I *made* myself forget." A terrifying thought suddenly assailed her. She sought the truth. "Is something wrong with my mind?"

"Are you crazy, d'you mean? Of course not. What you are experiencing is very usual, I think. I believe you said you have no one to worry about except yourself."

"Yes." There was still James, of course. Still killing himself with wine, but killing himself very slowly, it seemed. She had thought he was dead. It was important to believe he was dead so she could live. But he was alive, she'd learned—when? How? It didn't matter. He was no longer hers to worry about.

"What about that boy who was brought in last night with bronchial pneumonia?"

"Boy?" She had no boy. She disliked little boys. Did he mean Lester or Harold? Had the little pests followed her here to plague her?

"One of my little brothers? Here?" In her mind she was still fourteen, and they seven and nine.

"You told the intern on duty he was your son."

Her memory returned to the present with the speed of a space capsule. She was not a girl of fourteen, or a bride of eighteen, or a wife of twenty-seven; she was twice that age, and alone except for B.J.

"No, he's just a—a little friend. Is he all right, Doctor?" she asked anxiously.

"Not all right, but he should respond to treatment. He had a high fever, of course, but that's not too serious in children, and it should come down. We have all those miracle drugs for bacterial infections now, you know. And when you're as young as he is, a little rest and nourishment can work wonders. Of course, if it had been let go a few more days . . ."

Her lips moved in silent thanksgiving.

"Why did you tell the intern you were his mother?"

"So they'd put his bill on my insurance. This place won't take people who can't pay, you know."

The salt and pepper brows knitted in a frown. "I also know what you did is illegal. It's called fraud."

She expelled a long sigh of relief when he added, "But I don't think I'll tell on you. I have a hunch that little fellow's recovery will have a lot to do with yours. I'll ask his doctor to look in on you this afternoon. Dr. Frankel, that's his name."

"Thank you, Doctor."

"In the meantime, I've set up a pretty busy program for you. A special diet. No snacks on the side, do you hear me? Stay away from the coffee shop. A series of tests, to see exactly what we have here. And then—"

She sat up indignantly. "But I want to go home."

"Don't you want to get well first?"

"I *am* well," she said. "I feel fine."

"Good," he said. "But I want you to stay long enough for me to be absolutely sure of my diagnosis."

"You mean, I'm not sick, but you gonna keep me here till you find something wrong with me," she grumbled.

Most doctors would have gotten mad, but Dr. Kloster only laughed. "You really think I'm as bad as all that? No, I have my suspicions, but I want to be sure."

"Suspicions of what?"

"First let me examine you a little. Shut your eyes. Do you feel this? This?"

The touch of cold metal on her foot made her withdraw it. A needle jab produced a stronger reaction. "Ow! What are you trying to do to me?"

"Examine you, Mrs. Ricks. Close your eyes again, please. What do you feel now?"

"Nothing." She opened her eyes and was shocked to see a needle sticking in her forearm. Suddenly scared, Miss Lena began to cry. That, in itself, was disturbing. She had never cried this easily in her life. "What's wrong with me, Doctor?" she asked between sobs.

"Don't you know?"

She shook her head.

"Well, we can't be sure until we see the test results, but from all the signs, I'd say you've had a mild stroke."

Stroke! The sudden blowout in the brain that had killed both her parents.

The shock must have shown on her face. "I said a *mild* stroke," he emphasized. "If you follow my program, you should make a good recovery."

"And if I don't want to go through all that nonsense?"

He stroked his chin thoughtfully. "Well, I can always tell the cashier's office I know for a fact you have never borne children."

It was blackmail. Though her independence was affronted into rebellion, she had no choice but to submit.

There were tests, tests, and more tests. She was hooked up to tubes, plugged into machines, probed, poked, thumped, and photographed. Things were stuck into her and other things were drawn out. She was never told what was going on, and was not allowed to walk to her appointments with torture. She was pushed here and wheeled there; left to wait in lonely corridors for hours, then suddenly given instructions. The worst was not the tests, not even when they tapped her spine for a look at its fluid or when they injected something in her neck and took pictures of her head. The worst part was never knowing what would happen next, and always being treated like a retarded child.

Only Dr. Kloster treated her like a grown-up individual who had not stopped being Miss Lena just because she was ill. Only Dr. Kloster and Mamie, who came around a lot more often.

Mamie was a practical nurse on the day shift, and practical was the word that best described her personality. Mamie always did the practical thing, never caring whether it conflicted with hospital rules. "They can't fire me, girl," she declared with a flash of gold teeth. "I'm the cheapest help in the hospital, and I do the most work." She was about Miss Lena's age and complexion, but three times her girth, resembling, in her tight girdles and nylon uniforms, a sausage in its sheer casing. Almost immediately they became good friends.

Mamie liked to spend time in Miss Lena's room because the white women patients on the floor annoyed her, she said. Miss Lena gathered that they were mostly rich, spoiled rotten, and used to getting their way. They also had a habit of treating Mamie like a servant. Miss Lena, who'd had to play the self-effacing role of "the little dressmaker" to too many grand ladies, sympathized.

Mamie had a more pungent way of describing the grand ladies. They "thought they peed Chanel Number Five" when, in actuality, they "smelled like wet dogs in the morning."

"It's all that hair," she explained one morning, arranging a bouquet that she had diverted from another patient's room to Miss Lena's. "White folks got so much hair they can't help needin' all them deodorants and anti-stink sprays. When they get in here and can't shampoo that stuff every day, they really got a problem."

Mamie's cheerful theft made Miss Lena uncomfortable. "Don't you think you ought to put those flowers back where they belong?"

"No, girl," Mamie said, calmly arranging the bouquet of fairy roses. "She got so many flowers there's no space in her room for more. She'll never miss these little roses. They won't make her smell better anyhow. Besides, they remind me of you. They're little, pretty, and tough."

Miss Lena did not feel pretty or tough; she felt ugly and weak, and said so.

"You got to stop that kind of thinking right now," Mamie commanded, and brought a mirror. "Put on some makeup. Comb your hair."

"What for? Nobody's coming to see me."

"How you know?" Mamie winked. "Something tall, dark, and handsome might walk through that door any minute. This place is full of African doctors, you know. There's a Sudanese psychiatrist upstairs I'd love to go crazy for."

Miss Lena tried, then said, "I can't do it, Mamie." She could not raise her right arm above her shoulder.

"All right, I'll do it for you this one time. You got to start doing things for yourself soon, though. You still got some nice waves," she said, and sniffed. "Smells clean, too. Thank the Lord we don't have to wash our hair as often as they do. We'd go broke from all them beauty appointments."

"Broke and bald," Miss Lena said, pleased by what she saw in the mirror. After the application of lipstick and powder by Mamie, she did not look like an old woman or even a sick one.

"I've got to go to the bathroom," she announced next.

"Go, then."

It was down the hall. "But I'm afraid to walk that far by myself." She might fall again as she had at home.

"Look," Mamie said with elbows jutting from her wide torso like jug handles, "I can comb your hair for you, maybe, but I sure can't pee for you. If you afraid of falling, don't look down."

It worked! Holding her head high, keeping her steps small, Miss Lena made steady progress to the bathroom and back.

But when Dr. Kloster arrived that afternoon and found her walking around the room, he said sternly, "I didn't give you permission to get up yet."

"What's a person supposed to do when Nature calls? Wet the bed?"

"Look, Mrs. Ricks, I'm glad to see you walking so well. But I want you to stay in bed till you've been seen by the neurosurgeon I've called in. He won't be free to look at you until tomorrow morning."

Seventeen

The neurosurgeon was a tall, slim, unsmiling man with eyes so pale they seemed colorless and blond hair cropped like a closely mown wheat field to reveal patches of white scalp. Even without his jacket he would have been the whitest white man she had ever seen. Miss Lena thought this nearly hairless man would disprove Mamie's theories about white folks' odors. But when he bent to touch her neck with fingers like icicle radishes, she thought she smelled blood.

Miss Lena was grateful that Dr. Gerbner did not deign to talk to her. He spoke only to Dr. Kloster. But she overheard him say something about a thrombus in an artery, and gathered that he was mentally sharpening his knives.

She was right. After the great man left, Dr. Kloster said, "He thinks there's a blood clot blocking one of the arteries in your neck, cutting off some of the circulation to your head. He wants to remove it and repair the artery."

"I don't want that man cutting my throat. He looks like he needs blood."

"That's ridiculous," her doctor said. "You make him sound like a vampire."

"He's a surgeon, ain't he? Same thing. He must like cutting folks, or he wouldn't do it."

Dr. Kloster sounded exasperated. "Mrs. Ricks, I can assure you Dr. Gerbner is not desperate for patients. He has all the surgery he can handle. He only agreed to take on your case as a special favor to me."

"A German doing a favor for a Jew? That ought to make news."

Dr. Kloster flushed, his cheeks darkening from their normal apple red to beet color. But he said calmly, "No, a doctor helping another doctor."

"Well, don't ask for any more favors like that for me. I ain't never been cut in my life and I'm not about to start now. Operations can kill you."

Dr. Kloster looked as if he were about to have a stroke himself as he explained in a choking voice, "Dr. Gerbner is a very careful surgeon as well as a very good one. He would never suggest a procedure like this if you were a high-risk patient—say if you were older, or obese, or in poor general health. But he feels there's very little risk in your case, and he thinks there's a very good chance you may be helped immensely by the operation."

He feels. *He* thinks. She looked at him sharply. "What do *you* think, Doctor? You don't agree with him, do you?"

Dr. Kloster looked embarrassed. His flush, which had faded, began to deepen again. "I'm not qualified to disagree with him. I'm only a general practitioner. Dr. Gerbner is one of the finest specialists in his field."

"You're qualified enough for me," she declared. "Now tell me why you think he might be wrong."

He said hesitantly, "Well—mainly that you didn't report any episodes before this one. Strokes of this type usually come in a series."

Miss Lena, who had not been able to remember when he questioned her the first time, was wondering now about that dizzy spell on the street and that week of confusion in her shop. But she kept silent.

"Also, you don't have much trouble talking clearly,

even though your mouth is a little lopsided when you speak. That's not usual."

Miss Lena picked up her hand mirror to verify his observation. Her mouth looked all right to her. But she did remember that her voice had been so thick when she spoke to the telephone operator that she had been forced to repeat her address twice. She was too scared of the operation to mention it, though.

"Is there a chance I might die from the operation?" she asked, and watched her mouth go crooked. She put the mirror down hastily.

"There's always a risk with any surgery," he admitted. "But the only serious danger in this case is from the anesthetic. And we can eliminate that."

"Humph. And if I live through it, will I be scarred?"

"Very slightly, perhaps, on the side of your neck here." He touched the place, just under her left jaw. "Makeup should cover it. Or you can wear scarves, or change your hairstyle. But you should be asking Dr. Gerbner these questions. I'm afraid I may have confused you."

"I'm not confused. I needed to know the facts."

Dr. Kloster smiled sadly. "In medicine, there are no hard facts until patients are dead. While they're alive, we can only make educated guesses."

"Well, you doctors already got enough education, I guess. You don't need to get any more at my expense."

"Does that mean you've definitely decided to refuse the operation?"

Her answer surprised her. "No. It only means I want to think about it."

"But Dr. Gerbner wants to operate as soon as possible."

"It's my life he's messing with. And *my* throat he wants to cut. So he'll just have to wait till I'm ready."

Eighteen

It was Mamie, not B.J.'s doctor—whom Miss Lena never saw—who brought her news from the pediatrics ward. Two days after he was admitted, she said, B.J. was sitting up, talking, and eating everything he could get his hands on. The next day he was running all over the ward, asking fresh questions and making a general nuisance of himself. The day after that Mamie risked her job to find out when B.J. was scheduled to go down to X-ray, intercept him at the elevator, and detour him to Miss Lena's room for a forbidden visit.

B.J. did not ask how she was feeling, but it didn't matter. Miss Lena felt much better as soon as he walked in. He was healthier-looking than she had ever seen him. His gigantic bush was disgraceful, at least five inches long, but beneath it his face was no longer like a shrunken little nut; it had plumped out so well most of the wrinkles were gone. Perhaps they had been due to malnutrition all the time.

He was fairly bursting, he was so full of himself and his new well-being. He was, it seemed, the most important patient in the hospital. After the infection had subsided, a bone surgeon had looked at B.J.'s legs and had been amazed that he could walk without crutches.

"He asked me how I learned to do it. I told him some big guy tried to beat me up one time, and I had to break my crutches over his head, and after that the damn things wasn't no more good to me."

Mamie and Miss Lena had a good laugh.

"But that ain't all!" B.J. cried. "Listen!"

After the bone doctor's visit, a gland specialist had looked at B.J. "He's got some new magic shots that make people grow. He wants to try 'em out on me. I might can be any height I want, six feet, ten feet, even twelve. But first you got to sign permission for me to get the shots."

"Permission for six feet or twelve?" Miss Lena asked, restraining a smile.

"I figure I might as well be big as I can. Fourteen feet tall, maybe."

"You'd be a giant, B.J. You wouldn't even be able to walk through a door."

"I know it. I was only kidding," B.J. said with a giggle. "Six feet will be tall enough, I guess. Six feet plus three or four inches. Will you please sign, Miss Lena? It won't cost you anything. This gland doctor's got all the money he needs. A grant, he calls it. He says, if he can make me grow, it'll help him get more money next year."

Miss Lena said she would have to think about it. The mention of money to be made on experimenting with B.J. had aroused her suspicions. Besides, she might get in deep legal trouble.

"You didn't tell anybody I'm not really your—"

"Of course not," B.J. said indignantly. "What kind of fool you think I am? Please say you'll sign the papers, Miss Lena."

"I told you, I have to know more about it first."

"Oh, well," he said with a heavy sigh of frustration, "you still got time. He don't want to start till I'm good and cured. Cured enough to leave here. Boy, will I be glad to get out of this stinky old hospital. When do you get out, Miss Lena?"

"I don't know," she said. "When do *you?*"

"Soon," he said. "Tomorrow, maybe. If the X-rays don't show nothing wrong with me."

"That reminds me, boy," Mamie said. "I got to get you downstairs right away."

"Where will you go, B.J.?"

A shadow crossed his face. "I dunno. My old man was pretty pissed when the cops came for me. I guess he thought they was gonna lock us both up."

"They should have, you know."

"I know," he answered, admitting it all in those two words: his guilt, his betrayal, his complicity in causing her loss.

"Are you going to do something like that again?"

"I hope not, Miss Lena," he said, his eyes steadily on her face. "I couldn't seem to stop myself then, but I think I could another time. See, I wasn't helping my old man, just this friend of mine, 'cause I thought he was great, but—well, I don't think he's so great any more."

Oddly, she had more faith in this uncertain answer than she would have had in a positive promise. "What's my birthday, Mamie?" she asked suddenly.

Mamie gave her an odd look. "What?"

"Can you look up my records and tell me my birthday? I can't remember it right now, and I need to know it."

"You were born on Christmas Day," B.J. said. "You told me so."

"I know that. But what year?"

Mamie, with the same odd look, handed her her purse. "Look in here. You must have an I.D. card or something. Maybe a driver's license?"

Miss Lena shook her head. "I never learned to drive. Listen, B.J., there's a new lock on my cellar door. The combination is my birthdate: 12, 25, and the year. Mamie, you've got to look up the year and tell him so he can get in."

Mamie was indignant. "I'll do no such thing. You practically said this boy was a thief, and now you want me to tell him how to get in your place? Them drugs you're on must have really messed with your brain."

"Did I say he was a thief?"

"Not exactly," Mamie admitted.

"Well, then, what are you talking about?" Miss Lena demanded. "Anyway, I don't believe he'll do it again."

"You sure you want me at your place again, Miss Lena?" His sad eyes said, *She's right, you know. I can't be trusted.*

"Shut up, B.J. *Do* it, Mamie."

Mamie grumbled a promise and whisked him away, not a minute too soon. As soon as they were gone Dr. Kloster passed in the hall. She called to him, and he came in.

"What is it, Mrs. Ricks?"

She was smiling until she noticed the odd expression on his face. "I wanted to tell you I'm ready to have the operation. What are you staring at me like that for?"

"I can't get over what I just saw."

"What?"

"You were holding your right arm above your head and waving your hand."

Dr. Kloster had plenty of reasons to regret that remark. It turned Miss Lena completely around. She could move her arm now, couldn't she? She could even wave her fingers. Well, then, why did she need an operation?

To make matters harder for the doctor, he was outnumbered and didn't even know it. Dr. Kloster hardly knew of Mamie's existence, because she always managed to be elsewhere when any of her superiors on the hospital staff were in Miss Lena's room. But she was a very real influence, and she was dead set against surgery.

"Girl, you crazy if you let them white folks cut you. Most of the patients who go down to O.R. come back worse off than before. And on your throat, too? You know what our folks will say about you if they see you with a throat scar. They'll think you've been in a knife fight."

That point had not occurred to Miss Lena, but she knew it was true. A scar on her neck would plummet her straight down from her hard-earned middle-class respectability to vulgar lower-class status.

It was a distressing prospect, but Miss Lena was not totally convinced she was well, either. "I still have cramps in my fingers, Mamie," she whined, feeling herself close to tears. "Sometimes my whole arm goes to sleep on me."

Mamie looked at her contemptuously. "I have cramps in my fingers, Mamie," she mocked in the same whining tone. "You sound like Miss La De Da across the hall. Since when are black women allowed to complain about cramps?"

It was the springboard for a lecture on Mamie's personal theory of evolution, which differed with the standard Darwin in only one detail. "I've worked in hospitals all my life, and I know white folks are sicklier than we are. For one thing, they can afford to have all them fancy diseases that keep them in bed a long time. We can't.

"But there's something else. The way I figure it, if there was ever any weak black people in this country, they died out long ago, back in slavery times. Or maybe even on them boats coming over. Them boats were horrible, you know; everybody chained together with not enough food or water or even air. By now, all of us that are left are *stone* survivors.

"Take that kid. I really cracked up laughing when he said he started walking without crutches 'cause he broke 'em over somebody's head. Now you know no white doctor's ever gonna understand that story. That's why them doctors are so interested in him. They want to study him till they can come up with some fancy scientific explanation. But it's really very simple. *We* understood it, didn't we? He started walking because he *had* to.

"And you're gonna get up and start doing for the same reason. You got to, 'cause ain't nobody gonna do it for you." Finished with changing Miss Lena's bed, she stepped back and added, "Oh, I almost forgot. They're discharging him tomorrow morning."

Miss Lena felt tears rising in her eyes. Deserted was what she was about to be; deserted and abandoned. B.J. was leaving, and Mamie was offering such rough comfort it was no comfort at all. "Did you find out my birthday year and tell him?"

Mamie gave her an odd look. "I still don't see how a person could forget her own birthday. Sure I told him. I didn't want to, but I'd promised. You were born in '19. Same year as me. How come you look so much younger?"

"You can't mean it, Mamie. I feel a hundred years old. I must be wrinkled as a prune." The tears were coursing down her cheeks, as far beyond her control as a sudden rain.

They annoyed Mamie. "Stop that damn crying, will you? You know I can't stand weak sisters."

Neither can I, thought Miss Lena. I don't know why I'm acting like this. Lord, please make me stop.

"I was going to show you your young self in the mirror, but you know God don't like ugly, and that's what crying makes you. Uh-oh. I got to leave now. Here comes your doctor, and he's got that creepy surgeon with him. I hope you won't let them talk you into that operation. And I hope when I come back you've decided to be a woman."

But when she came back Miss Lena had already been moved downstairs for surgery.

Dr. Kloster had won out against the secret odds by bringing up his own reinforcements.

"I know you're feeling better, Mrs. Ricks," he began, ignoring her tear-stained face, "but that's all the more reason why you should have the operation now, before you have another stroke. I hate to scare you, but—"

Another stroke? Her troublesome blood turned to melted ice.

Dr. Gerbner interrupted him. "Then let *me* do it. Let me be Dr. Frankenstein, hmmm? I have the right accent for it." The quip brought a weak smile to her face, but it soon faded.

"Mrs. Ricks, I know you think you're fine now, but if that clot remains where it is, you will probably have a second stroke, and a third, and so on, and they might get progressively worse. You might end up permanently disabled. Or blind."

That dreadful word, *blind*, was all it took to convince her. Dr. Gerbner was standing on the left side of her bed, Dr. Kloster on her right. She knew because they had taken up those positions on entering her room. But she could only see the pale, bony form of the surgeon, who looked, in his white coat, like the angel of death.

The phantom on her right, whom she could not see

at all, spoke in a familiar voice. "The operation is nothing to be afraid of, Mrs. Ricks. It's a minor operation, really, and will only take a short time. You won't feel anything. But you'll know everything that's going on."

Miss Lena stared resolutely at the surgeon. He was spooky-looking, but at least she could *see* him. "I'll be awake all the time?"

"Yes. We don't want to depress your brain with a general anesthetic. A local will be safer. Also, I want to keep you alert so I can ask you questions."

Miss Lena was pleased. The thing she feared most was losing *control*—of herself, her life, and, above all, of her mind. Induced unconsciousness meant losing control. Staying awake meant she would still be in charge. She could give orders; she could even change her mind and tell them to stop the operation.

It did not work out quite that way, however. She was restrained by sheets and straps that made it impossible for her to move, and the injection made the formerly good side of her jaw so numb she spoke with great difficulty. When the surgeon asked if she felt various sensations, she managed to utter the vowel parts of "yes" and "no" clearly enough for him to understand her. Beyond that she said nothing, and felt nothing, either, except for a pleasant high from something that had been mixed with the numbing stuff in the needle. Since for the moment she was helpless, Miss Lena decided to shut her eyes until it was over. She did not care to see her own blood spurting around the room.

Whether it spurted or not, she never knew. The operation was over very quickly, just as they had promised. She did not open her eyes until after she was wheeled into the recovery room.

The room was drab, painted in that grim shade of

gray reserved for institutions and the U.S. Navy, and its only other occupants were corpselike forms swaddled in sheets on adjoining tables. But it was the most beautiful place she had ever seen, because she could see every crack and chip in the paint on its ceiling and all of its walls.

After she was returned to her room, Miss Lena refused to rest as she had been ordered. There were too many interesting possibilities to explore: the television, to which she found herself paying attention for the first time since she entered the hospital; the newspaper, which she had not read in a week because of poor concentration; and, most exciting of all, the restored obedience of her right hand. Like an infant discovering his extremities for the first time, she sat for long periods just holding it up in front of her and watching her fingers wiggle.

The author of the Necessity Makes Miracles theory came in with Miss Lena's dinner tray and almost dropped it when she saw her combing her own hair.

"Well, do! Look a' here!" Mamie exclaimed in delight, seemingly forgetting her opposition to the operation.

"If I had my irons here I'd curl it," Miss Lena lied with calm arrogance, knowing she probably could not lift the heavy curling irons, let alone twirl them. "But I don't, so this'll have to do." She picked up an eyebrow pencil next. Though her hand shook a little, she did a fair job.

"Look, your right hand's as good as it always was. You'll be back at work in no time. Soon I'll be coming around to order me some party clothes." Mamie winked, wickedness spreading across her broad, homely face, and swung into a sexy little finger-popping dance. "I don't just live for this gloomy old hospital, you know. I got my own thing on the outside. And it's a nice thing, even if it is somebody else's husband. You got yours too?"

Miss Lena shook her head.

"Well, what's the point of painting your face then? What's the point of anything, if you don't live a little? There's that kid, but what is he to you? Not even your own child, and I'd bet worrying over him was what put you in here."

Miss Lena did not dispute her.

"Well," Mamie said, subsiding into a chair, "different strokes for different folks, I guess. Me, I like the kind of strokes that make me feel good, and that's what my man steady deals in." She made her meaning extra clear, wiggling back and forth in the chair and groaning expressively. Miss Lena was amused. But Mamie went on, and she went too far.

"I could understand it if that boy was your own flesh and blood. Any mother will worry over her own. I know, I have children myself, but they're grown now, thank God, and you'll never catch me worrying myself sick over somebody else's. What for? What good is it? Face it—no matter how much you do for him, one day he's going to walk out of your life and tell you to kiss his black—"

"Mamie," Miss Lena said sharply, "shut up. You don't understand."

"I guess I understand one thing. I'm not wanted," Mamie said, and got up pretending to be hurt. "Go on and kill yourself raising somebody else's kid if you want," she said, flouncing out. "Me, I'm going to live a little. And have a good time till I die."

Miss Lena was able to laugh to herself over Mamie's

love life. The criticism of her relationship with B.J. bothered her a little, but it was the suggestion of going back to work soon that had really made her uneasy. In time, she was sure, she could train her hand to sew again. But what could she do about her disorganized mind? Assuming she had any customers left after a month of neglect, how would she organize her days and hours and weeks to serve them? The whole business of arranging schedules and juggling appointments and completing work on time to meet them, all once so automatic, now seemed hopelessly beyond a woman who had not even been able to remember when she was born. What would she use for a memory, now that hers behaved like a rusty old tub with more holes in it then a sieve?

Nineteen

The answer to her question sat cross-legged on the foot of her bed a week later, doing a jigsaw puzzle upside down. In the week since he had been discharged from the hospital, B.J. had been efficiently smoothing over her customer relations and keeping the fires of her business banked until she returned.

"That old lady, that Mrs. Lewis, she was pretty mad after you stood her up two times in a row. But when I told her you got hit by a car, she didn't mind so much."

Miss Lena, who had been concentrating painfully on crocheting a circular doily assigned to her by the occupational therapist ("We must keep busy, you know. The busier we are today, the better we'll be tomorrow!"), dropped her work suddenly. "Why did you tell her that, B.J.?"

"Car accident sounds better. Makes 'em feel sorrier for you if they think you all banged up."

So that was why the gorgeous glass bowl of red and purple anemones had arrived that morning with Mrs. Lewis' engraved card. Miss Lena grimaced in irritation. "You know I hate lies, B.J. Why can't you tell the truth?"

"If I did, your customers would never expect to see you again, except maybe in a wheelchair. Most people think a stroke kills you."

It made sense, like all his stratagems. But she was still outraged. "But don't you see you're forcing *me* to be a liar too? That's not right, B.J. I don't like to lie. Where was I supposed to be hit, and what kind of car hit me?"

"Right in front of your shop, by a big black Ross Rolly."

"Rolls Royce," she corrected automatically.

"That's what I *said.* Miss Everett said, if you had to be hit, you sure picked the right kind of car. She wanted to send a lawyer over to help you collect a lot of money right away, but I told her you was still unconscious. I think you better get conscious again now and call her, though. You can tell her you already got a lawyer. Main thing she's worried about is her wedding dresses, and she ain't got much patience. After you talk to her, there's a couple other people to call."

"Who?"

He pulled a dirty sheet of scrap paper from his pocket and consulted it. "Mrs. Johnson. She had an appointment with you today. I think her husband wants to see you too, about some choir robes. And Dr. Norman. She was going to pick up her dresses and take them to somebody else to finish, but I told her you would finish them."

"Even though I'm unconscious?"

"Oh, I told *her* the truth. Almost. I said you was in the hospital for your high blood pressure. That's what I told Mrs. Johnson, too."

Miss Lena clapped a hand to her forehead to ward off a headache. Now, when the realities of life alone seemed too much for her to cope with, she would also have to sort out the tangles of B.J.'s lies, remember what he had said to whom. She must have been mad to plan on a continued association with him. It would never, never work. His standards were not hers. They were ghetto standards, survival-at-all-costs standards: devious, dishonest, outrageous. She had risen above the swamp of ghetto life, and kept herself above it, by staying uncompromisingly straight and honest. Unless she allowed herself to be sucked down again, she and B.J. would be in constant conflict. But she could not carry on alone any more. She needed someone to help her. And who else was there?

Unaware of her dilemma, he bent to pick up a shopping bag. When she saw Dr. Norman's red Liberty print silk on top, she turned her face away.

"You expect me to work on that here?"

"Why not? You ain't got nothin' else to do."

Miss Lena had progressed remarkably in two weeks, from almost total helplessness in her right arm to writing clearly enough to sign checks and pay the bills which B.J. brought with her daily mail; from passive exercises to movements she performed faithfully alone; from stringing large beads to crocheting with a small hook. But the thought of manipulating a needle and thread again threw her into a panic.

"Not now, B.J. Put it away."

"Afraid you can't do it?" he asked accurately. "How come? You been sewing ever since I got here."

"That wasn't sewing. That was crocheting. It's different."

He shrugged. "Well," he said with a calculating look, "you can always do what I said first."

B.J.'s first idea, which she had unconditionally rejected, was that Miss Lena should go on welfare. He knew a lady who would help her get a big welfare check, he said, and who would tell her how to collect Social Security disability payments too, without getting caught. All Miss Lena had to do was give the lady back part of the money every month, and she would be allowed to claim as many as six children. B.J. saw nothing wrong in it. She was too sick to work, wasn't she? She was used to living pretty good, though, and could hardly stand to be poor again, right? Then cheating on welfare was the only solution. People did it all the time. He couldn't understand why Miss Lena refused even to talk to his influential friend at the welfare office.

"I still think you ought to let her sign you up, Miss Lena. You can keep working on the side, just so too many people don't know about it. Do it at home or something. Then, if you don't happen to feel so good, you can always stop work."

"Hand the dress here, B.J."

"You don't have to claim six children if you think it's too many. Just me and a couple of others."

"What did you say? Claim *you?*" she asked. "Oh, never mind. Hand me the sewing."

He had to thread the needle for her, and the first hemstitches were sloppy, but soon she had the needle so well under control she wondered what she had been frightened of.

"If only I could remember my appointments," she murmured to herself. "How will I ever keep track of it all?"

"You don't have to remember nothin'," he said indignantly. "That's *my* job. Now call them ladies. Miss Everett first. Remember, she thinks you was in an accident. Then Mrs. Johnson and Dr. Norman. Then I'll play you a game of checkers till suppertime."

In spite of the conflicts between their standards, it was thanks to B.J.'s and Mamie's rough encouragement that she was getting back to normal so quickly. Oh, Dr. Kloster and Dr. Gerbner and their staff had done a lot for her, but none of them took the same intense personal interest in her recovery. The operation had helped miraculously, of course, and so had the medicine and the whirlpool baths and the exercises, but none of them were as effective in getting her moving again as Mamie's brisk "You can't lay up in that bed forever. You ain't no white lady. Look at that foot sticking out from under those sheets. You black as me. No rich man's gonna take care of you. Get up and do, girl, get up and do."

And no amount of occupational therapy could have gotten her back to work as quickly as B.J.'s assumption that there was no reason why she should not be working, even in the hospital. If anything, he seemed to be urging her to take on more work than before her illness.

"You need a new sample in your window, Miss Lena," he'd said one day. "I was thinking."

B.J. was always thinking, always coming up with new ideas for her to carry out. Just listening to them made her weary sometimes.

"What is it now?"

"How come all your samples are so little? Why you make 'em up in such little sizes, I mean?"

Miss Lena explained her practical reasons. "Because it costs less to make a dress in a small size. I can even use scraps sometimes. And if a sample doesn't sell, I can always wear it myself."

"I thought so," he replied. "But them little bitty dresses in the window make your customers mad."

"You think so?"

"I *know* so. Mrs. Johnson was fussing about them, and Dr. Norman was too. Even Miss Allinson was complaining. Most of your customers are big women, Miss Lena. It makes them mad when they see something in your window they can't wear, especially if they like it. It just reminds them how fat they are. Dr. Norman said she guessed you didn't plan on selling none of them sample dresses, 'cause you ain't got no customers that little, unless they children. And she ain't never seen no children in your shop but me."

Miss Lena paused to consider this new thought. She hated waste, hated to make a dress no one might wear, so always made her samples in her own diminutive size. But perhaps she had hung on too long to a penny-pinching habit left over from her lean days.

"I'll think about it, B.J.," she told him.

"Don't think about it," he ordered. "*Do* it as soon as you can. Make up a bigger sample to put in your window. It'll make the ladies feel a lot better. And somebody will buy it right off the dummy. You'll see."

"What's in the window now?" She had forgotten.

"Just a piece of yellow cloth I draped around the dummy. The people were tired of looking at that little bitty green dress. One lady said it looked like a doll's dress. She was joking, but I could tell she was mad. I heard another lady say nobody but you could wear it. On her it would look like a bathing suit, she said. It was making them jealous of you, so I took it down."

That had given her plenty to think about last week. This week he had an even more taxing idea.

"You know what you ought to do, Miss Lena? You ought to have a fashion show."

Miss Lena groaned. "I don't even know how I'm going to catch up with the backlog of work I have on hand, B.J. Now you want me to put on a production. You have no idea how much work that involves."

"I'll help you. You can get other people to help you, too, if you have to."

"Did somebody put you up to this?" she asked suspiciously.

B.J. had to admit that Mrs. Johnson had requested the fashion show to benefit a pet project of her church.

"Well, it's not the first time she asked me. And it won't be the first time I've said no."

He looked serious. "You oughta say yes this time."

"Why?"

"Some of your customers are still mad at you. I done my best to explain you been sick, but they still don't understand why you forgot 'em."

"What's that got to do with my having a fashion show?"

He answered her question with another. "Why do ladies buy clothes?"

"What?"

"You sell 'em, you must know. Why do they buy clothes? What do they like best?"

She could tell he was driving at something. "You tell me, B.J."

"Showing off, that's what they like. They want people to notice 'em. They want to be stars. Now, if you give 'em a chance to show off on a *stage*—"

"Most fashion shows use professional models, B.J."

"Well, this one won't. It'll use real people. Your customers'll be happy 'cause they'll get a chance to be stars. Everybody will know *you* made the clothes, though."

His argument was persuasive, but Miss Lena hedged. She had done all right without having a fashion show all these years, and she had fended off plenty of requests from churches, charity groups, and women's clubs. Why should she take on such a huge responsibility now, when she tired so easily she was not sure she could even complete the work on hand?

"How do you know I can do it, B.J.?"

"Because you *have* to," he said, sounding annoyingly like Mamie. "You ain't got as many customers as you think. Not any more. A fashion show would get you some of the old ones back, plus bring you some new ones."

A brutal change of subject was necessary. "We'll talk about it later, B.J. Tell me about yourself. Have you seen your father?"

His face knotted in an ugly scowl. "No. I don't go around bothering him, and he don't come around bothering me."

Miss Lena hoped fervently that this pattern would continue. "What are you living on? I haven't given you any money. What do you do for meals?"

"Oh, I'm eatin' good. My friends feed me. Mostly I have breakfast at Foot-Long's and supper at Mom Boggs'. And I have lunch here at the hospital every day with Dr. Robbins, the gland guy, before I come to see you. Sometimes I spend the night at Mom Boggs', but mostly I sleep in your basement. You won't know it when you get home, Miss Lena. I've cleaned it up real nice."

"There's one thing you haven't cleaned up, though," she said, wrinkling her nose as he came closer.

"What's that?" he asked innocently. A dozen long plaits hung from his scalp like snakes. He idly pulled two of them over his brow, crowning himself.

"Yourself. Here's two dollars. Buy yourself a large bar of soap and a towel, and wash all over. Wait. Here's another two dollars. Go to the barber and get a haircut. I'd like to know who braided it like that for you."

"King William did. He didn't charge me, neither. He's a friend of mine. I sweep up his shop sometimes."

"He ought to be ashamed of himself."

"But," he protested, "all the guys are wearing plaits and corn rows."

"They'll be wearing dresses next."

He pulled one of his braids forward and studied it. "You think it looks faggoty?"

"Yes."

"Hey," he said, "speaking of faggots, one named Leroy was by yesterday to see you. He said to tell you he decided to go to South America for Christmas instead of to the islands, and do you want to go too?"

His innocence, it seemed, was another of those imaginary things, like ghosts, that she could stop worrying about. "Are you going to get that haircut?"

"Yes," he said grudgingly after a long pause.

"Then tell him no," she said. "I'll be too busy getting ready for my fashion show."

Twenty

"You don't look too bad," B.J. said, squinting critically as they stepped out into the sunlight. "Just skinnier, that's all."

"This dress hangs off me like a shroud," Miss Lena said self-consciously. She was conscious, too, that her weight loss had lined her face, but didn't mention it.

"Make one that fits you, then," he said. "Make two. Make four."

As they started down the hospital steps, she suddenly caught his shoulder.

"What's the matter?"

"I get dizzy going down steps. It happens every time I look down."

"You don't *have* to look down. Look straight ahead. Look at me. I'm not looking down, am I?"

"I know," she said, and withdrew her hand. But the compulsion to see where she was placing her feet remained, and she continued to totter.

"I didn't say you couldn't hang onto me if you want."

Gratefully, she put her hand on his shoulder again. "What would I ever do without you, B.J.?" Even though she had just been thinking, what am I going to do *with* you? You're a thief, you're a liar, you're no good. But I need you.

"Why you asking? You know you don't ever *got* to do without me. You want a cab?"

"Yes," Miss Lena said, then changed her mind. Dr. Kloster had said she was to lead as normal a life as possible, and that included getting regular exercise. "No, wait. Let me see how far I can walk first. I won't get a cab till I need it."

They covered six blocks at a slow pace before Miss Lena admitted she was tired. When she gave the cab driver her apartment address, B.J. protested.

"Hey, what you goin' home for?"

"That's where I belong. I'm sick, remember?"

"No you ain't. You well, or they wouldn't of let you out the hospital. Let's go by your shop for a few minutes first. Huh, Miss Lena? Please? There's something I want to show you."

She had been looking forward to a long, lazy bath and a quiet evening. As it turned out, she was not going to have them. The door of her shop opened on bedlam.

"Surprise!"

"Welcome home!"

"We missed you!"

Half the neighborhood, it seemed, had crowded into her little salon. She barely recognized the room, it was so bedecked with paper festoons and gaudily dressed people. B.J. had to prompt her by whispering some of their names, but on her own she recognized King William, the barber; the old newspaper vendor, Bubba; Foot-Long, of course; and Mom Boggs, who was threatening to cave in Miss Lena's delicate love seat. Mamie was there, too, along with a sprinkling of Miss Lena's customers: Miss Allinson and Mrs. Johnson and Mrs. Johnson's best friend, birdlike little Mrs. Blackwell. Apparently B.J. had been selective, inviting only the ones he liked.

After greeting her guests, Miss Lena fortunately didn't have to make other conversation. Every mouth in the room was full, because the flock of church ladies who had come with Mrs. Johnson had apparently been busy for days preparing food.

"We got to fatten you up," the minister's wife declared, advancing on her with a paper plate heaped with chicken, spare ribs, and potato salad. "You ain't nothin' but skin and bones. Didn't they give you no food in that hospital? Finish this, and I'll bring you some more."

Less than two hours out of the hospital, and she was already breaking her diet. To make matters worse, B.J. brought one of Foot-Long's obscene-looking specialties, which the chef was cooking on a portable electric rotisserie near the door, and heaped it on her sagging plate.

Miss Lena was overwhelmed. But she perceived that none of her guests would leave until all the food was gone, so she determined to do her part. Not that they needed much help. Back in her work room, several well-padded churchwomen sat around the cutting table systematically devouring fried chicken and barbecued ribs as if they were being paid piece-work rates for their consumption. At the rate those sisters were polishing bones, the party wouldn't last long.

"I'll bet you thought you didn't have any friends," Mrs. Johnson said. "That's why we talked the little fella into letting us do this, so you'd know people cared. I'm sorry I didn't come to see you before, but I can't stand to visit anybody in the hospital. Those places depress me too much. That's terrible, I know, especially for a minister's wife. Henry gets after me about it all the time. But I won't do it. I'd rather see people at home."

Miss Lena understood. Her hardest task, next to finishing off that plate, was convincing Mrs. Johnson she could feed herself after tonight and would not need to have platters sent to her daily from the church kitchen. She knew what those platters would look like—fried fish, fried chicken, more mounds of potato salad and baked macaroni, plump, pale pigs' feet nestling in grease and gelatin—and knew, also, that they would send her straight back to the hospital.

After declining future platters, she ate her present one. She also smiled, shook hands, and exclaimed with seeming tirelessness over a pile of Get Well cards and daintily wrapped gifts—three linen handkerchiefs from Miss Allinson; a bracelet of bells from Mrs. Cosgrove, who was happily cruising the Caribbean; a bottle of reeking gardenia cologne from Miss Everett; two yards of peach-colored double-knit polyester from Mrs. Johnson, who said, "I knew I couldn't buy you anything near as nice as you could make out of this for yourself." It would go well with the orange and gold striped scarf from Mamie, who knew she would have to begin collecting scarves.

She opened the gifts and thanked everyone from her uncomfortable perch on the love seat between Mom Boggs' massive hip and the delicate wooden arm, which felt like being crushed between a marshmallow and a toothpick. After she had opened all her other presents, B.J. handed her a small cube clumsily wrapped in the tissue paper she used to make patterns, and labeled with a large warning: "DANGER! Do Not Open Till Xmas!"

"Thank you, B.J. But you shouldn't have spent your money."

"How you know I spent any money? Maybe I got it free, the way you got that chair, and that rug, and that lamp, and—"

"B.J., hush! People might not understand."

"You mean they might think you stole your stuff? *These* folks wouldn't care. Mom Boggs has a whole cellar full of stolen dresses for sale, and Foot-Long writes numbers, and—"

"Hush!" Miss Lena said again, more severely. But Mom Boggs went on fanning herself without a break in her rhythm as if she had not heard. She had brought Miss Lena the best present of all: a series of colored drawings by the neighborhood children, all lavished with red hearts and featuring Miss Lena as a red-lipped, long-haired, glamorously attired stick figure. Miss Lena planned to display them in her window before taking them home to keep forever.

Mrs. Johnson, who seemed to be in charge of the party, was the first to leave. "I'm so glad you're going to have the fashion show for us, Lena. We announced it last Sunday. The whole church is looking forward to it."

Miss Lena shot a murderous glance at B.J., who managed to look blankly cherubic. After Mrs. Johnson's departure with half the Senior Choir in her wake, the gathering began to break up. Mamie had no difficulty persuading the lagging guests that it was important for her patient to get plenty of rest.

"I don't think you'll need a nurse," she said as she was leaving, "but in case you do, here's my number."

"I'll use it because I need a *friend*," Miss Lena said.

"*You* need a friend? With all these people here? Girl, you're the most popular old bag I ever seen. But I know what you mean; there are friends and friends. Real ones and jive ones. Sure, I'd love to visit you. Maybe I'll bring my gentleman friend."

"Make it soon," Miss Lena said sincerely, and pressed the hand of this gruff, kindly woman who had come to seem like a sister. No doubt about it, Mamie was one of the real ones.

"B.J.," Miss Lena said sternly when they were alone at last, "why did you tell Mrs. Johnson I'd have the fashion show?"

"You said you would, didn't you?" he replied.

"I said I'd think about it."

"I didn't want you to think too long. You might change your mind," he admitted.

"And I suppose you've already asked my customers to be models," she said, expecting the worst.

"Some of 'em," he admitted. "They all said yes."

"What am I going to do with you?" she exclaimed. She picked up the clumsily wrapped cube, held it to her ear, and shook it. "Let me see if this is ticking."

"Why would it do that?"

"Why else would I have to keep it so long?" she teased. "Besides, it says 'Danger!' That means it might explode."

He caught on. "I wouldn't give you a bomb, Miss Lena. I might give one to some people, like my father. But not you."

Miss Lena said very severely, "Don't ever let me hear you say another bad word about your father, B.J. And if you ever catch *me* saying anything bad about him, make me stop."

"But—"

"But nothing." She had done a lot of thinking on the troublesome subject of B.J.'s father, and had decided this was the only possible attitude for her to take. It was natural for a boy to identify with his father. If she were to encourage B.J.'s bitterness or, worse, augment it with her own, she would only teach him to hate himself. Of course James Ricks was a drunkard and a thief and a rotten husband and father—now. But she would have to forget all that, and help B.J. forget it, too. Otherwise he might decide to be just like him.

For the moment, though, the subject was closed. She stretched and yawned luxuriously. "It was a lovely party, B.J. I was going to scold you about it, but I really enjoyed myself."

"Sure you did. I knew you would. Now you got a lot of new friends."

"I don't know about that," she said realistically, remembering Mamie's remark, *There are friends and friends,* "but at least I know the people in the neighborhood now, and that's a good thing, I guess. What's more, I don't have to think about cooking tonight, or about working, either, except for cleaning up this mess." She looked around wryly at the room, usually so neat, which was strewn with paper plates and other party leftovers.

"I'll clean it up," B.J. said, and began gathering debris into a large paper bag. "But Miss Allinson is getting nervous about her wedding gown."

"She didn't mention it to me."

"Of course not. You're supposed to be re—, re—"

"Recuperating?"

"That's it. So she told me instead."

"She told you, huh? Who's in charge around here, anyway? You or me?"

B.J. was discreetly silent.

"All right." Miss Lena capitulated with a sigh. "After I have a bath and a little nap, I'll come back and work on the wedding gown."

So the early-evening nap was re-established in Miss Lena's schedule. Before her hospital stay, it had been detrimental to her work, but now she found that it enabled her to get more done. After dark, with the shutters closed so that the shop seemed empty to passersby, she was not interrupted by phone calls or walk-in customers. B.J. had instructions to make no appointments for her before 11 a.m. If she needed to sleep late in the morning, he would be at the shop to greet walk-ins and take phone calls. On that first night and every other night, he had her work neatly laid out and waiting: Miss Allinson's gown and pattern, and the little file card on which Miss Lena had printed her measurements.

The second night, Miss Lena impulsively invited B.J. home with her for dinner.

Twenty-one

It was the first time he had seen her apartment, and she wondered as she opened the door whether she would regret inviting him there. She did, almost immediately, and not just because she might be inviting a second robbery.

She enjoyed his first excitement, his screams of delight on discovering that she lived in a place "just like on TV." But he seemed driven to destroy it by a ravenous curiosity that needed to touch and handle everything; that seemed compelled to discover what lay inside every drawer and behind every door. Wherever he moved, even when he touched nothing, he left a small trail of chaos behind. He was the evil genie she had always feared, whose entry into her elegant sanctum would turn it into a junk pile, and she had invited him there herself.

But she needed him there to straighten out the even more distressing disorder in her head. Miss Lena had always been a firm believer in a place for everything and everything in its place, but now she could not remember any of the places. She could not even assemble the simple ingredients for a meal. While she wondered aloud where she had put the paring knife? the cooking oil? he rummaged and rapidly found them. When she asked what on earth could have happened to her favorite skillet, the one she used for everything, he pointed it out, hanging on a hook right in front of her eyes. Without him, she was forced to admit, she would probably have starved.

He was just as essential to her functioning at the shop. Armed with her appointment calendar, her address book, her file box of customers' measurements, and a vast catalog of information kept only in his head, he organized her work for her. To fastidious Miss Lena, it seemed more like disorganization—but it worked. She did not ask again, not even jokingly, which of them was in charge of her shop. She did not want to contemplate the answer. It was B.J. who set her priorities now.

"Miss Allinson's things should come first; she's waited the longest," he dictated. "Then whatever Mrs. Lewis wants." And after that, Dr. Norman's dresses; mainly, Miss Lena suspected, because he was afraid of the educator. Not that there had been any mention, lately, of school. Miss Lena needed him too much at the moment to bring up the subject.

After finishing Dr. Norman's things, she was to make a skirt for a new customer, Mrs. Scharf, who deserved prompt attention because she was both pleasant and rich. At least that was B.J.'s opinion, and these days, his opinion carried far more weight than was justified by his age. Miss Lena had to defer to it, since she was no longer able to manage her shop alone. He was considerate enough to keep her secret, but she was now almost totally dependent on him to manage it for her.

She did not know where things were stored in her shop any more than she had known where to find them in her kitchen. Neither did B.J., but with frantic rummaging, he found everything and rearranged it in a way that made sense only to him.

"I'll put this pink stuff on the bottom of this pile. It's Mrs. Cosgrove's, and she won't be back till after the Christmas holidays. We got a postcard from her today. This gray dress is for Mrs. Johnson, but she ain't in no hurry; she'll wait all year as long as she knows you're gonna do that fashion show. This is the red velvet for Miss Everett's bridesmaids. I might as well put it away too. They ain't even been here yet to get measured. This is your week-after-next pile."

"Where's my right-now pile?"

"There ain't none. I'll just keep on handing you the next thing till all the piles are gone."

"You think that will ever happen, B.J.?" she asked with a sigh.

"I hope not," he shot back. " 'Cause then you'd have to close up."

"I guess you're right," she said. "But I wish I understood your system better. I wish I could remember more things myself."

"What for?" he asked suspiciously. "I ain't goin' nowhere."

"You're making sure of that, aren't you?" she said.

"What you mean?"

Miss Lena did not choose to explain. She turned back to her machine to finish off one of Miss Allinson's going-away dresses, and made an annoying discovery. "I'm out of blue seam binding. That's what's wrong with counting on you to remember everything, B.J. That's what's wrong with working at night, too. No stores are open at this hour."

"It's quittin' time anyway," B.J. declared like the boss he had become. "Ten o'clock. Why don't you go home? Unless you want to stay and watch this good program on TV with me."

"What's it about?" Her insurance check had come through and enabled her to buy another TV set—not color, though, and not as large as the stolen one. She figured since she had refused to pay off that obnoxious policeman, that it was just as well to offer less enticement to thieves.

"Oh, dope smuggling and spies and karate and murder and a whole lot of other good stuff."

"No thank you," she said with a small shudder as her shop began to reverberate with explosions. "What appointments do I have tomorrow?"

"Nobody but Miss Allinson at eleven and Mrs. Lewis at eleven-thirty," he replied without a glance at the calendar.

"Don't you write appointments down any more, B.J.?"

"Sure."

But when she studied her big wall calendar, all she saw were some hieroglyphics that were totally incomprehensible to her. Either he was using a kind of shorthand he had invented, or he had never spent enough time in school to learn how to write.

With his eyes fixed on the TV, he paid no attention to her. "What time you coming in tomorrow?"

"I think I'll try to get here by nine and finish Miss Allinson's dresses."

"Good. Then I can run out right away and get the seam binding and your coffee."

"Get some thank-you notes, too. We have to send them to all the people who brought gifts." And I, she was thinking slyly as she put on her coat, have to find out whether you can write.

"O.K. Say, Miss Lena?"

She turned with her hand on the doorknob. "Yes, B.J.?"

"You didn't open your present, did you?"

"No." It still sat inviolate on her bedroom dresser, surrounded by the juvenile drawings that had just been replaced in the window by a size 14 sample.

"Good," he said, already absorbed in the groans and

screams emerging from the electronic box. "I wanted it to be a surprise."

Miss Lena was faithful to her promise all that week, which included the long Thanksgiving holiday, and for four weeks thereafter, even though B.J. spent Thanksgiving with the Boggs family while she ate her slices of delicatessen turkey roll alone.

After the holiday, B.J. returned to her dinner table and they settled into a smooth-functioning routine at the shop. It had been slow going at first, but by the end of her second week out of the hospital, she began to believe she might get caught up on her work after all. She could never have done it without B.J.'s fantastic memory and his intuitive understanding of people. He knew where to reach all of her customers at any time of day and what to tell them. He also had an uncanny talent for sensing which women required urgent attention and which could be cajoled into accepting delays.

Two weeks more, and she felt free to indulge in her favorite pastime, creating and sketching original designs, a much more pleasurable process than the painstaking execution of a dress. It seemed incredible, but her work was caught up enough to grant her a brief breathing spell. Mrs. Lewis had been pleased with the replacement for her stolen gown, an evening dress and coat in a pale blue and silver brocade selected for her by B.J. He had become such a skilled shopper for the business that Miss Lena seldom needed to visit the fabric stores any more, especially now that the owners knew B.J. and were willing to trust him with samples.

Even the brides had been outfitted on schedule. Miss Allinson's dresses were finished first, well ahead of time. As for Miss Everett and her party, once their measurements had been taken, it had been a simple assembly-line procedure to cut and stitch six identical velvet gowns, one white and five red.

Christmas was less than a week away, but Miss Lena was not suffering from her annual depression. On the contrary, her imagination was soaring and pulling her spirits along with it. Designing for a fashion show allowed her to throw away all the conventional rules. Mrs. Cosgrove would look like one of her own favorite fantasies, a Caribbean chorus girl, in a green satin sarong and matching turban from which three peacock feathers would sprout to make her nine feet tall. Mrs. Johnson would be even more dramatic, an African queen in a stiff, towering headdress like Nefertiti's and a long robe with huge batwing sleeves. The robe would be in a spotted orange print bordered in black, and when Mrs. Johnson raised her arms, she would look like a gigantic monarch butterfly. So would her daughter Monica, robed identically in spotted yellow.

. . . No, wait, Miss Lena would dress several other girls in yellow as winged bridesmaids. If she could get some of that white-on-white embroidered Peruvian cotton, Monica's robe would climax the show as an ethnic wedding gown.

While she was still mentally clothing her models, Leroy dropped in to chatter about his forthcoming trip. She hardly listened to his raptures of anticipation.

. . . The same shade of peach Mrs. Johnson had given her would flatter Mrs. Roderick Lewis. Miss Lena would put her in something daring for a change: everything covered except one leg and hip, bared by a high slit in the skirt. Sure, Mrs. Lewis was an old girl, but she was as slim as a young one, and there was nothing wrong with her legs except prominent veins that could be concealed by flesh-colored tights. Mrs. Lewis would wear anything, anyway, even a Lady Godiva costume, if it was for charity.

Yes, she replied absently to Leroy's questions, she was well enough to go to South America. And, yes, she could afford the trip. Mrs. Weinberg had brought back the duty-free tweeds from England as promised, and the new customer, Mrs. Scharf, had bought all but one piece. Miss Lena's profit on the deal would more than cover the cost of a week in Venezuela.

"You ain't even listening to me, girl," Leroy said with a petulant pout. "You act like you're a thousand miles from here already. What's on your mind?"

"Uh . . . I was just dreaming up some designs for a fashion show I'm having in the spring." Lord, why had she said *that?* He would want to be one of the models.

But he was more intent on persuading her to accompany him. "Well, why can't you do your designing in Venezuela? You'd get tons of inspiration there. You'd see native costumes, high fashion from Europe, and everything in between. You could take your sketch pad down to the beach at Macuto, bask in the sun, and design for *days.*"

"I'm sure I could," she said absently. She was seeing Dr. Norman in a crisp tent of tomato red, the fieriest shade of near-orange, fine-pleated from yoke to hem and from shoulder to wrist, like a walking flame. Whoever first said black people should not wear red had to be color-blind. Blazing colors suited them best; what most black people should avoid were muddy shades like beige and brown.

"I don't understand you," he complained. "You always go away at Christmas."

"Yes, that's true." She had always *needed* to be away at Christmas. But this year, for the first time in her life, she was thinking of an apartment-sized Christmas tree with a heap of presents beneath it, perhaps a set of electric trains. Was B.J. too old for trains? No, a boy was never too old for trains. Men liked them too. It was part of the male nature to be in love with everything mechanical that moved.

"Stop holding back," he said firmly. "You're going, and that's that. You need it. You can afford it. And you deserve it, Lena. I'll call up and make your reservation right now."

She intercepted his hand as it reached for her phone. "No, Leroy."

"All right. I'll send you so many postcards you'll hate yourself," he promised cheerfully, and left.

Miss Lena had no regrets for an entire hour. Then B.J. came in from his errand, breathless with excitement, to announce that he had been invited to spend all of Christmas week with the Boggs family too.

"Earl Junior is getting a motorcycle. He's getting a new rifle, too. And he's gonna teach me how to shoot. Says I'm old enough to know how to handle a gun. Says he knows a place in the country where we can get pheasants, rabbits, maybe even deer. . . ."

It was a fine opportunity for the boy, of course. It was wonderful of her neighbors to take such an interest in him. At his age, he needed the companionship of a man. It would be wrong of her to say that she was terrified of guns and shooting and even more afraid of motorcycles; wrong to impose her silly feminine fears on him. Even more wrong to admit that she dreaded spending the Christmas holidays at home alone, that in the past she had always made elaborate arrangements to avoid being beached on a desert island in a sea of tinsel, and that it was because of B.J., and only B.J., that she had just refused an invitation to go away.

Thinking such high-minded thoughts, exercising such noble restraint, she did not even know she was angry until she heard herself screaming like a crazy woman, "All right then, don't bother coming home with me any more. Eat your dinner with them tonight and every night, till they get good and sick of you. And I hope that's soon, and I hope you starve!"

At home, she snatched up the young children's drawings and ripped them to shreds. Picked up the older child's clumsily wrapped package and tossed it into the garbage can. Then dropped to the floor and did exercises to work off her dangerous anger before it blew up again in her head. Her last weekly checkup had been perfect. She would be a damn fool to risk another stroke now by letting her emotions get out of control.

Finally calmed by exhaustion, she retrieved her gift from the garbage can. She had better open it now, lest B.J. see it with its wrappings stained with grease and coffee grounds. As she unwrapped the many layers of tissue paper it got smaller and smaller, like a loose head of lettuce, until she wondered if it were empty. Then she reached something that felt hard, even through its cocoon of tissue.

It was a small, brilliant flame set in a circle of thin platinum. A real, flawless, blue-white diamond, at least a quarter-carat, that caught all the light and sprayed showers of sparks around the room.

Twenty-two

Boldly, she wore the ring to her shop the next morning on her right hand.

It was conspicuous as a spotlight, but B.J., bent over her worktable and writing with painful concentration, did not notice it. She picked up the top envelope from the completed stack at his left, turned it over and studied it critically. It was neatly addressed, in a round, clear, childish hand, to Mrs. Edward Cosgrove at the Valley View Apartments.

"Those are the thank-you cards," he said without looking up through his thick lashes. "They're all finished. I left 'em unsealed in case you wanted to write something on 'em. I'm doing the Christmas cards now."

"Christmas cards?" she asked blankly, as if she had never heard of such things.

His hand darted into an opened box on his right, plucked out an envelope, then shoved the box toward her for inspection.

B.J. had chosen well. The card was not gaudy and not ordinary either, yet it was clearly not cheap. It pictured a golden partridge in a tree dripping with golden pears, and was suggestive of opulence and sophistication, but not blatantly so.

Inside its single fold was a one-word message: *Greetings.* Nothing more; nothing religious to offend the various creeds of her customers.

"You like it?" he asked without looking up.

"Very much. I couldn't have chosen a better one myself."

"Sure you could. You could even draw your own; that would be best of all. But you don't have time this year, so I figured I'd save you the trouble. You want me to leave these unsealed too, or you want me to sign 'em for you?"

"Nice of you to offer, B.J. I thought you couldn't write."

The sarcasm in her voice brought his head up as if jerked by a string. "Sure I can write. Why'd you think I couldn't?"

She snatched the large calendar off the wall and thrust it under his eyes. "Because of this. What do all these markings mean?"

He looked genuinely amazed. "Can't you understand 'em?"

"No, and neither could anybody else."

"Geez. I thought any old dummy could figure this stuff out. It's just like those easy puzzles they have in the paper for kids." He pointed to a blob with legs; a bloated animal. "This stands for Mrs. Johnson."

The Hippo. Of course.

"She had an appointment that day in November. And this Jewish star stands for Mrs. Weinberg."

"And this crossed-out bell?" she asked, flipping to the December page.

"That's Mrs. Cosgrove, of course."

"Of course," Miss Lena echoed as if it made sense to her.

" 'Cause she always makes so much noise. 'Rings on her fingers, bells on her toes; she makes a racket wherever she goes,' " he improvised. "I crossed her out when we got the postcard saying she wouldn't be back till after New Year's. I need to start filling in January now. When you gonna get a big calendar for next year?"

"When my insurance agent sends me one, like he always does."

"We can't wait for him, Miss Lena. Besides, you got a different insurance company now, remember? Maybe they don't send out calenders like the other one did. I started to buy a big calendar in the card shop, but I didn't have enough money left after I got the cards. I think you ought to let me go back and get one, though, before your appointments get all messed up again."

"*Your* appointments, you mean. *I* certainly can't read these doodles of yours."

"Why not? Didn't I just explain 'em to you?"

"Can't you just write them down in *words?*"

"Takes too long. When I write fast, my handwriting's so messy *I* can't even read it later. I have to write real slow to make it clear. Took me three hours this morning just to write these cards."

There were only twelve in the finished stack. But she did not quite believe him. She still felt he was using code messages on her calendar to make himself so indispensable she would never dare get rid of him.

Her next remark was a surprise attack. "How much money do you have left in your bank now, B.J.?"

"Enough," was his non-answer.

"How much money did you have before I went to the hospital?"

"Hey, look what you made me do, asking all them questions." He held up a smeared envelope, then tore it up. "Now I got to write this one all over again."

He was trying to distract her, and she knew it. "Stop writing a minute, B.J. I want to talk to you."

"I got to get these done in time to take 'em to the post office. It's December twenty-first *already,*" he grumbled.

"B.J., *they can wait,*" she said in her no-more-nonsense tone of voice.

"O.K.," he said reluctantly, and swiveled in the chair to face her.

"I asked you how much money you had left in your bank, and how much you'd spent."

"I don't know exactly. I had a lot once. Now I got five or six dollars left, I guess. The cards were twelve-fifty. Ten for the Christmas cards and two-fifty for the thank-yous. I bought 'em with your money, but if you think they cost too much, tell me what you wanted to spend and I'll make up the difference."

"I'm not worried about the cards," she said, conscious that he was dodging the issue. "They're worth whatever they cost. What I'm wondering is where you got the money to buy this."

She threw her fist at his face so suddenly he ducked. Then he saw the diamond.

His face contorted with rage. "But you promised!" he screamed. "You promised not to open it till Christmas!"

"You won't be around at Christmas, remember?"

"I know you mad about that, Miss Lena. Mom Boggs and Pop Earl would have invited you, but they was afraid you'd say no. They ain't got a nice house or nothing fancy. You're a high-class, refined lady, and they're just ordinary people."

"We're all ordinary people around here, B.J. Ordinary people who can't afford diamond solitaires."

"How you know it's a real diamond?"

"I know," she said quietly. "I've seen enough real jewels to tell them from fakes. Where did you get it?"

"I bought it."

"Where?"

"I promised I wouldn't tell. But I bought it with my own money."

"Have you been paying yourself that ten percent I promised you?"

"Sometimes, when I remember. Mostly I forget. But I had plenty of money left from before you went in the hospital. All that money your customers gave me. Remember?"

"Enough to buy this ring?"

"Yes."

"B.J.," she said sharply, "this diamond had to cost at least two hundred dollars."

"Not at the place I bought it from."

She was relentless. "What place was that?"

He wriggled uncomfortably in the chair, as if he had to go to the bathroom. "I can't tell you. You just got to believe me, Miss Lena. I paid for it with my own money."

"How can I believe you, if you won't tell me the whole story? Half the truth is the same as a lie, B.J., and you know I can't stand to be lied to. You've lied to me about so many things I can't believe anything you say any more. You told me you lived on Mole Street when you were really staying in my basement. You said you didn't know how my shop got robbed last month, but you were the one who let the thieves in. Did they pay you two hundred dollars to help them rob me? You said you knew who robbed my shop last spring, too, but you wouldn't tell me their names. How about telling me now, B.J.? Who were the thieves?"

"If it'll make you feel better, I won't go to the Boggses for Christmas. I'll stay here."

Her blood was pounding a warning drumbeat in her ears. She disregarded it and went on with her lecture. "No, it won't make me feel any better. Nothing will make me feel better but the truth. The *truth*. Do you even know what that means?"

"I didn't know you was *that* mad about me going away for Christmas."

"That's not what I'm mad about," she said, conscious that she was telling a partial truth herself. "I'm mad about all your little tricks and lies. I swear, B.J., you've got more angles than that star you put on my calendar. I don't believe you have to draw pictures on my calendar, either. I think you just do it to make sure I'll always need you. And why didn't you tell me who your father was? I know he sent you here. Don't deny it, B.J. James Ricks put you up to coming here. He was going to use you as a wedge to open the door so he could walk back into my life."

His eyes were almost closed, screwed up in pain, and his fists were clenched. "Miss Lena, you're wrong. I swear I didn't know you was ever married to my father."

"I don't believe you. And I don't believe you bought this ring, either. Prove me wrong. Show me the sales slip."

He shook his head. "I can't. I ain't got none."

"Of course not, because you didn't buy it."

"I didn't buy it in a *store!*" he shouted.

"Where did you buy it then?"

He was silent.

"I think you stole it, and you know how I feel about stealing. If you don't tell me who you stole it from right now, I'm going to call the police, and they'll *make* you tell."

His face, faded from black to ashen gray, looked older than when she had first seen it. His voice was choking. "I just wanted to give you something nice instead of some old dumb junk like toilet water or costume jewelry. But the trouble is, you don't trust nobody. Maybe you can tell real jewelry, but you can't tell when people are faking and when they're real." Looking up at the ceiling as if addressing an invisible third party, he complained, "Aah, what's the use talkin' to somebody who don't believe nothin' you say? Ain't no use. No use at all."

She thought he was crying as he ran out the door, but he moved so swiftly she could not be sure if she had seen wet spots on his ashy cheeks.

She followed him, holding his hat and coat. "It's cold out, B.J.!" she called. "Come back! You forgot your jacket."

But the street was empty of both pedestrians and traffic, and eerily silent as it whitened swiftly with the winter's first snow. No one answered.

Well, good riddance, she said to herself. He was nothing but trouble anyway.

But the echo of her own lecture was still ringing in her ears as it must have sounded to his. Already it seemed pompous, self-righteous, perhaps even grossly unfair. She was still standing just inside the door, foolishly holding the hat with its earflaps and the warm plaid jacket. She laid them carefully on a chair. He would be back for them, she told herself, as soon as his temper cooled. She would apologize for her barrage of accusations and ask him again, gently this time, to explain about the ring. This time he would tell her the whole story, and she would believe him. She twisted the ring on her finger as if it had magic powers to bring him back and make it happen.

But the day lengthened and grew even quieter, the snow continued to fall, and B.J. did not appear. Nor did anyone else. She peered at the controversial calendar, saw no squiggles or doodles in the block labeled Friday, and concluded that she had no appointments today. She might as well leave.

But there *was* that stack of cards to be finished and mailed. Calling on her self-discipline not to desert her now that B.J. had, she sat down and resolutely addressed herself to the task.

Almost immediately, she knew she needed B.J., with or without his codes. She spread out the thank-you cards and stared at them. She could not remember which women had brought her which gifts. She had to settle for an all-inclusive phrase—"Thank you for your thoughtfulness"—which she wrote on each card before signing her name.

Addressing the Christmas cards required even more discipline. For her, it was always the most depressing chore imaginable, but this year it shrouded her in an extra blanket of gloom. Her reluctance made it slow work. When the last envelope was sealed, the room had begun to grow dark, and there was still no sign of B.J. She had just enough time to mail the cards. She pulled on her boots, closed up her shop, and headed toward the post office. Afterward she would go straight home and make some cheerful holiday plans. She would not waste another minute of her life running after that wayward child. She had just been gravely ill. She might not have much time left on this earth. She had better enjoy it.

But it seemed she had forgotten how to enjoy herself alone. It had happened so insidiously, she had not realized she was growing accustomed to constant companionship, to lively questions that required answers, to keen ears that listened and a quick mind that responded even when she was talking to herself. Her cozy apartment no longer comforted her, and her gadgets did not invite her to pleasure. Side by side, the television and the eye-level oven stared at her with blank, doleful eyes like an idiot's. Before she might begin to cry, she called Leroy's office.

The girl who answered sounded giggly; sounded as if she were being tickled; sounded, in fact, drunk. No, Mr. Harris was not in. He had gone out to lunch earlier and had not returned. No, that was not usual—but, after all, it was the Friday before Christmas. "Merry Christmas," she laughed, and Miss Lena replied hollowly, "The same to you."

"Merry Christmas." The two most depressing words in the English language. Miss Lena preferred "terminal cancer."

She dialed the hospital and asked for Mamie. It seemed that Mamie, too, was out to lunch. On the Friday before Christmas, everyone was out to lunch. Whenever you really needed people in this world, they were out to lunch. Or out to shop, or celebrate, or fornicate, or something.

Feeling herself grow hysterical, Miss Lena pulled herself up rigidly and asked herself: since when had she needed anyone? People were nothing but a plague. If she didn't keep them at a distance, they'd infect her with their idiocy.

But that philosophy, which worked for her so well the rest of the year, would not help her get through the dreadful, artificially cheerful holidays. She called Leroy at home.

He was just finishing his packing. "Child, why didn't you call me sooner? I might have been able to do something even last night, but today there isn't a seat left on any plane. I just tried to get one for another friend of mine. I'm *so* sorry, but I've got to dash to the airport now."

He'd tried to sound disappointed and sympathetic,

but there was no disguising the undertone of elation in his voice. In an hour he'd be airborne, his plane nosing toward the coast of another continent. He was already anticipating a week of new experiences: new scenery, a new climate, new foods, new friends.

As for the other so-called friends who had crowded into her shop a few weeks ago, where were they now? Packing for honeymoons, rehearsing their weddings, or busy decorating and provisioning their already-cozy nests. Buying gifts to stuff like pack rats into the void of loneliness that ached worse on December 25th than on any other day of the year. Filling that hollow place to the brim would insure that on this one day they would be surrounded by a close circle of love and gratitude, however distant and indifferent the circle might be on all the other days. Any other time, people could stand loneliness, indifference, even hostility. But on December 25th, when happiness was practically required by law, even a circle of greed was better than none at all. If she called her married friends, they might take pity and make room for her at their holiday tables. But Miss Lena did not want charity. She was too proud to admit she was desperate—except to someone likely to be as lonely as she was.

She dialed Mamie at home and, miraculously, connected. The husky, familiar voice said "Hello" as if it were saying "Go to hell" on the third ring.

"What are you doing over the holidays?" Miss Lena asked.

"Trying to live through them, just like all the other lonely old bags. What else? I tried to get work straight through New Year's, but they didn't need me. So I'll just have to sit here and endure it. They'll need me after the first, though. The place always fills up with attempted suicides over Christmas. I just have to hang on for ten days and try not to be one of 'em."

"I thought you said you had children."

"*Grown* children, honey! The boys are overseas in the Army, and the girl's in California. They ain't about to fly all this way just to see an old lady."

"What about your gentleman friend?"

"Christmas is one time a married man's got to spend every minute with his family. Leaving me high and dry." She chuckled with the rich humor Miss Lena was sure would always keep Mamie from becoming a suicide statistic. "If I'm dry, how the hell can I be high? I sure wish I could afford to stay drunk the next ten days."

"How'd you like to get drunk with some company?"

"Who?"

"Another lonely old bag. Me."

Mamie pretended to hesitate. "You ain't exactly my type." There was a long pause, then a hearty chuckle. "But you'll do. Listen, no offense, I just meant I'd prefer to be with a man. You understand. The truth is, I'd go out with King Kong tonight, or *Mrs.* King Kong, for that matter, but I ain't had no offers from either of 'em. You look better than they do. Act better, too. Stay where you are. I'll be over as soon as I put on some glad rags."

Miss Lena had not planned to go out, only to offer Mamie the hospitality of her apartment and her food and wine hoard. But to keep her Christmas depression at bay, she was ready to do almost anything, even break one of her most basic survival rules: Always stay home after dark, especially on weekends and holidays.

"Put on the finest thing in your closet. Maybe we can

go out and stir up some action. If we can't, at least we ain't too old to dream."

Miss Lena searched her closets for something that would come up to Mamie's expectations. Though many of her neatly tailored business dresses were colorful, she was sure none of them would do. "Fine" meant sexy, gaudy, eye-catching. *Male* eye-catching.

She rooted in the box at the bottom of her closet where she kept her samples and pulled out the purple velvet minidress and matching shorts that had spent last October in her window. Well, why not? she thought recklessly. Her legs were at least as good as Mrs. Lewis', if not better. Mrs. Lewis had borne children and was a quarter-century older besides. She hung the velvet outfit in the bathroom and turned the hot shower on full to steam out the wrinkles. Then, with wild inspiration, she used grape juice to dye a pair of pantyhose to match and dried them in the cap of her hair dryer.

She was already so far out of character she decided to go all the way. She smeared her eyelids with purple shadow and purpled her lips as well. Then she doused herself with the gardenia cologne Miss Everett had given her.

When she opened the door for Mamie, both of them burst into spontaneous, mutually self-deprecating laughter. Mamie's large swollen feet were crammed into gold sandals, and her body was bursting the seams of an orange satin sheath that was so shiny it seemed fluorescent. Her breasts rose above its scoop neckline like a pair of floating coconuts, and she smelled like a hothouse full of gardenias.

"Lord, girl, I sure hope we can find us a couple of things in pants to pair off with quick! At least we smell the same. But—purple and orange! I never saw a worse clash of colors in my life. —Oh, what the hell, who's going to see us? It's dark as a cave in Susie's anyway."

"What's Susie's?"

"A nice place. You'll like it. Let's go."

Twenty-three

Earl Junior laid down the law to B.J. as soon as he let him in. Not hollering like Jayjay, but sweet-talking like he would to a woman. Smiling easy talk that was somehow meaner than his old man's yelling.

"A visit is one thing, Short Boy. A long-term stay is something else. If you got no other place to go, playtime is over, my friend. Do you understand? You got to hustle plenty if you plan on living here awhile."

"And if I don't?"

He regretted the fresh words as soon as they were out of his mouth. Earl Junior was starting to remove his belt.

"Then that means you must be sick. And if you sick, we have to cure you. Back in olden times, the slaveowners had a name for your disease. They called it *Dysaesthesia Aethopiis.* Translation is lazy niggeritis. Symptoms are goofing off, acting stubborn, and trying to run away every time you don't like it where you are. Cure is rub the patient down with oil and work the oil in with a good, strong leather strap. Any time you show symptoms of *Dysaesthesia* around here, I'll help you get well in a hurry." Earl Junior swung his belt by the pointed end, clanging the big silver buckle against the wall. "I won't use the oil, though. Mom needs it to baste the turkey."

The Boggs house was filling with rich cooking smells, just like the last time, but B.J. already knew this holiday was going to be different.

"Naturally," Earl Junior continued, smiling scarily with his mouth but not his eyes, "I'm hoping you won't get sick on us. 'Cause we're all mighty fond of you around here, Short Boy. Course if you don't want to cooperate with us, there's the door. It's plenty cold out there, though."

"What you want me to do, Junior?"

"*Mister* Junior to you." Earl Junior replaced his belt slowly, still smiling with his mouth while steadily staring at B.J. with those hard unreadable eyes. "Exactly what I tell you, exactly when and how I tell you to do it, and nothing else." He glanced at his chunky gold watch. "Tall Boy should be here any minute, and then I'll give you your first assignment. Probably send you and him out together to peddle some merchandise."

Bobo burst in just then without knocking, looking more untogether than B.J. had ever seen him. One jacket sleeve was so badly torn it was half hanging off him, and a trickle of blood ran down from his scalp and branched out over one side of his face like a skinny red hand.

Mom Boggs waddled in from the kitchen. "Don't bleed on my brand-new carpet, boy. That's all I ask." She settled with a sigh into her specially built wide rocker, which had been pulled into a corner to keep it from damaging the new high-pile rug, which was lettuce green, Mom's favorite color, the color of money.

There was something funny about Mom Boggs. She could see and hear as well as anybody else, but she only seemed to notice what she wanted. Like those three monkeys in a row.

"Get a rag, Junior," she said.

Earl Junior passed the job to B.J. "You heard what she said, boy. Hurry."

The only thing he could find in the kitchen, which smelled so lushly of beans simmering with fat meat on top of the stove and turkey and yams roasting in the oven, was a damp dishrag that stank of mildew. He came running back and mopped Bobo's face with it.

The older boy pushed his hand away. "Damn, that stinks. What you got on it, rotten cabbage?"

"Dishwater," B.J. replied calmly, parting the long hair to dab at Bobo's bloody scalp. The hair had gone so nappy at the roots he couldn't tell whether Bobo might need stitches or not. Probably he did, though; blood was still welling up under the naps.

"That's enough. Quit before you mess up my do. You want to do something, go get a clean rag and tie my whole head up."

B.J. glanced questioningly at Earl Junior, who said firmly, "This ain't no barber shop, Tall Boy. This is my house. What's your problem?"

"We got to get up some cash in a hurry. He swears he'll kill me next time."

"Who?"

"That cop."

Earl Junior remained calm and smiling. "I thought you had the cops under control, Bobo."

"Not this one. Not my regular boss, a different one. A big pig named Oliveri."

"I still don't understand what he's got to do with you and me. We only deal with DiLuca, you know that."

"You know that job I did across town? The dressmaker? DiLuca ain't got no connections in that precinct. Oliveri was on the case. He thought the lady was gonna cut him in on her insurance check, but she didn't. So he came after me. Mad as a pig smellin' garbage he couldn't get to. Tore my new threads. Just look at my jacket." Bobo's fancy jacquard-weave sleeve, ripped from shoulder to cuff, fell away from his arm as he raised it.

"That ain't nothin'. You oughta see your head," B.J. remarked, dabbing again. Once more his hand was pushed away, but feebly this time. He kept on dabbing.

"That's right, son," Mom Boggs approved. "Keep on doin' like you doin'. This is Mom's house, and in here you do like Mom wants."

The rag was getting more red than not. "I think he might need some stitches," B.J. said.

"Fuck that. No doctor's gonna shave off my hair. Took me three years to grow it this long. My head sure hurts though. That cop went upside it with the butt of his gun like he was playin' jungle music." He buried his face in his hands, increasing the flow of blood.

"Hold your head up and keep it still," B.J. ordered.

"Money," Bobo moaned. "I need money. If I don't lay a thousand dollars on that cop by Monday he gonna use the other end of his gun on me."

"A thousand. Well, well," Earl Junior crooned. "I guess you and Short Boy really got some hustlin' to do over the holidays."

Bobo jerked his face up at him. The smooth mahogany color had fled from his cheeks, turning him ashy with fright. "You mean you ain't gonna help me?"

"Son," Earl Junior said pleasantly, "I do anything I can to help people, you know that. I even help strangers, and you and Short Boy are more like sons to me. But the kind of help you're askin' for, I can't give."

"You ain't got a thousand?"

Earl Junior shrugged. "If I did, should I throw it away on you? Nobody told you to go way over there on Berkeley Street and mess with that lady. You got in this trouble on your own. Now get out of it on your own."

"You took all the stuff off me," Bobo reminded him.

"And you got paid for it."

"But I can't make a thousand in a weekend!"

"This is *Christmas* weekend," Earl Junior pointed out.

"I still can't do it. I'll be dead by Tuesday."

"There's always Gerardo," Earl Junior suggested. Bobo groaned. That was a sure recipe for sudden death. Gerardo was a six-for-five loan shark; three for two if you were desperate enough, and if you didn't pay, he didn't play. Feeling sorry for his friend, B.J. offered to help him.

"You? What can *you* do? You the one got me in this mess in the first place," Bobo said scornfully. "Listen, Junior, I thought of a plan in case you couldn't help me. Jayjay had something to tell me today, so I asked him to meet me here."

"Jayjay coming here? When?"

"Any minute."

"Hide the liquor, children," Mom Boggs ordered. After several vain attempts, she managed to heave her bulk up from the chair and began gathering cut-glass decanters into her apron. "Not that I ain't hospitable, but we got to have something left around here for the holidays."

It was B.J.'s turn to be terrified. "Where can *I* hide?" he cried, looking around the square, immaculate room. It had no nooks or dark corners; everything was plastic, shiny, and right out in the open.

Earl Junior shoved him toward what looked like a solid wall of paneling under the stairs, and opened a paneled door. "In here."

The closet was cluttered with old raincoats and umbrellas and rubbers and shoes and God knew what else, maybe dead rats and snakes and lizards that Mom Boggs used for her conjure work. There was not enough room to either stand up or sit down. When he tried to move, things came crashing down on him, so he just stayed uncomfortably bent over. The space under the stairs was airtight and soundproof, filled with the stale funk of sweaty old clothes and shoes. About to suffocate, B.J. shoved silently and cracked the door open enough to breathe. And hear, and see.

Earl Junior was speaking. "You must of caught some brain damage from that beating, if you think you gonna get a thousand bucks from ol' Jayjay."

"He has fifteen thousand saved up. You heard him say so yourself."

"I hear a lot of things. Doesn't mean I believe 'em."

Bobo began talking fast, the words spilling all over each other like alphabet blocks falling out of a box. "Yeah, well, seeing is believing, right? Ain't that right, man? You know he always sees me at his house. You don't never go there, man. But me, I go there all the time, and I know he got money. I seen it. Why would I lie? I even know where he keeps it."

Earl Junior's laugh was nasty and mocking. "In his mattress, right?"

"How'd you know?"

B.J. felt sick because Bobo didn't even know Junior was laughing at him.

"Well, look here, Tall Boy," Earl Junior said, still laughing, "suppose our old friend Jayjay does have all this cash stashed in his mattress, what makes you think you gonna get some of it?"

"There's more ways than one of getting it."

Earl Junior was suddenly serious. "Shut up. You said too much already."

Bent over in the closet, aching so bad Junior might as

well have gone ahead and given him that beating, B.J. felt a cold-water trickle of fear down his spine. Then the water turned to ice as his father's voice filled the room.

"Merry Christmas, men," thundered the world's most unlikely Santa Claus. "How are you all this Christmas Eve?"

"Fine, Jayjay," Earl Junior answered. "How are you?"

"Fine, fine, splendid. Bursting with Christmas spirit. Happy to share it with my employees."

Jayjay had been tasting before he got there; B.J. recognized the signs. The old man was in his grand mood—lordly, expansive, generous. He had even been known to give his son a dollar for dinner when he was like this.

"How come we got demoted to employees? I thought we were partners," Earl Junior objected playfully.

Bobo overrode him. "Boss, we was just wonderin' if you might be plannin' to hand out a little Christmas bonus."

"That might be forthcoming, if you have a little Christmas cheer to hand out first."

There was an embarrassed silence. Mom Boggs had locked up every drop of spirits in the place. And for some reason Earl Junior and his father were both scared of her. Maybe it was the nasty roots and things she always carried around in her apron pockets.

Jayjay cleared the huge sewer of his throat of about a pint of phlegm. "In that case I guess we'll talk business first and Christmas later."

"But this *is* business, Jayjay," Bobo pleaded. "If I can't get the bonus I need, I won't be around to do no more business with you. I'll be dead."

Through the crack in the closet door B.J. could see his father, a towering, impressive figure even in his rags.

He reached inside his tattered layers and pulled out some change. "Certainly, son. I know what it is to be hungry. Get yourself a decent meal. Though why this selfish family won't feed you is beyond my understanding."

No one took the coins from his hands; they fell to the rug and sparkled there, unwanted.

"A meal ain't what he needs, Jayjay. What he needs is a certain sum to protect his life."

"Insurance, you mean?"

"That's a good word for it. Listen, Jayjay, we've never bothered you with all the details of our operation, but the fact is, we have a large amount of overhead for coverage."

"Coverage? Speak plainly, Junior. Speak English, if you know any. And where's your father?"

"Out. But he'd tell you the same thing. If we didn't pay off the cops, our whole operation would collapse."

James Ricks swayed, a colossus astride a wavering world.

"Cops? *White* cops?"

Junior countered with, "You know any other kind with the power to protect us?"

B.J. wished his father would move out of his narrow line of vision, but he couldn't help being fascinated to see his old man stop swaying and stand motionless, leaning like a wind-struck tree.

"You mean to tell me white men are siphoning off our profits, draining our capital?"

"I'm telling you we have to give them some of it or we wouldn't have any at all. We wouldn't even be able to stay in business."

B.J. thought he saw his father giving off a green glow like decay, like an upright corpse. Resembling, with his glowing red eyes, a dying Christmas tree. "Why hasn't somebody told me about this before? Because you knew I'd object?"

Bobo could not restrain himself any longer. "What's wrong with the old fool? I thought he knew everything, but he don't know *nothin'.* Don't he know you can't even run a *legal* business in this town without payin' off the cops? If you don't pay they'll break in and rob you theirselves, and shoot up the place besides. Shit, you can't even have a shoeshine stand around here without some cop coming around with his hand out. You can't stay alive two days in a row without fattening up some guinea pig."

The mixed aromas of rich cooking and musky incense told B.J. that Mom Boggs was back in the room. "Hush, boy, you just got the old heebie-jeebies is all. You stared old Bro' Death in the face today, and you still seeing him. Mom's got the cure for that. Take this."

"What is it?"

"It's a cross carved out of black cat bones. The life cross, not that old long-handled death cross. That old sword-shaped cross ain't no good for nothin' but dying. This one helps with living, and it's sprinkled with certain essences for extra power. Carry it on you all the time to be safe."

"Pay them no mind, Jayjay," Junior said. "The reason we didn't tell you is we didn't want to bother you. You're the brains, right? We wanted to leave you free to think and plan."

"Quite right. But if you had any faith in my plans, you wouldn't have wasted our money. My plans are so perfect there is never any need to bribe the police. If my instructions are followed, no one who works for us runs any risk, because I do not make mistakes. I do not leave margins for error or trails for the police to follow.

"For example," he continued, beginning to sway again with the rhythm of his oratory, "tonight you will acquire a certain amount of prime beef. But the entire operation must be conducted between eight twenty-nine and eight forty-five post meridian. And you must confine yourself strictly to the prime cuts of sirloin, not the rump or the rib. Also, I know how the hog calls out to your primitive blood, but you must restrain your craving for sausage and spare ribs, trotters and jowls. There will be no time for anything but the pick of the prime sirloin, and only that amount of it which you can pick up in sixteen minutes."

"Why?" Bobo asked.

"How many times must I tell you not to ask 'why'?" Jayjay thundered. "Just do as I tell you, and you'll stay out of trouble. Obey my instructions to the letter, and you won't have to worry about the police. The trouble with you is, you want to think you can think. But, just to satisfy your curiosity, I know our supplier and I know our market. The supplier can only give us sixteen minutes within which to work safely, because that is the length of time it takes him to make one complete round of the warehouse. And our market, in spite of its peasant roots, wants nothing but the best. Also many of them are now adopting strange creeds. "Me no eat pork" is a cry fast becoming as common as "Gimme a pig's foot" used to be. But this is still America, where no one says, 'Me no eat steak.' They may tie up their heads and talk that vegetarian talk, but don't be deceived. There's hardly an American alive who can resist red meat.

"As for me, I only crave red wine, or white if no red is available. Come, let us toast the baby who is about to be born to die for us three months from now."

"I'll die sooner, if you don't get up off some money," Bobo complained.

"Shut up, Bobo. Go ask Mom if she can spare us a little port. Oh, never mind. I'll go myself," said Junior.

Jayjay seemed not to hear either of them. "Speaking of infants, have you seen that creature who claims to be my son? I always felt a mistake was made in the hospital. A son of mine could never be that small. That was one time I had to take what the white man gave me. But the only time in twenty years."

Trying to get even smaller in the closet, B.J. jarred loose some hangers that came crashing down on him.

"What was that?" Jayjay demanded.

"Oh, just Mom in the kitchen," Earl Junior explained. "Her goofer dust fell off the shelf and got mixed in with the giblet gravy, so she had to throw it all out and start over again. Here's your wine, Jayjay. Drink up."

"Your mother is a root worker? Maybe she can help me get rid of my hants. They are with me even in the daytime, but the nights are the worst. That is when they climb on my chest and sit around grinning at the foot of my bed."

"She's good at that sort of thing," Earl Junior said.

"She didn't put anything in this glass of wine, did she?"

"Of course not, Jayjay."

"I don't see anyone else drinking it."

"That's 'cause she could only spare one glassful."

Jayjay held the glass to the light suspiciously. "There's some funny-looking sediment in there. It seems to be wiggling."

For the first time in his life, B.J. saw his old man refuse to touch a glass of alcohol.

"What's wrong, Jayjay?" Bobo asked. "Why don't you drink it?"

"A conjure woman cursed me once. Me and any sons I might have. I can't risk that happening a second time. Not until I get the first curse removed."

B.J. was sure there had been something in that glass. Not conjure powder, though. Maybe some kind of sleepy dust. Earl Junior had all kinds of pills he peddled—prescription stuff, not the hard foreign stuff.

"Sorry you don't trust my hospitality, Jayjay. Tell you what. I'll get you a brand-new bottle."

"That would be better."

"Jayjay, you don't understand my problem. This cop is after me. He's dangerous. He—"

A snap of Earl Junior's fingers cut him off. "Shut up about your problem, boy. Go to the liquor store and bring back a jug for our boss's Christmas."

Bobo went.

Jayjay was getting the shakes, his clothes flapping like pennants in the wind. He was getting hoarse, too, but he was still eloquent. "If I had known you were paying the police, Junior, I would have broken with you and your father long ago. There is no need to pay tribute to Caesar's centurions. There is only the need to discipline ourselves. If my plans are followed to the letter, no police will ever know or interfere. You cannot ask me to share my capital with white bloodsuckers. I have been in conference with this supplier. He is ready to supply all the meat for the club we are going to open after the first of the year. A class restaurant—do you understand, Junior? Not another grits-and-grease joint smoking in the pit of Hell, but an exclusive club where our best people can be accommodated. A quiet, carpeted sanctum for our lawyers, doctors, judges, respectable businessmen."

"I follow you, Jayjay. Those people want nothing but the best."

"They are *accustomed* to nothing but the best. At lunchtime they go with their white colleagues to private clubs where they have poached salmon and prime sirloin served with deference and skill. When they go out at night without white companions, why should they have to eat Sister Sue's barbecue or Minnie Mae's greasy fricassee? Rubbing elbows with raunchy barmaids and raucous garbage men? Having their appetites spoiled by the smells of stale grease and rancid armpits? Our club will have no aroma except Russian Leather, piped in through a central blower system. And the real leather of its chairs."

"You sound serious this time, Jayjay."

"I'm always serious."

"You plan to move on this soon?"

"First of the year. I have already signed the lease."

"Did you, er, put up any money yet?"

"Only a small deposit. The rent is two thousand dollars a month, and well worth it. I will deliver my half, my thousand, on the first of January. I will expect you and your father to come up with your half on the same date. Will there be any problems?"

"No, no problems, Jayjay. Here's Bobo now. Bobo, give the boss the bottle so he can break the seal himself."

"Will you drink with me?"

"It's your bottle, friend."

"Then I invite you to share it. Drink with me to seal our deal."

The old man's hands were shaking so, Earl Junior had

to step forward and pour the wine for him. "To our future success," Jayjay said, draining his glass in one desperate swallow and holding it out for more.

"To our future," Earl Junior echoed, touching his glass to his lips without sipping.

The next glass of wine felled Jayjay like a giant mahogany tree. B.J. saw Earl Junior stoop down beside him and place a deceptively tender arm around his shoulders.

"Get down on the other side of him, Bobo," Earl Junior directed. "Come on now, Jayjay. Put an arm around each of our shoulders. Attaman, Jayjay. Here we go, now. Upsy daisy."

Together the two of them raised James Ricks to his wobbly feet. "All right, Jayjay, here we go, man. Don't forget the bottle, Bobo. Our boss may want a nightcap to help him sleep."

"We gonna take him home?"

"Sure. He may need some assistance in getting to bed. We'll tuck him in."

"Maybe even turn his mattress so he'll be more comfortable?"

"You're slow to catch on, Bobo, but I think you're beginning to get the idea. It's a cold night. We may even have to light a fire to keep him good and warm. Get the door open, Bobo! Take it easy, Jayjay, we're starting down the front steps."

"Man, but he's heavy."

"Dead men always are."

Jayjay struck up "We Three Kings of Orient Are" in his ragged baritone, and his helpers joined him in three-part harmony. A frigid gust of wind blew back their voices.

Mom Boggs's lush scent had been in the room a long

time. "Don't forget to buy the cranberry sauce, children," she sang out cheerfully before she shut the door behind them. B.J. slipped out of the closet as soon as he heard her pad back to the kitchen. Her scent went with her, but the city's icy breath was still in the room, stinking like a skull full of rotten teeth. Something white gleamed on the pale green rug. It was a small pair of bones polished like ivory and tied together with loops of hair to form a square cross with knobbed ends. Bobo must have dropped it when he bent to help lift Jayjay. B.J. would give it back to him.

On second thought, he would keep it for himself. He was going to need all the luck he could get from now on. He slipped the charm in his pocket, his fingers gathering comfort from the contrasting smoothness of bone and roughness of hair. In the kitchen, Mom Boggs was singing a Christmas spiritual:

What month was Jesus born in?
Las' month of the year.
Well, Lord, we got January,
February,
March, April, May and June, Lord;
We got July, Augus' and September,
October and November;
And the twenty-fifth day of December,
In the las' month of the year.

Bad as he feared what might happen to his father, bad as he wanted to cry for him, he knew he would have to be like Mom Boggs. He had heard no evil, he had seen none, and he would tell none.

Twenty-four

And here she went, blithely breaking another of her cardinal survival rules: *Never go into a bar unless escorted. And never, even then, unless it's a* nice *bar.*

Susie's met Mamie's criterion of a nice bar, but not Miss Lena's. She could hardly complain, since she had already broken Rule Number One: *Never be so desperate for company you're forced to lower your standards.*

Miss Lena's standards did not condone loud conversation; a jukebox that was just as loud, but drowned out none of the more offensive words; ragged linoleum floors with curling edges that provided a dangerous footing for high heels; or loose, tilted bar stools that threatened to dump their occupants. Not that her code let her sit on a bar stool anyway. Ladies, she believed, always sat at tables. Females who sat on bar stools were not ladies, she explained to Mamie. They were women asking to be picked up.

"Well?" Mamie demanded. "Why you think I brought you here?"

When Mamie also pointed out that most of the booths were already occupied by men sleeping off too many drinks, Miss Lena rapidly shed her ladyhood, climbed aboard a shaky stool, and tightly wound her purple-clad legs around its pedestal.

"What you drinking?" the young, sweet-faced barmaid asked.

Miss Lena, never a big drinker, said, "A glass of white wine."

"We ain't got nothin' but tokay, sherry, and muscatel."

"We're both drinking champagne," Mamie declared imperiously.

Miss Lena reached hesitantly for her purse. Champagne was expensive. "I didn't bring much money with me, Mamie. I never carry much cash."

"You ain't s'posed to. Put that pocketbook away, fool. Don't you know those men down there are buying our drinks?"

"What men down where?"

Mamie nodded her massively bewigged head to the right. "Those two at the far end. They'll probably be over in a minute."

"That's what I'm afraid of."

"Afraid? Why? Don't tell me I'm out with a fifty-four-year-old virgin."

"Not exactly," Miss Lena said with a smile. "I've just lived like one for twenty years."

"Well, you better relax and act like you thirty-four again. 'Cause that's what age you look, and they been starin' at you ever since you walked in. It's them legs that did it, I think. Them crazy purple legs."

As her eyes grew accustomed to the dim lighting, Miss Lena recognized the two men: one of them tall, broad-shouldered, and lean-waisted, the other shorter, and as wide below as he was above. Earl Junior and his father.

She returned their raised-glass salutes and whispered, "I know them, Mamie."

"Well, that always helps. They don't look too bad. They favor each other. Are they brothers?"

"Father and son," Miss Lena said.

"No kidding. They both look to be in their forties."

"It's dark in here."

"Not too dark for them to see you. What ages are they, then?"

"I don't know them that well, but I'd say one's in his early thirties, and the other one's in his early fifties."

"Married?"

Miss Lena shrugged. "I think the father is. I don't know about the son."

"Who cares?" Mamie said gaily, draining her champagne glass. "They men, ain't they? Listen, girl, I play, you know that, but I play fair. They saw you first, and you knew them first. You can have the young one. I'll take the old one."

"Take them both," Miss Lena said, too late. Pop Earl had slid onto the stool at Mamie's right, and she had already turned her back on Miss Lena to greet him.

And on her own left, Earl Junior was snaking an arm around her shoulders as if he had paid for that privilege along with the champagne. She did not draw away from his touch because she was repelled, however. She drew away because she was attracted.

Trying to turn off the disturbing feelings she thought her nerves had forgotten how to produce, she reminded him that she was old enough to be his mother.

He laughed easily, revealing a full mouth of perfect, even teeth. Miss Lena wished he had not smiled. Miss Lena found perfect white smiles against dark lips nearly irresistible. Black men—and women, too—with full sets of teeth were so rare.

"I already got a mother," he said. "And you already got a son."

"I wish you had a few missing teeth," she mumbled, and took a nervous sip of her champagne.

"What was that?" he asked, and leaned closer.

"Never mind. Have you seen him?"

"Who?"

"The boy you call my son."

"Oh, he was by for a few minutes tonight, to grab a bite and get a sweater he left at our house. But then he had to make a run. Said he might be back later." He chuckled. "Smart for his age, that kid. A regular little man. Always wheeling and dealing. I see you're wearing your ring." He stroked her hand sensually, letting his fingertip linger just above the ring. "You must like it. I'm glad."

She jerked her hand away in sudden surprise. "Did he get it from you?"

"Not exactly. Hey, why you so jumpy?"

"What does 'not exactly' mean?" she asked crisply.

"You've hardly touched your champagne, lady. Don't worry, there's plenty more. We bought a whole bottle. And when that's gone, there's more in Susie's icebox."

They were big spenders, then. How could they afford it? Warily, she sipped from her glass. She didn't want to get drunk. If she had ever needed to be alert, this was the time. As soon as she set down the empty glass, it was refilled like magic.

His fingers were stroking her left hand now, stimulating feelings she had thought long dead. "You ought to have another ring for this hand."

She had downed only one drink, and her head was swimming. Was this suave street bandit proposing to her? In the dim light, he was handsome; his scars invisible, his hair well combed, his eyes clear and sparkling.

"I might like one," she said.

"You can have it for the same price he paid. Twenty-five dollars."

In spite of the champagne, Miss Lena instantly became as alert as if ice water had been thrown in her face. Earl Junior was not wooing her. She had been an old fool to think so. He was merely using his considerable charm to persuade her to buy. But she toyed with her ring, pretending to be deceived. She needed to find out what B.J. was mixed up in.

Earl Junior seemed to sense her indignant feelings from the sudden rigidity of her back. He began to stroke it. "You know, I'm not just interested in selling you jewelry. A man my age gets tired of living with his folks. He'd rather have a place of his own, and his own woman." He ran his fingertip down the line of her jaw, from earlobe to chin, as if to remind her that she too was scarred now, and it did not spoil her appearance for him. "His own *beautiful* little woman."

It was a little easier not to respond to him now that she knew his attentions were all salesmanship, but not much. "I don't understand how these rings can be so cheap. Are they hot?"

He smiled again, lighting up the room. "Do I really have to answer that question? My parents and I, we have a lot of friends who bring us nice things. And we have a lot of other friends who want nice things. We just help them get together, that's all. You might say we're in the retail business."

"Where do your friends get these things?" she persisted.

"Why do you ask so many questions, pretty lady? I never ask questions like that. I just accept the good things that come my way, like manna from heaven. The good Lord provides, and I thank him." He raised his arms to illustrate his pious speech. "It's getting cold out. Couldn't you use a nice, warm fur coat?"

Miss Lena was sure the good Lord had nothing to do with it. "No," she said, trying not to react to the warm, steady pressure of his hand against her back.

"Oh, come on. Every woman wants a fur coat. Every woman *needs* one. When your lover's arm isn't around you, like mine is now, you can snuggle into your fur and feel just as good. I'm not talking about something cheap, now. I would never suggest something cheap to a high-class woman like you. I'm talking about something nice, something that would suit your personality. Come on, now. What's your favorite fur? Sable? Ermine? How about a beautiful jet-black mink? I could get you one, brand-new, for only four hundred dollars."

He was breathing in her ear. He was brushing her ear with his lips. In spite of knowing it was all part of the sales talk, she was reacting as any woman would. Enough was enough, Miss Lena decided. "You mean a coat with sleeves, or one without?" she asked boldly. The remark made him flinch, but not withdraw. He only tightened the pressure of his arm.

She nudged Mamie so violently she almost toppled from her stool.

"Hey, ouch! What's wrong with you, girl?"

"I want to leave. I know a nicer place."

"Just when I was getting comfortable," Mamie grumbled. But something on Miss Lena's face stopped her from more complaining. She said something to Pop Earl, stuffed an object in her purse, snapped it shut, and climbed down awkwardly from the stool.

"Leaving so soon?" Earl Junior asked with a semblance of a stricken face.

"The night's young, and so are we. We'll be back later," Mamie promised with a wink, and followed Miss Lena to the street.

She was panting when she caught up with her. "Hey, what's the hurry? What'd that cute young stuff do to make you so mad?"

"He was trying to sell me something. Furs. What did his father try to sell you?"

"French perfume." Mamie opened her bag to reveal a frosted glass bottle, then snapped it shut. "We didn't agree on a price, though. I said I'd pay him when I see him. That's one way to make sure I *do* see him."

"I hope you don't," Miss Lena said grimly.

"Oh, I get it. You thought you was getting all that attention for free. When you found out it wasn't free you got mad. You too proud to pay for it. Right?"

"Aren't you?"

"Sometimes. But sometimes I ain't too proud," Mamie admitted humbly. "What's this 'nicer place' you mentioned?"

Miss Lena, who did not know any nightclubs, cast about frantically in her mind for the name of one. "The Lorelei Lounge," she said, because it was the only place she could think of.

"Well, what you walking me down this cold street for? It's in the other direction. That boy really must have upset you. You got to get used to these hustlers out here. Some of 'em can be real nice company, if you don't take 'em serious."

Miss Lena had never been inside the Lorelei Lounge, but it turned out to be closer to her idea of a "nice place" than Susie's. The patrons were well-dressed, the noise level was subdued by thick carpets, and they were immediately led past the bar to a table.

Miss Lena felt comfortable there, but Mamie was quickly bored into a state of restless irritability. "What is this, a funeral home?" she demanded loudly.

"Where's the body? I've seen livelier crowds at some viewings."

Miss Lena had to admit that nothing much was happening at the lounge. The crowd would come later, she imagined, for the first show.

"Listen, girl, if they got a show, the prices in here are bound to be sky-high. Let's get back to Susie's before the Queen of Sheba comes back and does us the favor of taking all our money."

The woman Mamie called the Queen of Sheba was Marvel Scott, who had almost been Miss Lena's customer once. Someone else had made her that exotic paisley jumpsuit in which she looked so haughty—far too haughty to send a waitress over to a table occupied by two women as long as there were men in the place. Her prejudice was fortunate for them: they got away without spending a dime.

Miss Lena wanted to go home, but Mamie wouldn't hear of it. "You ain't given Susie's a chance," she argued. "It's not a bad bar. Nothing bad ever happens there. I wouldn't take you to a rough bar. It's a friendly sort of place, like a home away from home. The customers are just like family."

She was rushing back eagerly to see the Earls again, while Miss Lena was bracing herself to face them.

But she was relieved, and Mamie was disappointed. Earl Junior and his father were not there when they returned. The place had filled up with other people who seemed like the sort Miss Lena could be comfortable with, just as Mamie had promised. Middle-aged working-class men and women, some together, more alone, many drifting together and forming couples in the course of the evening.

Mamie introduced her to her friend, the proprietor,

a big tan woman who wore a blonde wig as massive and curly as her black one.

"You might as well have some more champagne," Susie said. "Earl Boggs paid for a whole bottle for the two of you."

"Now, wasn't it nice of her to tell us?" Mamie beamed. "Most club owners would never tell you a thing like that. They'd want you to spend more money. I told you this was a nice place."

Susie bustled back to the kitchen to serve some seafood platters. Miss Lena, smelling crab, was suddenly hungry.

With a plate of crabs and two glasses of champagne inside her, she began to feel good. Better than good: mellow. Tolerant of everyone, even the Boggs family and their way of earning a livelihood. They were operating according to their survival code, and even if it was not hers, it was all right for them. If Earl Junior and his father had come in at that moment, she would have told them so warmly.

But, much to Mamie's loudly expressed disgust, they did not return. Instead, the door opened and closed behind a series of other salesmen and sales-boys. Susie's was not only a pleasant place to get food, drink, and company; it was, it seemed, a department store where you could buy anything you wanted at a huge discount, especially at this time of year. There were peddlers offering hosiery, perfume, shoes, jewelry, and lingerie. One thoughtful salesmen even had a pen-sized flashlight to shine down into his shopping bag so prospective customers could get a better look at his cache of sweaters. Miss Lena looked and rejected them, but Mamie bought one.

Even a blender was offered to Miss Lena in its brand-new box. When she shook her head, another lid was lifted, and she was shown a small television set. She refused that too, and the persistent merchant offered her the catalog of a well-known national appliance company.

"There's got to be something in here you'd want, ma'am. Some beautiful gifts for your family."

"I don't have a family. I don't buy gifts," Miss Lena said truthfully.

"Buy something for yourself then," he said, riffling through dazzling pages of cameras, stereos, and stoves.

"You can really get me anything in this catalog?" she asked incredulously.

"Just name your pleasure, ma'am, and I'll name the price. I guarantee you'll be satisfied."

She lifted questioning eyes to Susie, who was studying the catalog upside down from behind the bar. "He's telling you the truth," she said calmly. "I bought my whole kitchen off him."

"And it's a nice kitchen, ain't it? Tell her," the salesman urged.

"The best," said Susie. "Double ovens, fifteen-cubic-foot freezer, everything. I'll take you back and show you later."

After the man moved farther down the bar, Susie explained how he performed his magic. "He works at one of their warehouses, loading and unloading. He ain't really taking no risks. Them men work so hard for such low pay, the company *expects* 'em to steal."

Miss Lena's first evening at Susie's was just one surprise after another. Even food, she learned, could be bought there—uncooked food, not just Susie's platters. As soon as the appliance salesman drifted out, he was replaced by a tall, long-headed boy with a shock of silky black hair. For a lad of only sixteen or so, he seemed to be doing well. He was better dressed than the other salesmen, in a real sheepskin jacket and beautiful brown boots. He was better-looking, too, with a strong, square jaw and that heavy tassel of hair decorating his long elliptical head. Only a large adhesive plaster on one temple marred his beauty. Miss Lena thought she had seen him before. He was such a striking figure, she should be able to remember where. But her memory was not as good as it used to be, and the dim lighting and the champagne she had drunk did not help.

Susie seemed to know him well, however. "What you got, Bobo?" she asked.

"Steaks," he answered with a brilliant flash of teeth that made Miss Lena wonder if there were a dentist in town who devoted his practice exclusively to thieves. Then the boy reached into the fuzzy recesses of his coat and withdrew a flat waxed-paper package, which he opened to show off a half-dozen lean, beautiful sirloin strips.

Mamie's eyes popped with greed. "How much?"

"Five dollars a dozen. Three dollars for six."

"I'll take those six," Mamie said quickly, reaching for her purse.

"Got any more, Bobo?" Susie asked.

"Four dozen, out in my car."

"I'll take 'em all," Susie said, and bent out of sight below the bar. Miss Lena could not see what she was doing down there, but she heard grunts and groans, and concluded from experience that Susie was reaching up under her girdle. When she straightened, a twenty-dollar bill was in her hand.

"Put 'em in my freezer," she ordered. "And if you can get another four dozen, I'll take 'em too."

"No problem," said Bobo. He was out of the door in three loose, loping strides.

When he came back, he was carrying one end of a portable ice chest, and a smaller helper was carrying the other end. A hat with a visor was pulled down over the smaller boy's face, and the turtle neck of a sweater was up over his chin, but Miss Lena recognized him anyway.

"B.J.!" she screamed, startling him so badly he let go of his end, scattering steaks and shaved ice in a slick, gory heap on the floor. Miss Lena hopped from her stool and slithered across the ice toward him. "What are you doing in here?" she demanded.

"What are *you?*" was his telling response.

"Don't give me any smart answers, you—" she fumed, reaching for the collar of his sweater.

B.J. ducked and twisted, neatly evading her grasp. Caught off balance leaning forward, she slipped and landed with her bottom in a puddle of melting ice. When she had recovered herself enough to look for him, he was gone.

The tall black boy called Bobo asked politely if she were hurt, then helped her to her feet. But before she could ask him any questions, Susie had given him the bill and a signal—a brisk wave of the hand that clearly meant "Out." He snatched the money with two long fingers and was instantly gone.

Miss Lena ran to the door and looked out, but saw only a cloud of smoke from a car turning the corner on squealing wheels. A fast, powerful car, judging by the speed of that takeoff; but then, she reminded herself sadly, she would not have been able to tell its make even if she had gotten a good look.

Defeated and aching, she went back inside the bar. Susie's employees, the barmaid and two men, had already retrieved the steaks and put them away, and were efficiently mopping up the last of the melting ice.

Susie, who admitted that she was worried about falls on her premises, ordered them to dry up the wet spot with towels after they'd finished mopping. She also brought Miss Lena a large, free gin and tonic to ease any possible aches and pains.

"If your back hurts tomorrow, see my chiropractor," she advised. "He'll fix it right up. Have him send the bill to me."

Miss Lena assured her that only her dignity had been hurt. Her most distressing ache was not physical, and sipping the drink would provide only a temporary cure. She kept this to herself, though, and sat revising her earlier conclusions. With each sip she grew more sober and her memory got sharper. That good-looking rascal was the boy B.J. had chased the day she visited his school. The day she was robbed.

Buying and selling stolen goods might be O.K. for some people. But it was not an acceptable way of life for Miss Lena, and by now she felt she had a right to say it was not O.K. for B.J., though that meant she would have to offer him an alternative.

Mamie placed a heavy, well-meaning hand on her arm. "Maybe you'll listen to me this time, Lena. You ought to forget about that kid. He's a hopeless case."

"Maybe I'm a hopeless case too, Mamie."

"What you mean?"

"I don't care what he is any more. I just know I need him around."

"For what? To drive you crazy?"

"No, to help me run my business. I'm fine now, you know, except for one thing. I can't depend on my memory."

"I couldn't believe it in the hospital when you said

you couldn't remember your birthday."

"Well, it was true. And it's still true. Phone numbers, appointments, *everything* slips my mind. He remembers things for me."

"Well, can't you get somebody else? Somebody you can trust?"

Miss Lena shook her head.

"What about a relative?"

"My relatives are scattered all over the country. But even if they were here, I wouldn't want them working for me. They're just a trifling bunch of parasites who want to sponge off somebody."

"A friend, then?"

"I've always been a loner, Mamie. I don't have any friends except you. Would you—?" she asked eagerly.

"No thanks, girl. I don't have any kind of head for business. All I know about money is how to spend it. Plus, I don't believe in mixing business and friendship. That's a worse mixture than booze and pills."

"So that leaves me right where I started, needing B.J."

"But he steals."

"I know. He stole from me," Miss Lena admitted calmly.

"You know what? You're not thinking with your head. And you sure ain't thinking about your business, or you'd know a kid who steals is bound to ruin it. You're just lonely, that's all. Took you all these years to find out you're lonely, so it just hurts worse. That doesn't mean you have to stay with the first person who came along and showed you how lonely you was."

"Maybe you're right, Mamie," Miss Lena sighed. "All I know is, I need him."

"Sure, like you need another stroke," Mamie said

roughly, shaking Miss Lena's shoulder as if to wake her up. "Face it, that kid won't bring you nothing but trouble. And no matter how many times he breaks your heart, you'll never be able to say nothing to him about it. He can always turn around and tell you, 'You ain't my mother.' I ought to know what I'm talking about. I raised three step-kids for my husband along with three of my own."

Miss Lena did not acknowledge Mamie's advice. All she said was, "My bottom is wet."

Mamie had the good sense to smile and say nothing in return but, "Then you better go straight home and dry it off. I got to get home myself, anyway, and put these steaks in the freezer."

Twenty-five

Not surprisingly, very reasonably priced steak dinners were featured on Susie's menu the next two nights. Mamie, whose appetite never flagged, kept pointing out how tender and succulent they were. But Miss Lena refused to eat anything.

"What's the matter? You too finicky to eat meat that's been on the floor? Don't you know cooking kills most germs?"

Miss Lena gave her a hard stare.

"Sorry," Mamie said. But her sense of humor was irrepressible. "I seem to remember your behind was on the floor the other night, too. But I notice you still usin' it to sit on. . . . Well, it's about time I got a laugh out of you. You been in here two nights in a row lookin' like you just lost your best friend. And dressed for the funeral."

After feeling so out of character in that vivid, scanty outfit Friday night, Miss Lena had gone to the opposite extreme and decided to dress her age. She wore the sort of drab, modest outfit she used to make for Miss Allinson in the days before B.J.: a plain, full-skirted gray flannel dress that was much too long, sensibly ugly black oxfords, and a crocheted black cloche that hid her ears and all of her hair.

"At least you could take off that old-lady hat," Mamie complained. "Ain't nobody gonna look at you in that thing."

I don't want to be looked at, Miss Lena felt like saying, just as she had wanted to reply to Mamie's remark about looking like she'd lost her best friend: I have.

But she remained silent, and the hat stayed stubbornly on, while Susie came over and joined Mamie in some rough, affectionate kidding.

"Don't give her nothing to drink tonight, Susie. She might decide to go ice-skating again and put on another floor show."

"Lord, we don't want to let that happen. But at least she can have some food, can't she? She doesn't have a weight problem like us."

"Hell, no, she has an *under*weight problem. But she won't eat one of your platters either. I told her we could stay home tonight; I even offered to cook, but she insisted on coming here."

"Well, at least she likes my atmosphere," Susie said with a gold-starred grin.

"Yeah, but she needs to understand you have to pay for atmosphere, too."

"I'll pay half the bill. You can eat and drink for both of us, Mamie," said Miss Lena, who didn't mind any of the joking except the suggestion that she was a freeloader.

Mamie ruefully rubbed her distended stomach. She had already had two steak dinners, including bread, salad, and french fries. "Lord, ain't it the truth. I'll have to start my diet after the first of the year."

"Let's be honest for once, and stop making those jive New Year's resolutions," Susie said with a deep laugh that jiggled her own well-cushioned rib cage. Obviously the two of them had known one another well for a long time. "Why be hypocrites? We both know we gonna keep right on eating."

"And sinning, too, every time we get a chance," Mamie added.

"I guess it's a good thing I haven't had any offers

lately," Susie said frankly. "This place keeps me so busy I don't know how I'd find the time."

"What's your excuse, Old Miss Young?" Mamie demanded of Miss Lena. "I happen to know you've had an offer, and you got plenty of time."

"I'm choosy," Miss Lena said with a smile, and wished she had said nothing at all. She didn't want to feed their laughter. It only made her more depressed, and she had to wait for it to die down before she could ask Susie some vital questions. Finally an opportune moment came.

Yes, Susie knew Bobo. She'd known him for about a year. And B.J., too, just as long. The two of them used to always come in together, selling things. For a long time they'd seemed inseparable. Then Bobo had started coming in alone, without B.J. She had been surprised to see B.J. last night. Bobo was a regular, but the younger kid hadn't been in with him in a long time.

"How long?"

"Oh, I ain't seen him in three months. Maybe more."

It was three months ago, roughly, when B.J. had first appeared at Miss Lena's shop.

That Bobo was a real smart kid, Susie continued with apparent pride. He'd been hustling his way up the business ladder ever since he was twelve or thirteen. By now he must be making more money than most men twice his age.

—No, of course he didn't drink in her place. What kind of fool did Miss Lena think Susie was? She'd lose her license if she served minors. No, Bobo just came in on her busiest nights, usually holidays and weekends, peddled his wares, and left. She guessed she was taking a slight risk letting him come in at all, but a lot of her customers would miss him. To tell the truth, so would she.

"He always has the very best merchandise. Look at this." Susie showed Miss Lena a watch she was wearing, a fine brand with an expensive movement. "And this." A ring with a ruby and several diamonds. Both purchased from Bobo.

No, Susie didn't know where Bobo got such fine stuff. Maybe from legitimate store owners who wanted to unload excess stock.

"Oh, come on, now," Miss Lena said with raised eyebrows.

Well, such things had been known to happen in here, Susie said indignantly. Of course, she admitted, those peddlers in her bar who acquired their goods from legitimate dealers usually had nothing but junk to sell, while Bobo always had the best. But Bobo might have better contacts. He was a sharp kid. Big for his age, and smart, and smooth—easy-talking, a debonair dresser. He would go far. She thought B.J. hung around with him because he looked up to him.

Miss Lena got the impression that Susie looked up to Bobo, too.

For some reason Susie started talking as if she needed to impress Miss Lena with her high standards. "Listen," she said, "I know what you're thinking, but this is not the kind of place where anything goes. There's two things I won't let anybody sell in here, and that's drugs and tail. And believe me, the pressure is always on me to let them in. I have to pay off plenty to keep them out. This is a decent place, nice folks come here, and I mean to keep it that way. I'll close it up and go back to peddling my own ass before I'll let prossies and pushers operate in my bar."

"She ain't lying," Mamie interjected with a chuckle. "I seen her damn near kill a couple of hookers that strolled in here one time."

"That's 'cause they were white," Susie said calmly. "If they'd been black I'd have just asked them to leave politely."

"And if they hadn't?"

"Then I'd have helped them leave like I helped them other two."

No, of course Susie didn't know whether B.J. helped Bobo steal his loot. Who had said anything about stealing, anyway? For all she knew, she repeated emphatically, Bobo came by his wares legally. He was known to be friendly with Earl Junior and Senior, but they were not known to go in for stealing. Only selling. Other than that she didn't know anything about Bobo's friends or habits, or B.J.'s, either. She didn't know where either of them hung out or lived. She didn't even know their right names.

Miss Lena perceived that the conversation was beginning to make Susie nervous. She also perceived that knowing people in Susie's did not mean the same thing it did elsewhere.

"I know 'em and I don't know 'em," Susie explained with a wave of her hand that took in all of her patrons. "I let them tell me whatever they want, but I never ask questions or pry in their business. It might not be good for me to know too much about some people. You know what I mean? Other people might be too interested."

She slid her eyes meaningfully toward the booth nearest the door. It had been vacant a minute ago, but it was now occupied by a giant black policeman in uniform.

"Coffee, Charlie?" Susie sang out sweetly.

"Coffee and *food,*" he replied emphatically. "What's on the menu?"

"How you like your steaks?"

"Medium well and *big,*" he said. "I'll take my coffee right away."

"I wish I could bring you something stronger."

"So do I, but I'll have to take a rain check. You know I can't drink on duty. I'll just have an extra steak to make up for it."

"Coming up right away," Susie promised, and whispered to Miss Lena, "Sorry I couldn't be more help. That one's an honest cop. Pays for his food. I can't trust him. I ain't seen those boys since they were in here Friday night, but I'll ask around. Somebody might know something."

She bustled off to the kitchen, leaving Miss Lena convinced she was sincere in wanting to help, and that her answers had been truthful as far as they went. Susie had told her all she knew, Miss Lena believed. It was just her survival strategy not to know too much.

Mamie had been silent on the subject of B.J. for almost forty-eight hours, with an extreme tactfulness Miss Lena appreciated because she knew it must have been a great strain; but after overhearing that conversation, she could hold herself back no longer. "I should've known that was the reason you kept wanting to come back here. Any fool could see you ain't been looking for a good time. You're just running after that worthless kid." She waved her hand to silence Miss Lena before she could speak. "Oh, I know, I know, I should shut up and mind my own business."

"It's all right, Mamie. I know you're just trying to be a friend. And you are, a good friend. But you're wrong about B.J. He's not really a bad boy."

"No, he's just a nice little con man and hustler and thief. Ever ask him how many times he's been in jail?"

Miss Lena flinched at the idea. "No. But I don't believe he's ever been arrested."

"Hah!" Mamie said skeptically. "I'll bet he shows up down at Precinct Headquarters so often they got a special cell with his name on it. And I'll bet he's down there warming it up right now."

Miss Lena began to shudder so violently Mamie became concerned. "You catching cold or something? Did you get a chill in here the other night?"

Miss Lena shook her head.

"All right, I apologize," Mamie said. "I oughta show more understanding, I guess. I know lonely women like us do all kinds of simpleminded things to give 'em an excuse to go on living. Some of 'em raise cats and dogs. Some write letters to the newspapers. Some go batty about plants. Me, I'm the worst kind of fool, the kind who chases men, all men, any men she can find. So what right have I got to jump on you if you get attached to some kid? What I should be doing is help you find him."

An illogical hope brightened Miss Lena's mood. "How?"

"By using my head, that's how. Does he have a mother and father?"

"No mother. A father, yes." Miss Lena shuddered slightly. "But I don't ever want to see him again."

"I won't ask why," Mamie said. "Everybody who reaches our age got at least one somebody they want to forget. *I* got four or five. Didn't you tell me he was friendly with those two slick hustlers? The son and the father?"

"Yes, he spent Thanksgiving at their house, and he was supposed to spend Christmas with them too."

"Well, then?" Mamie asked impatiently.

"I asked Susie. She said they haven't been in since we saw them Friday night."

"Don't you know where they live?"

"Yes, of course, but—"

"But what? You got the perfect excuse. You could pretend to be interested in them furs."

"I don't want to go to their house looking for him. I want him to come to me." I don't want that Earl Junior to think I'm chasing him, either, she thought.

Mamie was hotly indignant. "Well, if that ain't the lick that killed Dick. She's not only simpleminded about this kid, she's got the nerve to be proud. If you ask me, that's the curse of our race. Too much pride. Thinkin' we're it when we ain't shit." Then, repudiating her harsh words, she patted Miss Lena's shoulder. "All right, girl, do it your way. Wait it out, if that's what you have to do. I'll tell you what I think. I think he *will* come looking for you soon's he gets some wrinkles in his belly. And I think that's gonna be pretty soon."

But, as Miss Lena soon learned, B.J. was not able to come looking for her. Susie had made the rounds of her patrons, getting nothing but blank stares and head-shakes in response to her query, until she reached the policeman. That tall, imposing person, like a uniformed Watusi with lethal hardware hanging around his waist, left his supper to cool and came over to talk to Miss Lena.

"Maybe you'd rather hear this in private," he said, indicating his booth.

It was inconsiderate—his food was getting cold—but Miss Lena shook her head. She was so apprehensive about his news, she felt if she stood up, she might fall.

"You were asking about a kid called B.J.? A cripple?"

She nodded.

"They're holding him at the Tenth Precinct. He was picked up Friday night. Suspicion of burglary."

Miss Lena's throat was so dry she could not speak.

The officer mercifully filled in the details for her without requiring her to ask more questions.

"They found him inside a meat-packing house that had just been burglarized. Several hundred dollars' worth of beef was missing. Choice steaks. He denied all knowledge of the theft. Said he was just waiting for a friend who worked for the company to come back for him. His story was, this friend asked him to help load some meat in his car to deliver to some restaurants for his boss. But there was no sign of the friend. I figure he took off as soon as he tripped the burglar alarm, and left this kid B.J. there to take the blame."

Susie had kindly provided Miss Lena with a drink, a rather strong one, three parts vodka to one of ginger ale. After downing it she found she was able to speak.

"Did you believe him when he said he didn't know they were robbing the place?"

"Ma'am, it's not important whether I believed him or not. What's important is what the *judge* believes. I didn't make the arrest, anyway. I just happened to be in the station when they brought him in. But if it will make you feel any better—yes, I did believe him. It looked pretty bad, his getting caught right on the premises. But I asked myself, if he knew he was doing wrong, why didn't he run? I figured he was telling the truth. Besides, I never saw a more innocent-looking kid in my life. Not that that means anything. Some of these kids are the greatest actors in the world."

Miss Lena, who knew all about B.J.'s acting ability, asked, "What will happen to him, Officer?" She wished for another drink, but shook her head when Susie offered it; strong liquor was against Dr. Kloster's orders, and besides, she knew she had better keep her wits right now.

"He'll have a hearing Monday morning. Unless somebody shows up in the meantime to claim him, he'll probably be sent up to Juvenile Hall to take out some time."

She was shocked. "Even if the judge finds him innocent?"

"Ma'am, more than half the kids at Juvenile Hall are innocent. They aren't even *suspected* of committing any crimes. They're just problem kids or homeless kids, kids nobody wants. It's a crime to put them in with real offenders, but what else is the state going to do? They can't put them back out on the streets with no place to go and nothing to do but get in trouble."

She might as well know the worst. "How long would they keep him there, do you think?"

"How old is he?"

"Fourteen."

"In a case like this, where there's no parent to assume responsibility, the judge usually puts them away till they're old enough to be responsible for themselves. In his case, that means four years."

"And no one's been there to claim him?"

The policeman shook his head. "No, and I doubt if anyone will. He says he's an orphan. Says both his mother and father are dead. It's a shame. If he had a parent who wanted him, he'd probably get a light sentence, maybe just probation, since it's his first offense. But since he's an orphan—"

Mamie had been giving Miss Lena a hard, steady stare as if all her 180 pounds were straining to say, "I told you so."

But it was Miss Lena who said triumphantly as she started purposefully toward the door, "Didn't I tell you so? It's his first offense. He's never been arrested before."

"Where the hell you think you're going?" Mamie asked.

"To police headquarters, of course."

"Lena," Mamie said, "you're *not* going to claim that boy."

"Yes, Mamie, I am."

"Didn't you tell me you thought he had something to do with you getting robbed?"

"I am almost certain he did," Miss Lena replied with dignity.

"And you *still* want to bail him out?"

"Yes."

Mamie threw up her hands in an I-give-up gesture. "They need to lock *her* up on the top floor of the hospital," she said to Susie.

"Well," Susie advised Miss Lena, "at least come back and find out what you have to do."

That made sense. Impatient as she was to help B.J., she had no idea of how she was going to go about it. Miss Lena let go of the doorknob and came back.

Only the policeman seemed happy about her decision. "I'm sure glad somebody's taking an interest in that kid, ma'am. To tell the truth, I've been thinking about him all weekend, and it's been bothering me. So if you'll just wait till I've finished eating, I'll drive you down to Headquarters. It's real lucky we ran into each other tonight, believe me. Once he got sent up to the Hall, there'd be no way you could help him."

Miss Lena slid into the booth beside him. Mamie and Susie quickly joined them for a conference.

"They'll let you see him tonight," the policeman said between bites of his steak, on which the grease had congealed, "but you won't be able to take him home till tomorrow."

"Why not?" she asked, dismayed.

"Bail hasn't been set yet. It won't be set till the hearing tomorrow morning. At least I think it's tomorrow morning. It could be Tuesday. They're allowed to hold him seventy-two hours without a hearing, but they usually try to speed things up in juvenile cases. After the hearing, you can post bail and take him home."

Seeing the lack of comprehension on Miss Lena's face, all three of them began explaining at once.

"Bail is money the prisoner puts up to get out of jail, to guarantee he'll show up for his trial," Susie said.

"The judge sets the amount at the hearing," Mamie added.

"It's like security deposit for a loan," said Charlie, who was now on a first-name basis with all three of them. "You leave them the security, and they lend you the prisoner."

"Without the money they wouldn't dare let them out," Mamie said. "Nobody in his right mind would appear for his trial unless he had something to lose, like a whole lot of money."

"How *much* money?" Miss Lena asked dazedly.

"We don't know yet," the officer told her again, patiently. "The judge hasn't set the amount of bail."

"I wonder if I'll have enough," she worried.

"You don't have to have it *all.* Just ten percent. The bail bondsman puts up the rest," Mamie explained. " 'Course you have to sign over your life to him before he'll do it. And if the kid jumps bail, you lose everything. Are you sure you want to go through with this, Lena?"

Miss Lena didn't bother to answer such a ridiculous question. Once she would have said no, but she was no longer ruled by good sense and caution. She was ruled by her feelings.

"What's a bail bondsman? I don't understand."

Charlie explained, "It's a man who makes his living putting up bail. It's a good business; they're covered by insurance, and they always get to keep some of your money. There are a half dozen of them right near Precinct Headquarters. You just go see one, and he makes all the arrangements."

Miss Lena's head was spinning; she was learning too many new things too fast. But none of this strange talk solved her most urgent problem.

"What am I going to do tonight?" she asked plaintively, staring blankly at a wall.

"Get her another drink, Susie, please," Mamie requested. "What do you mean?"

"I mean, how am I going to get B.J. out tonight? I can't leave him there overnight again. It's not nice there, is it, Officer Charlie?"

"It's not supposed to be, ma'am," he said gravely.

"Then what am I going to *do?*"

Susie returned with another glass of what looked like ginger ale. "Drink this."

Mamie said, "Stop playing around with all these fancy legal methods. They're for white folks anyway. Let's get black, and practical, and look for a short cut. Don't you know your ward leader?"

Miss Lena choked on the fiery liquid, which was almost pure vodka, and set her glass down. "My what?"

Susie amplified. "You know. The man who comes around to you for a contribution at election time."

Miss Lena's memory brightened. "A contribution? Oh, yes. I remember him. Short, bald, with a little moustache and wire-frame glasses. Black, but with a big hooked nose, like an Indian's. And a peculiar name. Oh, what is wrong with me?" She drummed her temples furiously to prod her sluggish memory back to life. "I can see his face, but I can't remember his name. It's an odd name, a Greek name, Phil something—"

"Theophilus, ma'am?" the policeman put in helpfully. "Theophilus Shaw?"

"That's it!" Miss Lena cried, and almost kissed him.

"He's mine too!" Susie shouted. "That little mother hits me for a hundred bucks every year. How much did he get out of you?"

"Why, nothing," Miss Lena said innocently. "Why should I give him anything?"

Both women groaned.

"No, wait," Miss Lena said. "My memory is terribly unreliable, but now it's coming back to me. At first I never gave, but I seem to recall that I gave him twenty-five dollars the year before last, because he told me his candidate would reduce taxes. But my tax bill was not any lower. Then he said that was because his candidate didn't get in. He needed more campaign funds, he said. So this year I gave him thirty-five. Will it help, do you think?"

"It's helping now," Susie declared.

"Whew," Mamie said with a massive sigh. "Girl, you had us scared there for a minute."

"Phone's in the back," Susie said, pointing. "Here. I'll even give you a dime. Go call him."

"At this hour?"

"At any hour. That's what you paid him that sixty dollars for, the right to wake him up whenever you need him."

"I see," Miss Lena said, but she did not see at all. Nor did she move, until Susie gave her a sharp push and said, *"Go!"*

The policeman, Charlie, rose from his seat like a human Eiffel Tower. "I've got to leave now, Susie. I should've picked my partner up ten minutes ago."

Susie abandoned all the deference with which she had treated him earlier. She shoved him back down into the booth with the same firm hand she had used to push Miss Lena toward the phone. "You can wait five more minutes, till she calls. I'll bring you a fresh cup of hot coffee."

It was past midnight, Miss Lena noted, passing an illuminated clock that advertised Red Lion Beer. She dialed timidly, expecting Mr. Shaw to be angry, as she certainly would be if a stranger awakened her at that hour.

But he was calm and benign, as if it happened to him all the time. He had a deep, mellow voice like a radio announcer's, which was comforting, though Miss Lena scarcely trusted it, it sounded so *trained.* "Of course I remember you, Mrs. Ricks. You are the lovely little couturière. How's business? Thriving, I hope. What can I do for you?"

Miss Lena explained.

She was on her way to Tenth Precinct Headquarters now? Good, he would meet her there. All he needed was the boy's name.

"I don't know what they have in their records," she said. "They might have him down as either B.J. Riggs or B.J. Waters."

Mr. Shaw did not seem perturbed. "What is his *right* name, madam?"

She did not hesitate. Without being aware of it, she must have made this decision a long time ago. "His name," she said, "is Bruce James Ricks."

"And your relationship to him?"

That answer, too, came instantly, as if long determined. "I am his mother."

Twenty-six

When she made the same statement to the sergeant behind the desk at Tenth Precinct Headquarters, it caused a slight flurry of confusion.

"B.J. Brown was the name we booked him under," the sergeant said.

"Yes," Miss Lena replied with a sweet, serene smile. "But you see, his father married again."

The middle-aged policeman was left scratching his bald pate in bewilderment. "How's that again?" he asked. Then he thought better of his request for a repetition, said, "Never mind," and held up his hand to keep her quiet.

So far, so good. Miss Lena was relieved. She had never been inside a police station before, and had clung to the cop Charlie in terror when he announced he was letting her off around the corner instead of taking her inside. He was not supposed to be doing this at all, he explained; he was supposed to be on duty. Now that she had called in a politician, whose interference might offend his fellow officers, he had better not appear to be involved. He gently disengaged her hand from his arm, helped her out of the car, and wished her good luck before speeding off.

Once inside, a surge of confidence had come from somewhere to sustain her. Perhaps it was the vodka. But Miss Lena thought it was her dowdy, old-fashioned costume. It cloaked her in respectability, and seemed to give her immunity from the rough treatment she had expected in this cavelike place of concrete and steel and huge, rough-voiced men. If she had come in looking like a hussy in skimpy velvet, she would have been treated like one.

"I'll have the boy brought in so you can see him," the sergeant said. "You can't take him home, though."

But Mr. Theophilus Shaw had already assured Miss Lena that she would be able to do just that. That obliging person had arrived at the station ahead of her to get the important piece of paper called "a copy of the charge." He had already called Judge Lawson, he said, and the judge had expressed a willingness to do what he could. Judge Lawson was a very good friend, and inclined to be very grateful to good constituents like Mrs. Ricks. It was a serious charge, a felony, but since the boy was a juvenile, and since it was his first offense, and since Miss Lena impressed everyone as such an upstanding citizen . . .

(Especially in this dress.)

. . . the judge would probably sign that all-important paper with instructions to release B.J. into her custody.

Miss Lena was very impressed that Mr. Shaw and the judge were willing to do so much for her for nothing. She said so.

"Oh, it's not for nothing, madam. I hate to put it so crudely, but politics *is* expensive."

Miss Lena nodded. She had no money in her purse; a practical precaution, especially in a bar.

"Excuse me," she said, turning her back on Mr. Shaw. She bent and began a series of wriggling, twisting, and groping movements. The desk sergeant's face again acquired an expression of alarm. "Are you all right, lady?" he asked, apparently shocked to see a respectable little old lady performing the movements of an exotic dancer.

"Perfectly all right, thank you." In the course of the evening, the little roll of bills she had tucked into the top of her all-in-one girdle had worked its way down to her waist. At last she was able to grasp it. She straightened and turned around with two tens and two twenties concealed in her right hand.

Opening her hand, she said, "Will this be enough?"

Mr. Shaw's large eyes became moist behind the thick glasses. He took them off and wiped them on his handkerchief, revealing that his eyes were really small and squinty, then replaced the glasses, the better to see the denominations, probably. He reached out and took both the twenties, put them in his pocket, hesitated, then came back and snatched the tens.

"Just to be certain the judge will be accommodating," he said. "After all, it is a serious charge. A felony."

Miss Lena already knew that. She also knew already that politics was expensive, and wished Mr. Shaw had spared her the repetition of both statements. She was glad she had kept the rest of her weekend cash, another pair of twenties, concealed in her left hand. That greedy little bald-headed buzzard would surely have taken them too.

But really, at this moment, she did not begrudge him her money. She even regretted her harsh thoughts. Mr. Theophilus Shaw did not look like a buzzard in his bedroom slippers, with his white pajama top creeping up above the velvet collar of his elegant black Chesterfield coat. No, he looked more like a pigeon-toed penguin waddling off on his errand of mercy and corruption.

Corruption. She rolled the word silently on her tongue. It had a voluptuous feel and taste, like a tempting platter of slightly tainted meat. Underdone roast pork, perhaps. Or stolen, gamy sirloin steaks. Why, the whole society was corrupt, and so was Miss Lena Ricks. Was she not buying a favor from a judge? Then she could hardly presume to criticize anyone else.

B.J. looked in no shape to stand criticism, anyway, when the guards brought him in. Two gigantic Neanderthal men to guard one small, sleepy-looking boy! Miss Lena was indignant. B.J. didn't need all that much guarding.

What he needed was a big hug, and that Miss Lena instantly provided, without regard for the musty smell that emanated from his clothes or the possibility of germs, lice, chinches, etc. "Why didn't you call me, B.J.?" she cried.

"I thought you wouldn't want to hear from me. You said I was a liar, and a thief, and—"

"I know what I said. I was wrong, B.J."

"Maybe you wasn't wrong. I guess I proved you right, now," he said with the saddest of smiles.

"Hush," she said, mindful of where they were and who might be listening. "You thought you were working for your friend Bobo, helping him do an honest job. Isn't that right?"

"That's what I told the cops," he answered obliquely. "I said Bobo told me he worked for the meat company. He had all these deliveries to make, and he wanted to get off early next week for Christmas; that's why he needed me to help him load the meat in his car."

"This is very important, B.J.," she whispered. "Did he break into the place, or did he get in with a key?"

"I didn't see how he got in. He told me to wait in the car till he called me. When he did, the back door was already open. You still mad at me, Miss Lena?"

"Of course not. I found out you were telling the truth

about the ring. Earl Junior told me you bought it from a friend of his."

"Why couldn't you believe me in the first place, Miss Lena?"

She shut her eyes tight against his calm, accusing stare. "I don't know. Maybe what you said was right. I never trust anybody."

"Maybe you're right not to."

Their eyes locked.

B.J. was the first to look away. Almost casually, he said, "Take that Earl Junior and his Pop. I thought they was my friends, but they ain't. Not really. They invited me for the holidays, but after I left your place, they said I would have to work for them if I planned to eat and sleep there permanent. I had to get out and hustle stuff every night to pay for my room and board. But they ain't been down here to try and get me out. Ain't even been to see me."

"You had to work for me, too, remember?" she reminded him.

"Working for you is different. It ain't gonna get me locked up. Worst thing can happen to me at your place is, Dr. Norman might put me back in school.

"And I found out something in here, Miss Lena. School ain't nowhere near as bad as jail. If I ever got out of here and found myself back in Hale, I'd be so happy, I'd never call it 'Jail' again."

Maybe the experience hadn't been the worst thing that ever happened to him, she thought. If only it didn't have to be prolonged.

"Ain't nothin' to do in here but sit in that stinking little cell and listen to them bad guys tell stories. They all murderers, and most of 'em say I'll be sent to Juvenile Hall and be locked up with a bigger bunch of murderers for four years. Is that true? Is that what's going to happen to me, Miss Lena?"

"I hope not." She was conscious that the police might be only pretending indifference; might be listening alertly to every word. She bent and whispered, "But if you want to get out of here, you better start calling me 'Mother'."

"Yes, Mother," he said instantly, as if he'd been rehearsing for months.

Got no right to call her that, not now. Only a junkie steals from his mother. And I ain't no junkie, 'less I'm a dream junkie, like my Pop. Yeah, that's what I been. A dream junkie. Dreamin' I could be partners with Bobo again. Dreamin' I could be actin' cool like Bobo, walkin' tall as him, lookin' good like him. Dreamin' I could be Bobo instead of miserable messed-up me.

Wonder how she can like me the way I am?

Miss Lena had been right about the guards. "I thought you said your mother and father were dead, boy," one of them said.

B.J. responded quickly, "My real mother and father, yes. This is my other mother."

"Your grandmother, you mean?"

"My mother."

The desk sergeant looked up wearily. "Look, I've already got a headache. Don't ask them to run through *that* again. I don't care if she's his *god*mother. If she wants him, she can have him."

"*Do* you want me, Miss Lena, I mean, Mother?"

She answered his question with another hug and asked another, "Do you want me for a mother?"

His response was hardly what she'd hoped for. Pulling back from her embrace, he said, "I dunno. I mean, I dunno if I can be good enough for you. I done too many wrong things in my life."

"It hasn't been such a long life."

"Yeah, but I'm almost grown. And I grew up wrong."

"It's not too late for you to change, if you want to."

Bobo would scorn the straight life she wanted him to live. Wherever he was now, he was laughing at straight people and hustling them. Tall, laughing, dapper, cool. . . .

"Do you want to?"

"Uh . . . lemme think about it."

Maybe she didn't know B.J. at all. This was a hard, sad little stranger. She changed the subject. "Why'd you say your father was dead?"

"Because he is."

She looked at him wonderingly.

"Remember I told you he knew how to turn on the gas without calling the company?"

She nodded.

"Well, he must have tried it again when it got cold, only this time he didn't do it right. I heard about it, so I went down there and looked. I don't know exactly what happened. Maybe his head was too bad this time, maybe he was smoking, or maybe the company had messed with the valve, I don't know, but the whole house blew up with him in it. The one next door to it, too. Ain't no houses left on Mole Street now. Just a bunch of holes."

Wasn't no accident, I know that. Bobo and Earl Junior killed him. But I got to pretend I didn't hear them planning it. I made up that other story, and I got to stick to it. Otherwise they'd kill me and anybody I told.

"How do you know for sure your father was killed?"

For the first time in that calm, chilling recital, B.J. showed emotion. He gulped and looked sick. "I found some parts of him. A foot, and some teeth, and a—a finger with a ring he always wore."

"A silver ring with a blue stone?" she asked suddenly.

"That's it. One time he hit me and cut my face with it. But I kept the ring anyway. The cops tooken it off me though. They thought I stole it, I guess."

"I'll try to get it back for you," she promised. "It was my wedding present to him. It was a good ring, a sapphire. Funny, he never pawned it in all those years, hard as things must have been for him sometimes."

"He never even took it off. Maybe he still loved you, Miss Lena."

"Maybe he did." She caught him by the shoulders. "Listen, B.J. I want to tell you something. I know it's going to be hard for you to believe, if all you can remember is the way he treated you lately, but deep down inside, your father was a good man. He did something a lot of people can't do."

"What's that?"

She found, at last, that she could use the word. "Love. I think he loved the people close to him too much. The first time his habit came down on him was after his mother died."

"And the next time was when *my* mother took sick and died."

"That's right. So please don't let yourself feel bitter toward him, B.J."

"I don't hate him no more, Miss Lena. In fact I been wishin'—"

"What?"

He gulped. "Wishin' . . . there was enough left of him for a funeral."

She gathered all her strength to answer him. "That's not important, B.J. The important thing is to remember him right. Remember him right, and try to grow up right."

"I don't know if I can, Miss Lena. Told you, I done too many wrong things. I *know* too many wrong things."

"Well, B.J.," she said slowly, "if I've learned one thing this weekend, it's 'Don't blame people for what they have to do to survive.' "

"This time I didn't have no choice. It was either hustle or starve. But it *was* wrong, wasn't it?" he insisted on knowing.

"Hush, B.J.," Miss Lena said in alarm. But the police were not listening any more; they were too busy overpowering two unruly prisoners who had just been brought in still fighting. While the men were being subdued and handcuffed, Mr. Theophilus Shaw returned with the paper signed by Judge Lawson, ordering the police to release the juvenile B.J. Ricks, a.k.a. B.J. Brown, in the custody of his mother, Mrs. Lena Ricks.

The police were kept so busy handling the new prisoners, they had no time to pay much attention to her or B.J. The sergeant glanced at the paper Mr. Shaw handed him, grunted, and asked Miss Lena, "Do you promise that this juvenile will appear at his hearing?"

"Yes, sir," she said, and scribbled her name on the other piece of paper he shoved at her. He took it, nodded, and waved them outside.

Freedom. Miss Lena gulped great lungfuls of cold, crystalline air. She had never in her life expected to see the inside of that grim building, and, once inside, had been afraid she would never see the outside of it again. She gripped B.J.'s hand tightly, sure he was feeling the same way.

"When will the hearing be, Mr. Shaw?" she asked.

"Don't worry about it," that amazing person said. "The judge has a large backlog of other cases. In the meantime, he has confidence in your ability to keep this young man straight. Do you understand?"

"I hope they catch that Bobo," Miss Lena said.

"I hope they don't," Mr. Shaw responded instantly. "Because in that case there will have to be a hearing, and this young man will have to appear and face charges."

Now Miss Lena understood. With luck, there would be no hearing at all.

It was late, well past two a.m. Mr. Shaw, for all his magical powers, was human. He did not even bother to stifle his yawn. "Can I give you folks a lift?" he offered as they reached his mammoth car.

At this hour, the quiet, snow-filled street was inviting. The snow had stopped falling, but the city was carpeted wall-to-wall with bright white. It would be gray slush by morning.

"No, thank you," Miss Lena said. "You've done enough for us already, Mr. Shaw. We'll walk."

"They ain't never gonna catch Bobo," B.J. assured her as their benefactor drove off. "He's too smart."

"Why'd you pick him for a friend, B.J.?"

" 'Cause he's smart, like I just said. He's the biggest, smartest kid out here. I knew he'd been makin' it on his own since he was twelve, so I knew he could help me. Plus I was crippled, and he could protect me. The other kids were always getting picked up for doing dumb things. Bobo never did anything dumb, and he never got caught."

She was dismayed at the undercurrent of admiration in his voice. She would have her work cut out for her. "He left you to take all the blame for a robbery. Do you still think he's your friend?"

He had good legs and I didn't. He could run and I

couldn't. That's just the way it was. Nobody's fault.

He answered with only a slight hesitation. "No . . . but I don't blame him for that, Miss Lena. See, when things get tight out here, a guy's got to make it, best way he can, without thinking about what might happen to somebody else."

He was reciting her own philosophy back to her, Miss Lena thought with chilling recognition. The only difference was that she had always operated within the law.

She sighed. A crowd of disturbing questions was clamoring in her mind. Does Bobo work for Earl Junior and Senior? Did they plan the meat company robbery? Did you help them plan it? Did your father?

Before she could ask them, they were offered their second ride of the evening. This time it was a police car that pulled up beside them. What must have been the tallest, blackest man on the force stepped out.

"Hello, ma'am," Charlie said. "Glad to see things worked out all right for you. Can we give you a lift home?"

"No thank you," she said. "We like walking."

"B.J.," he asked, "do you know a big kid called Ulysses Bobo Jones? About six-one, dark complexion, straight hair, with a recent wound on one side of his head?"

B.J.'s answer was barely audible. "Yeah, I know him."

"Well, I hope he wasn't a good friend of yours. We found him tonight, dead, in an alley. Shot in the back with a police bullet. He was reported running from the scene of a crime."

Bobo never got the money to pay off that cop, then. My father must not have had that much money. Why'd they have to kill him, then? 'Cause he was getting in their way? 'Cause he didn't understand about payoffs and all that side of the business? 'Cause he had all them big-shot dreams they didn't understand? 'Cause he lived in his dream world and they lived in the real world? Shoot, that's not enough reason to kill a man. Why'd they have to kill him? Why?

B.J. blinked back the tears. He would have to wait till later to cry for his father.

"Well, behave yourself now, young fella. Do like she tells you, and stay out of trouble."

The police car drove off.

"Do you want to come home with me?" Miss Lena asked.

"I ain't got nobody else."

It was hardly an enthusiastic answer, but it would do. "Neither have I. Let's go home."

"To your shop?"

"To my apartment," she said. "We'll stop at the shop first, to pick up the cot, because I don't have a bed for you yet. But this time I'm taking you home, Bruce."

"What did you call me?" he asked in wonderment.

"Bruce. A mother has a right to name her son, and I've named you Bruce James Ricks. Bruce for me, and James for your father, and Ricks for both of us."

"I like it," he said after a minute of deliberation.

"Although," she teased, "it might be simpler just to change one initial and call you B.W."

"What for?"

"For Boll Weevil. That's the pesky little bug that's always looking for a home."

She's right. I didn't know it, not even when I moved in her basement, but that's what I was looking for all the time. A home.

"Well," he admitted cheerfully, "I guess I bugged you enough, all right."

The little joke got more laughter than it deserved; they were both giddy with relief and exhaustion. Finally silent, they plodded through the snow, leaning against one another for support, like a two-legged stool. Shaky and badly balanced, but still upright, still triumphantly surviving, which was more than could be said for the scores of solitary drunks and strays sleeping in doorways and alleys this freezing December night.

"Well, I guess I found one," he called to her later from the dining room, where his cot had been arranged. A dining room was just another luxury she would have to give up now. She told herself it was simpler to eat in the kitchen, anyway.

"One what?" she asked sleepily.

"A home."

"Yes, I guess you did. Good night, Boll Weevil."

"Good night. Say, Miss Lena?"

"Yes?" she murmured, drifting down toward sleep beneath the covers.

"I have a sister," he said. "They put her in a foster home when my mother died, 'cause they said my father couldn't raise a girl by himself. Brenda doesn't like it there, though. She says the people are mean."

The announcement had shocked her upright and thoroughly awake. "You *had* a sister, you mean," she growled, hoping she had been dreaming.

"No," his relentless voice piped clearly, "she's still around. She's only twelve, but she's real grown-up for her age. She wouldn't be no trouble at all, Miss Lena. She could help you lots of ways. She can cook and clean real good, and she loves to sew. I'll bring her here tomorrow."

"You will *not!*" Miss Lena shouted. With all possibility of sleep destroyed, she lay awake wrestling with this new piece of information, balancing common sense and self-preservation against the ease with which more space could be found in her closets and another bed could be put in her bedroom.

Gripped by sudden panic, she called out, "There aren't any more of you, are there? Just you and Brenda. That's all, isn't it?"

Her only answer was a soft, contented snore that seemed to be coming through a cloud of cotton. And, from the carillon in the church on the square, the chimes of the Christmas carols which always started playing at dawn.